Robert Muchamore was born in 1972 and spent thirteen years working as a private investigator. *CHERUB: Man vs Beast* is his sixth novel in the series.

The CHERUB series has won numerous awards, including the Red House Children's Book Award. For more information on Robert and his work, visit **www.muchamore.com**

Praise for the CHERUB series:
'If you can't bear to read another story about elves, princesses or spoiled rich kids who never go to the toilet, try this. You won't regret it.' *The Ultimate Teen Book Guide*

'My sixteen-year-old son read *The Recruit* in one sitting, then went out the next day and got the sequel.' Sophie Smiley, teacher and children's author

'So good I forced my friends to read it, and they're glad I did!' Helen, age 14

'CHERUB is the first book I ever read cover to cover. It was amazing.' Scott, age 13

'The best book ever.' Madeline, age 12

'CHERUB is a must for Alex Rider lovers.' Travis, age 14

BY ROBERT MUCHAMORE

The Henderson's Boys series:

The CHERUB series:

MAN vs BEAST

Robert Muchamore

*Hodder
Children's
Books*

A division of Hachette Children's Books

A Catalogue record for this book is available
from the British Library

ISBN 978 0 340 91169 3

Typeset in Goudy by Avon DataSet Ltd,
Bidford-on-Avon, Warwickshire

Printed and bound in Great Britain by
CPI Bookmarque Ltd, Croydon, Surrey

The paper and board used in this paperback by
Hodder Children's Books are natural recyclable products
made from wood grown in sustainable forests.
The manufacturing processes conform to the
environmental regulations of the country of origin.

Hodder Children's Books
a division of Hachette Children's Books
338 Euston Road, London NW1 3BH
An Hachette UK company
www.hachette.co.uk

WHAT IS CHERUB?

CHERUB is a branch of British Intelligence. Its agents are aged between ten and seventeen years. Cherubs are mainly orphans who have been taken out of care homes and trained to work undercover. They live on CHERUB campus, a secret facility hidden in the English countryside.

WHAT USE ARE KIDS?

Quite a lot. Nobody realises kids do undercover missions, which means they can get away with all kinds of stuff that adults can't.

WHO ARE THEY?

About three hundred children live on CHERUB campus. JAMES ADAMS is our fourteen-year-old hero. He's a well-respected CHERUB agent with several successful missions under his belt. KERRY CHANG is a Hong Kong-born Karate champion and James' girlfriend. His other close friends include BRUCE NORRIS, SHAKEEL DAJANI and KYLE BLUEMAN.

James's sister, LAUREN ADAMS, is only eleven, but is already regarded as one of CHERUB's best agents. On campus she's inseparable from best friend BETHANY PARKER. She's also very friendly with GREG 'RAT' RATHBONE, who was recruited by CHERUB after becoming entangled in James and Lauren's last mission.

CHERUB STAFF

With its large grounds, specialist training facilities and combined role as a boarding school and intelligence operation, CHERUB actually has more staff than pupils. They range from cooks and gardeners to teachers, training instructors, nurses, psychiatrists and mission specialists. CHERUB is run by its chairman, Dr Terence McAfferty, who is commonly known as Mac.

CHERUB T-SHIRTS

Cherubs are ranked according to the colour of the T-shirts they wear on campus. ORANGE is for visitors. RED is for kids who live on CHERUB campus but are too young to qualify as agents (the minimum age is ten). BLUE is for kids undergoing CHERUB's tough 100-day basic training regime. A GREY T-shirt means you're qualified for missions. NAVY – the T-shirt James wears – is a reward for outstanding performance on a single mission. LAUREN wears a BLACK T-shirt, the ultimate recognition for outstanding achievement over a number of missions. When you retire, you get the WHITE T-shirt, which is also worn by some staff.

1. MORNING

Andy Pierce's bed felt *fantastic*. His duvet was wrapped around his chin, his muscles felt relaxed and his warm pillow fitted snugly under his head. But the gash of sunlight leaking between the curtains was tormenting him.

The fourteen-year-old didn't have the heart to crane his head up and look at the bedside clock, but he knew he had to get up. In less than an hour he'd have his elbows propped on a desk and a tie around his neck for the waking nightmare that was Monday morning: English, French and drama. Today would be even worse than usual because Andy was going to get nailed for not doing his Macbeth homework.

He pictured the dirty look he'd get off Mr Walker as his bedroom door swung into the room.

'I called you three times already,' Andy's mum shouted, as she bounded across the carpet towards the window.

Christine Pierce looked like a sour-faced angel: dressed for work in a white polo shirt, white trousers and white canvas plimsolls.

'There's toast on the table downstairs. Stone cold now, I expect.'

exploded with light as Christine swished the
apart, then whipped away the duvet covering her
son.

'Mummmm,' Andy moaned, as he shielded his eyes with
he hand and put the other over his privates.

'Oh, give over,' Christine grinned, giving her son a friendly
slap on the ankle. 'You've got nothing down there I haven't
seen a thousand times before.' Her expression turned to
revulsion as she caught a whiff of the duvet hanging over her
arm. 'When *exactly* did you last change these sheets?'

Andy shrugged as he rolled on to his bum and grabbed a
pair of clean boxers he'd set out the night before.

'I dunno . . . Last week I think.'

'Pull the other one. Those pillowcases are yellow and I
don't even want to think about the smell.'

'It's not *that* bad.'

Andy watched his mum's lips thin out as he yanked a
school shirt sleeve up his arm. Thin lips meant he had to be
careful: she was on the verge of going thermonuclear.

'When I get home from work this evening, I expect to see
that *disgusting* bed linen washed and hanging on the rotary
line out the back. And you can do your brother's while
you're at it.'

'*What?*' Andy gasped. 'Why have I got to do Stuart's bed?'

Andy recoiled as his mother jammed her pointing finger
under his nose. 'You claim you're old enough to stroll in
from the cinema with your mates at a quarter past eleven. In
my book, that makes you old enough to start taking more
responsibility around this house. This isn't a hotel, and I'm
your mother, not your cleaning lady.'

'Yes, your majesty,' Andy said sullenly.

Christine glanced at her watch and sounded more friendly as she backed away. 'I've got to run. You know, it would make my life easier if I got a *little* bit more cooperation out of you.'

Andy had heard this guilt trip before and wasn't buying it. 'Where's my lunch money?' he asked, as he kicked both feet in the air and hitched black school trousers up his legs.

'There's bus fare on the kitchen worktop. Ham, tomato and mustard sandwich in the fridge.'

'Can't I get chip money?'

'Don't start on that one again. You know I haven't got thirty quid a week for you and Stuart to spend on junk food.'

Andy tutted. 'Everyone goes round the chippy. Sandwiches are totally embarrassing.'

'Go whine to your father. His wife's driving round in a new Focus, while I'm maxed out on three credit cards.'

This guilt trip worked better. Andy had grown to realise that his dad was a total scumbag. His mum had to put in a ton of overtime just to keep their heads above water.

'I should be home by seven,' Christine said, leaning forwards and kissing her son on the cheek. 'And I'm *not* joking about changing those beds, you hear me?'

Leaving a smudge of lipstick on her son's face, she backed out of the room and set off downstairs. The teenager was half a minute behind, threading his belt into his trousers as he walked.

Stuart was in the kitchen and irritated his big brother by being perky and neat as usual. The eleven-year-old had his hair combed, blazer and tie on and Bugs Bunny blaring out of the portable TV. As Andy grabbed a triangle of cold toast, the two boys exchanged grunts.

'Mum's stressed out,' Stuart said sourly. 'Why you gotta keep winding her up all the time?'

Andy wasn't proud of the way he got into rows with his mum, but he didn't mean it. It just kept happening, part of being a teenager or something. Whatever his true feelings, Andy wasn't going to give his little brother the satisfaction of a straight answer.

'Why don't you mind your own?'

Stuart sucked air through his teeth. 'You're so selfish.'

'Piss off.'

'Don't *start*, you two,' Christine shouted from the hallway. She had a bag over her shoulder now and the car keys in her hand, all set to leave. 'You've got ten minutes or you'll both be late for school. Don't forget to turn the deadlock in the front door as you leave.'

Andy gave his mum a nod. 'Later Mum, have a good day at work.'

'Not much chance of that,' she answered gloomily.

Andy waited for the front door to close before scowling back at his brother. 'You're asking for a punch with that smart mouth.'

Before Stuart could think up a comeback that was nasty enough to sting but not so nasty it earned him a dead arm, a scream erupted out on the driveway.

It could only be their mum and it wasn't an *I've seen a spider* scream or the way she'd screamed at their father when they were getting divorced. It came from deep inside, like she was in a lot of pain.

4

The two lads bolted out of their seats at the dining table and raced down the hallway towards the front door.

A Balaclava-clad man smashed Christine's car windscreen with a mallet as Andy burst out on to the driveway. Christine writhed in the gravel, screaming and spitting. Her face and hands glistened with red paint that had been thrown in her face.

The man popped two more windows along the side of the car, but Andy fixed on his accomplice, a stocky dude looming over his mother. He wore camouflage trousers, a black Balaclava and looked ominously like he was about to stick the boot in. Andy didn't even have shoes on, but couldn't stand there while someone laid into his mum.

'You're dead,' Andy screamed as he charged forward.

He was stocky, but the teenager wasn't up to fighting a grown man. The masked dude wrapped an arm around Andy's neck and planted a gloved fist hard into his face.

'I'm not the killer here,' the dude snarled, as Andy's nose exploded in pain.

Andy toppled backwards into a hedge, before a giant boot sank into his belly, pushing him deep into the tangled branches. As Andy wiped a bloody nose on his white sleeve, the Balaclava-clad men jogged off towards a battered Citroën parked across the end of the driveway.

The little getaway car lurched as Andy experienced the most desperate feeling of his life. It wasn't just the pain in his nose, or worrying about his mum, but a feeling of total inadequacy: he'd let the thugs who'd attacked her get away and hadn't been able to stop them because he was only a kid. As Andy untangled himself from the branches and staggered on to his feet, he could hear her moaning.

'I can't see,' Christine sobbed.

Stuart stood on the doorstep, chalk white and rigid.

'Don't just stand there, moron,' Andy yelled as he stumbled towards his mother. 'Get inside, call a bloody ambulance.'

As Stuart came to his senses and raced for the phone, Andy noticed that a hangman's noose had been spray-painted on to the garage door and a message written alongside it:

QUIT YOUR JOB AT THE ANIMAL LAB
NEXT TIME YOU DIE
BY ORDER – THE ANIMAL FREEDOM MILITIA

2. PUTTY

'*Doctors fear that the thirty-six-year-old woman may have suffered permanent damage to her eyesight. This is the latest in a string of increasingly violent attacks by the Animal Freedom Militia. Avon police say they are doing all they can to protect employees of Malarek Research, but with more than two hundred workers at the laboratory, their resources are stretched to the limit . . .*'

The news item came from a screen hanging on the wall beside James Adams' head, but he wasn't listening. He was in the dining-room on CHERUB campus and those of his mates who weren't away on a mission sat around their usual table: Kerry, Bruce, Callum, Connor and Shak.

It had been a couple of minutes since Bruce had gone arse over tit, spilling a tray of macaroni and 7up over a girl sitting a couple of tables across, but everyone was still winding him up about it.

James had a stack of chicken bones on the plate in front of him. His bloated tummy dug into the waistband of his jeans and he was content to sit back and let the conversation pass him by. Kerry had finished eating as well and she'd sprawled out in her chair, slipped her feet out of her sandals and rested her ankles across James' lap.

She could have put her feet on one of the empty chairs at the next table, but she hadn't and James appreciated the affectionate gesture. It meant Kerry was in a good mood and with luck they'd be heading upstairs for snogging and homework once their food settled.

Shak sat on James' right and took a quick glance at Kerry's feet. 'Your feet're really small. Kerry. What size shoe do you take?'

'Size two.'

Shak nodded. 'I found out why women have smaller feet than men the other day.'

Kerry looked baffled. 'On average, women are smaller than men all over.'

'Who wants to know why women have smaller feet than men?' Shak asked, breaking into a grin.

The kids around the table didn't look enthusiastic.

'Is this another one of your lame jokes?' Bruce asked.

Shak grinned. 'My jokes are *quality*.'

Everyone except Shak either spluttered or shook their heads.

Callum summed up the mood. 'If you say so, dude.'

'Fine, if you don't want to hear it . . .'

Bruce tutted. 'Tell us the stupid joke, Shak. Otherwise we'll never hear the end of it. Why do women have smaller feet than men?'

Shak's grin grew until it ate up his whole face. 'So they can stand closer to the kitchen sink when they do the washing-up.'

The joke was as bad as everyone expected, but it raised a laugh because the boys were already in a jovial mood. James managed a quick grin before he turned and caught the frosty look on Kerry's face.

'Male chauvinist pigs,' Kerry snapped, as she pulled her feet off James' lap and faced him off with her hands on her hips.

'Hey, I didn't tell the joke,' James said, raising his palms defensively.

Kerry glowered. 'But you laughed.'

There was a loud crack as she slapped James across the cheek.

'*Jesus*, Kerry,' James said, raising his arms in front of his head to stop her getting another shot in. 'Keep things in proportion, why don't you?'

'You'd all better wipe those smirks off,' Kerry said, shooting thunderbolts at the other boys around the table. Then she zoomed in on Shak. 'You reckon sexist jokes are so funny? How would you feel if I sat here telling Paki jokes?'

There was a tense silence as Kerry grabbed her food tray and steamed off. James sheepishly rubbed the stinging red mark on his face.

Callum and Bruce creased up as soon as she was out of sight. 'Did you hear that crack!' Callum yelled.

'That was *baaaad*,' Bruce said, as he exuberantly slammed his hand against the table.

James turned sourly towards Shak. 'Thanks for winding my girlfriend up.'

'No snogging for Mr Adams tonight,' Callum grinned.

The lads all snickered at James' expense.

'I don't know what you're all looking so happy for,' James said. 'Where have all your girlfriends got to tonight...? Oh, wait, I remember. None of you losers *have* girlfriends.'

'I've got Naira,' Callum said.

Bruce laughed. 'You had two snogs and she's been away on a mission for six months.'

'Still counts,' Callum said, glowering at Bruce. 'She e-mails me almost every day. Who have you ever snogged?'

'I've kissed girls.'

James laughed. 'Like who?'

'Not here,' Bruce said. 'Out on missions and stuff.'

Everyone groaned because they didn't believe him: Bruce was shy around girls.

'He snogs that little blue teddy he always sleeps with,' Shak giggled.

'Piss off,' Bruce said angrily. 'And I don't sleep with Jeremy. He fell off that shelf over my bed one time and Kyle went and told the whole world.'

'What the hell kind of name is Jeremy for a teddy?' James smirked.

'Yeah,' Connor nodded. 'You'd at least think he'd snog a teddy with a girl's name.'

Bruce exploded out of his seat and glowered at Connor. 'Wanna try repeating that in five seconds when I've punched all your teeth out?'

James backed up his chair and grinned at his mates as he stood up. 'I'll leave you four pussies to sort your squabbles. I'd better be in my room when Kerry comes knocking.'

'You reckon?' Shak said. 'That's really gonna happen when she just cracked you one.'

'I *happen* to have an ace up my sleeve,' James grinned. 'Little Miss Perfect is failing algebra. She needs my massive brain to sort out her Xs and Ys.'

Connor tutted. 'You're totally jammy, James. You always get lucky with girls.'

James looked smug as he walked away from the table. 'What can I say guys? Chicks can't resist me – they're putty in my hands.'

*

James went up to his room, stepped over the dirty laundry and sat on his double bed reading the copy of *Great Expectations* his English teacher had inflicted on him. He was supposed to be two hundred and fifty pages in already, but he was mired in the low seventies and couldn't concentrate because he expected Kerry to knock at any minute.

But he was having doubts by the time he reached page 106 and when a knock finally came, it was a triple.

'Lauren?' James yelled, as his sister's long blonde hair dangled inside the door.

'Ha-*haa*,' Lauren smiled, pointing at James as she stepped into the room. 'Your face is well red. Kerry said she gave you a good stinging.'

James slid his bookmark in and straightened himself up. 'You saw Kerry? Is she coming over?'

'Doubt it,' Lauren said. 'She's just been up in my room getting help with her maths homework.'

'You little traitor,' James gasped. 'What did you do that for? I'm way better at maths than you.'

'She's in a right mood with you, James. And I might not

be as good at maths as you, but I still get all As and I'm ahead of Kerry. Anyway, it serves you right for cracking a sexist joke.'

'Shak told the joke, I barely laughed.'

'Whatever,' Lauren shrugged. 'You and Kerry are such drama queens. It'll be hands all over each other again by tomorrow.'

'So, did you just come here to gloat about me getting slapped?'

Lauren grinned. 'Came to ask a favour, actually.'

'Sounds ominous.'

Lauren sat on the edge of the bed. 'You know Kirsten McVicar?'

James shook his head.

'Yes you do, James. She was at my birthday party. She's Bethany's friend, but she's a year younger. She was wearing those black tights with the green spots on?'

'Nah,' James said. 'Your mates all talk the same crap and you're always swapping clothes. Why's it matter anyway?'

'Kirsten dropped out of basic training last week. And you know Bethany's brother Jake is doing his training as well?'

James nodded. 'How's the little dude getting on?'

'Kirsten says Jake's struggling. He's only just turned ten. He's sprained his thumb and he's not exactly huge for his age, so he's having a hard time carrying his pack on long runs and stuff.'

'Pity,' James said. 'I hope Jake doesn't fail. He's a bit full of himself at times, but—'

'Pot calling kettle if ever I heard it,' Lauren interrupted. 'Anyway, me and Bethany made up a plan to give Jake a boost. We want to take him a little pick-me-up package. You know, chocolate bars for energy, dry boots and underwear, a padded strap to make carrying his pack easier.'

James looked shocked. 'Lauren, you can't just waltz into the basic training compound. The gates are alarmed and there's barbed wire and surveillance cameras everywhere.'

'Me and Bethany have it all worked out, but we could do with someone older coming with us.'

'No, no, *no!*' James laughed. 'Don't look at me. We'll get hammered if we're caught. Jake's a nice little kid, but he'll just have to suffer through basic training, same as we all did.'

'*Please*, James.'

'Besides, why do you care? I mean, I can see Bethany would want to risk her neck for her little brother, but you? I've never heard you say a good word about Jake. You battered him that time he blocked your toilet up with popcorn.'

'Bethany's my best friend. I'm doing it for her.'

'Hang on,' James gasped, as his face lit up with realisation. 'You're not doing this for Jake at all. Lover boy's in training as well, isn't he? You're doing this for Rat.'

'No,' Lauren gasped. 'I mean, Rat *is* Jake's training partner. But he's *not* my boyfriend.'

'Look Lauren, I know you've got the hots for Rat, but I'm on top of everything now. All my homework is up to date and my grades aren't bad. I must have spent a thousand hours running punishment laps and scrubbing toilets since I came to CHERUB. I'm not sticking my neck out for anyone unless it's life and death.'

'I thought you might say that,' Lauren grinned. 'So I'll have to call in the favour.'

'What favour? I don't owe you squat.'

James felt his heart jolt as Lauren gave him her evil smirk. Her face had altered since she was a toddler, but that expression hadn't changed a bit. It was the look she used to get right before jamming an ice-cream cornet in your face. It was the look she had when she broke the video and told their mum she saw James do it . . .

'Remember last year, when we were in Idaho?' Lauren said airily. 'Remember cheating on Kerry with a girl called Becky?'

James nodded grimly.

'I never told anyone; but, I mean, that information could slip out at *any* time and Kerry would kick your arse. So, I just want one little favour in return for eternal silence.'

'You *what*?' James yelled. 'That's not asking for a favour, that's blackmail.'

'I suppose you *could* call it that,' Lauren smirked. 'But James, you like Rat, you like Jake. Is it really such a big problem?'

'What kind of scumbag blackmails their own brother?' James asked indignantly.

Lauren ducked the question. 'James, me and Bethany have everything planned out. There's no way we'll get caught.'

'You know what,' James said, trying to sound confident, 'I'm calling your bluff. That thing with Becky happened more than a year ago and Kerry knows I'm no angel. She'll understand.'

Lauren grinned as she headed for the door. 'Fine, I'll go tell Kerry about Becky now then.'

James acted casual as Lauren headed out into the corridor and turned towards Kerry's room, but he couldn't keep up the act and scrambled after her.

Kerry's room was less than twenty metres away and Lauren was all set to knock by the time he'd caught up.

'OK, you win,' James whispered bitterly.

Lauren smiled contentedly. 'Thought I might.'

James huffed, 'But you can't keep blackmailing me. You've got to swear on our mum's grave never to tell anyone.'

'That's fair,' Lauren nodded. Then she broke into a grin and gave her brother a hug. 'Thanks, James.'

James was too pissed off to hug Lauren back, but he did have a grudging admiration for her cheek. Then Kerry's door popped open.

'Thought I could hear you two,' Kerry said. 'What's going on out here?'

'Nothing,' James said unconvincingly.

Lauren smiled at Kerry. 'I told this idiot to come and apologise to you.'

James was relieved to see that Kerry was smiling back at him. 'Guess I overreacted,' she said.

James shrugged. 'Sorry I laughed at that joke.'

'I'll live,' Kerry said as she stepped up and kissed James on the cheek. 'Did I hear you say you were behind on *Great Expectations* earlier?'

'Page one-twelve,' James nodded.

'That's further than me,' Kerry said. 'I'm never gonna catch up, so I got the film version out of the library. You want to come in and watch it?'

'Lifesaver,' James grinned, as he stepped into Kerry's room. Then he looked back at Lauren. 'Catch up with you later, sis.'

'I'll send you a text with the details,' Lauren said. '*Don't be late.*'

Kerry looked a bit confused. 'What's she up to?'

James moved in to kiss Kerry back. 'Don't worry about it,' he grinned, as he looped his arm around her back and kicked the door shut with his trainer.

3. DARK

Angst kept James awake and he rolled out of bed a few minutes before the 2 a.m. alarm. He put on clothes that would make him hard to see in the dark: navy blue tracksuit with a baseball cap and black Adidas trainers.

Lauren and her best mate Bethany were waiting for him six floors down in a crawl space under the fire stairs.

'Thanks so much for coming,' Bethany grinned. 'I don't know how Lauren persuaded you. I never thought you'd agree in a million years.'

'No worries,' James said sourly, as he scowled at his sister.

James couldn't stand Bethany. She was intelligent and funny, but her mocking tone and giggling fits drove him nuts.

'Are you sure nobody saw you sneak down here?' Lauren asked.

James shrugged. 'Not as far as I can tell.'

'Cool,' Lauren said. 'The shooting range is next to the training compound, so if we get stopped, we'll say we've been assigned to a mission and we're heading off to sign out some stun guns.'

'That's only gonna work if it's someone who doesn't know us,' James pointed out.

'Yeah,' Bethany said. 'But how many people are gonna be wandering around campus at this time of the morning?'

'S'pose,' James said. 'So what's our plan?'

'The less time we're out of our beds, the less chance that we'll get noticed,' Lauren said. 'So I'll explain as we run. Grab that pack and get moving.'

'Are you sure this fire door isn't alarmed?' James asked, as he reached towards a large blue backpack.

Lauren shook her head. 'Have some faith, bro. Me and The Bethster have every detail worked out.'

James felt his shoulder sag as he hooked the pack over his arms. 'Christ, I thought we were taking them a few bits of food and stuff. What's in here, lead weights?'

'Me and Lauren have the clean clothes and food,' Bethany explained. 'You're carrying all our equipment: wire cutters, electrical tools and three sets of waders.'

'We're the brains, you're the muscle,' Lauren grinned, as she pushed the fire door open. It was early summer, but the air still had a nip to it at this time of the morning. There was no alarm and Lauren looked back at her brother as if to say *I told you so*.

Knowing their packs would jangle if they ran, the three kids kept to a brisk walk. They cut across a squelchy corner of a football pitch, before heading into the woods that covered all of the undeveloped areas on CHERUB campus. After dealing with a tangle of undergrowth, their feet found a dirt path.

'This takes longer than walking across the open fields, but

nobody uses this trail except for running cross-country,' Lauren explained.

'And if we do come across anyone, we can use the trees as cover,' Bethany added.

James felt slightly reassured: the girls had obviously put in a lot of thought.

Once they were clear of the buildings, Lauren broke into a jog. But they couldn't run fast because the moonlight penetrating the branches was barely enough to make out the path. James moved up alongside his sister.

'We're going right up to the back of campus,' Lauren continued, breathing heavily. 'Remember when me and Kyle were on punishment and had to dig out all those ditches?'

'Uh-huh.'

'Most of them carry water off the farms that surround campus. They all feed into the stream that runs across the training compound. In a couple of places we cleared out ditches that join the stream *inside* the training compound. All that stops you getting in is a few strands of barbed wire and we can easily snip that.'

'Before you ask, we've checked and it's not electrified or alarmed,' Bethany added.

'What about video cameras?' James asked. 'They're everywhere. The instructors know if a squirrel farts inside that compound.'

'There's fifty-three cameras,' Lauren nodded. 'But they all run off a single circuit. If we pull the fuse the whole lot stops working.'

'How'd you find that out?'

'Martin Newman got punishment, cleaning out the

administration building,' Bethany said. 'We sweet-talked him into making a copy of the electrical plans for the whole of campus.'

Lauren giggled. 'And now you've got to go to the cinema with him.'

'Shut *up*,' Bethany gasped. 'Don't you worry. I know I promised, but I'll find a way to wriggle out of it.'

'Martin's gonna be so gutted,' Lauren said. 'Doesn't it crack you up the way one of his ears sticks out and one doesn't?'

'You can't talk, Lauren. You fancy Rat and he's no oil painting.'

Both girls were giggling at their little in-jokes, which irritated James.

'Make some more noise, why don't you?' he sneered.

'There's nobody around,' Lauren said dismissively, but both girls realised they were being dumb and calmed down.

*

It took ten minutes' jogging along the winding path to reach the back of the training compound. The three kids had slowly increased their speed as their eyes adjusted to the moonlight.

They were in good shape and none of the trio was seriously out of breath as they pulled up beside a ditch that was about a metre and a half deep. Lauren slid a torch out the back of her jeans and shone it around.

'This is the spot,' she whispered. 'James, get the waders out.'

James was relieved as he slipped the weight off his shoulders and unzipped the pack. It hadn't rained in a week, so they could find some hard ground to change their footwear, but they'd passed through a couple of boggy areas and their trainers were coated in mud.

After throwing two smaller sets of booted rubber trousers at the girls, James caught a whiff of feet as he wriggled the waders up his legs and hooked the straps that held them up over his shoulders.

'Where'd you get these?' James moaned. 'They're nasty.'

'Kyle had them when he was on punishment,' Bethany explained. 'He wore them every day for six weeks, so I'm not surprised they're a bit ripe.'

'Once you get down in that ditch, Kyle's smell is the last thing you'll worry about,' Lauren said, as she threw something at James.

He narrowly missed the catch, but realised it was a head-mounted lamp as soon as he picked it off the ground.

'The light's good for fifty metres, but don't use it any more than you have to,' Lauren said.

James slipped the elastic strap around his head and quickly flipped the tiny LED bulbs on and off to make sure they were working. Bethany was still struggling to get into her waders and Lauren sorted her out while James hooked on what was now a much lighter pack and set off towards the ditch.

He considered jumping into the muddy water, but it would splash up his arms and make a racket, so he took a cautious approach, sitting on the edge of the ditch with his legs dangling and gently lowering himself down.

There was a squelch as his waders sank into the twenty centimetres of mud that lay beneath the stagnant, thigh-high water. As his feet settled, James rested his palm against the clayish soil of the embankment to steady himself.

By this time, the girls stood atop the embankment and Bethany looked flustered.

'Maybe we shouldn't,' she said anxiously.

James rose to the tantalising possibility of Lauren's hair-brained scheme being called off.

'Maybe you're right,' he said, perhaps a little too eagerly. 'This is risky and the instructors are bound to punish Jake and Rat as well if we're caught.'

'We didn't come this far to quit,' Lauren said stiffly.

Bethany nodded apprehensively. 'Lauren's right – I always get the jitters.'

Lauren scowled at James. 'And don't *you* encourage her.'

James stared gloomily at the water as the two girls held hands and slipped down the embankment together. Bethany looked a touch wobbly as she took her first steps, but Lauren had months of wading experience under her belt and led off at a pace James and Bethany struggled to cope with.

It was less than ten metres from the spot where the path met the ditch to the tangle of barbed wire at the back of the training compound, but James' thighs already ached from pushing his legs through the swirling mud.

Lauren flipped on her head lamp to inspect the zigzagging strands of barbed wire. She tried pushing them, but they were taut.

'They've reinforced it since I was down here on punishment,' Lauren whispered anxiously. 'I hoped we'd be able to push the wires down and make a gap big enough to step through, but we'll need to cut it.'

James turned his back to Lauren so she could unzip his pack and grab the chunky set of wire cutters from inside.

'You know this is vandalism of CHERUB property?' James said. 'If they catch us, we're in serious trouble.'

Lauren sounded annoyed. 'Stop moaning, James. I'm trying to think.'

James watched as his sister artfully cut a single strand of wire. It left a gap of about half a metre at one corner of the ditch, right next to the embankment.

'We'll get a bit muddy, but we can squeeze through,' Lauren said.

She snipped off the loose strand of wire, before bending it up and hurling it into the trees. 'Nobody comes out here unless one of the ditches dams up, they won't miss one strand of wire.'

James agreed with his sister's logic, but wasn't in any mood to go around throwing compliments at her.

Squeezing under the wire was a palaver that involved going through one at a time and feeding their packs through afterwards. James was broader than the two girls and ended up with mud streaked across the back of his tracksuit.

Once they were through, it would have been quicker to climb out of the ditch and run along the embankment, but they didn't want to risk being caught on video so they carried on wading, keeping as low as possible with the white of their faces shielded by baseball caps.

Seventy metres beyond the wire, Lauren leaned against the embankment and quickly flashed the powerful beam of her head lamp. It caught one side of a concrete shed before she ducked down again.

'Party time,' Lauren grinned.

The ditch here was shallower than where they'd dropped in. The three youngsters stepped out and set off at a run towards the shed, with globs of mud sliding down the outside of their waders. When they reached the shed wall, Lauren and Bethany pushed the straps holding the waders up off their shoulders.

'Get them off and put your trainers back on, James,' Lauren ordered.

'What's the point?' James asked. 'We've got to go back the way we came.'

'No we don't,' Lauren explained. 'There's only ever one training instructor on duty at night. As soon as they see that the cameras have stopped working, they'll come down here. We'll run in the other direction to the main training building. We can hand the packages across to the trainees, then we'll sprint out via the front gate.'

'What about the alarm?' James asked.

'Doesn't matter,' Bethany said. 'They'll find out that it went off eventually, but the instructor won't be anywhere near the control room to hear it.'

'Doesn't it sound anywhere else, like the security console on the main gate?'

Lauren shrugged. 'Not as far as we know.'

James shook his head as he kicked the waders away and went into the pack for his trainers. 'You mean you *don't* know for sure?'

'It's pretty unlikely, James. I mean, why would anyone on

the main gate need to know if an alarm went off at the training compound?'

'But you're not sure,' James hissed furiously. 'You *guaranteed* that we wouldn't get caught!'

'Yeah,' Lauren shrugged, 'but I always knew there was *some* risk. I mean, I only said about the guarantee to make sure you came.'

The realisation that Lauren had lied on top of the blackmail made James furious. He had his trainers on now and he stood up and faced his sister off. 'I'll get you back for this. You're out of order.'

'If you do I'll tell Kerry,' Lauren grinned back.

'You swore on our mum's grave.'

'Tell Kerry what?' Bethany asked.

James and Lauren both snapped at her, 'Mind your own.'

Bethany knew James didn't like her, but she was annoyed with Lauren. 'We're in the middle of the training compound here,' she said acidly. 'Can't you leave the family feud till we're back in our rooms?'

She had a point.

'OK,' Lauren said, looking at Bethany, 'you put all the waders in the big pack. James, there's a plastic box with electrical tools in the front compartment of your pack. Grab that and come with me.'

James walked around to the front of the shed, happy at least that he hadn't landed the filthy task of cramming three slippery sets of waders into the pack. The shed door was aluminium with a yellow and black warning sign riveted to it.

ELECTRICAL HAZARD
640 VOLTS
QUALIFIED PERSONNEL ONLY
DANGER OF DEATH

'You said this was just a fuse box,' James gasped.

Lauren shrugged. 'There must be some other stuff in there, but I can handle it.'

James grinned with relief when he spotted the heavy duty padlock on the door. 'We haven't got our lock guns,' he said. 'And there's no way we'll manage to crack that monster off.'

'Don't need to,' Lauren said, as she slid a key out of her jeans and pushed it into the padlock. 'Good old Martin. It was in the same filing cabinet as the plans for the electrical system.'

They stepped into the shed, which hummed with the sound from a washing-machine-sized transformer. A panel mounted on the wall opposite had a dozen rows of switches with fuses lined up underneath.

'Open the box – I need an electrical screwdriver.'

James' fingers were numb from the water in the ditch and he fumbled as he peeled back the plastic lid.

'Which one's the electrical screwdriver?'

Lauren shot him a contemptuous look as she snatched it. 'The one that looks like a screwdriver, maybe? Point your light at me and keep your head still while I work.'

She looked along the rows of switches. Each one controlled a different system inside the training compound and they were labelled with strips of faded Dymo tape: SHOWERS, LIGHTS (INT), LIGHTS (EXT FLOOD), LIGHTS

(ASSAULT COURSE), WATER HEATER, GOLF BUGGY (RECHARGING). The circuit labelled CCTV was halfway along the third row.

'Here we go,' Lauren grinned. 'I'll replace the fuse with one that's blown. When the instructor comes in here, it'll look like the circuit fused because of a power surge or something.' She leaned in close and read the writing on the fuse casing. 'Fifteen amp, size C.'

Lauren reached into the box of electrical stuff and grabbed a chunky fuse with a green label. She flipped the main switch for the CCTV circuit to the off position before using the screwdriver to pop out the working fuse. After replacing it with the pre-blown fuse, she turned the circuit back on. A red warning light came to life, confirming that the fuse was a dud.

'OK,' Lauren said, grinning confidently. 'So far so good.'

They both flipped off their head lamps as they stepped outside. Bethany's hands and arms were covered in mud, a result of her struggle to get the waders back into James' pack.

'All done?' she asked.

Lauren nodded as she looked at her watch. 'Two thirty-one a.m.,' she said. 'I reckon we've got about ten minutes before the instructor gets here to replace that fuse.'

4. FEAST

Basic training is hell. A trainee can quit at any time, but if you want to become a CHERUB agent you have to get through it. Your brain and body are pushed to breaking point by instructors who don't care if you're crying, injured, hungry or sick. All they care about is toughening kids up so they can cope with all the bad stuff that might happen on an undercover mission. And if you make it through the one-hundred-day course, you'll be able to cope with just about anything.

James had an emotional flashback as he peeked between branches at the windowless concrete building where CHERUB trainees slept. He remembered himself two years earlier, huddled inside after an exhausting day of training, with the springs from the dank mattress jarring his back and rain plinking off the corrugated metal roof.

'I didn't see any instructor come out,' Lauren whispered.

Bethany shrugged. 'They *must* have noticed all the cameras going off.'

The threesome crept around behind the bushes until they came to the building's double-doored entrance. Lauren flicked her head lamp on and off, startling a bony-legged ten-year-old, who was being made to spend the night standing on one leg, back to the wall and hands on head. Trainees received punishments like this for the tiniest breach of the rules, sometimes even for no reason at all.

'Who's out there?' the girl asked, in a plummy voice that hinted at a rich background.

'Natasha?' Lauren asked, stepping out of cover.

'Get *back*,' Natasha squealed desperately. 'Mr Large will be out here at any second, there's a video camera pointing right at us.'

'No there isn't,' Lauren grinned, as James and Bethany followed her out of the bushes. 'We fused the circuit. He's probably out trying to fix it.'

As soon as Natasha heard that the cameras were off, she took her hands off her head, put her foot down and began to massage her aching calf.

'*Owww*,' she moaned. 'It's so painful standing on one leg like that. But I'm telling you, Large is still in there. I would have seen if he'd gone out.'

'Dammit,' Lauren said.

'How can he just be sitting there if we've blown up the cameras?' Bethany asked.

'Unless he's nodded off,' James said.

'What are you lot doing here?' Natasha asked.

'Rescue mission,' Lauren smiled. 'At least, we can't rescue you, but we brought you all extra food and dry underwear to cheer you up.'

'That's amazing,' Natasha said, bouncing cheerfully on the balls of her bare feet. 'You guys are so brave!'

Bethany went into her pack and pulled out a package wrapped in a cellophane freezer bag.

'Three Snickers bars, a flapjack, two cartons of orange juice and two fresh sets of underwear,' she explained. 'We've stripped as much packaging off the food as we can, but make sure the instructors don't catch you with anything you shouldn't have or you'll get punished.'

Natasha almost burst into tears as she broke the package open and bit a massive chunk off the end of a Snickers bar.

'Mmmmm,' she said. 'I am *so* starving. We spent three hours running around the assault course yesterday and all we got for dinner was that watery green soup.'

'Oh *god*,' James grimaced. 'I'd forgotten all about training soup. That stuff always made me gag, no matter how hungry I was.'

James, Lauren and Bethany looked at each other as Natasha started on her flapjack.

'What can we do if Large is still in there?' James asked.

'Well, he has to be asleep,' Lauren said.

'But we were planning for him to be on the other side of the compound,' Bethany said. 'He could burst out here any second.'

Half a minute earlier, James would have been arguing to quit and run, but the emotive sight of the training building and Natasha's ecstatic reaction to her package had changed his mind. 'We've come this far,' he said. 'I'm up for sneaking inside if you two are.'

Lauren and Bethany exchanged surprised looks before nodding in agreement. James opened the door of the accommodation building and crept into a gloomy corridor.

The smell was straight out of his training nightmares: sweat, antiseptic and damp concrete.

Three steps in, he came to the open door of the instructor's lounge and craned his neck inside. Sure enough, the monstrous figure of Norman Large lay slumped across a battered sofa, with static fizzing on the six black and white monitors stacked on a desk opposite him.

CHERUB's nastiest employee had let himself go since the humiliation of being demoted from head training instructor the year before. He now sported a ragged beard and a dozen kilos of fat around his midriff.

Then suddenly – 'Not fishfingers,' Mr Large begged, as James nervously edged backwards.

But it was just sleeptalking and Lauren grinned as if to say, *Who has nightmares about fishfingers?*

'Right,' James whispered to the girls. 'You two get in there and hand those packages out *fast*. If Large wakes up we're dead.'

The nine kids in the dormitory were aged between ten and twelve and they all slept solid, like you'd expect after sixty-three days of brutal training. James kept watch in the doorway as Lauren woke Rat, and Bethany rushed to her brother, Jake.

The only light came from the green EXIT signs over the emergency doors. James wasn't an especially sensitive soul, but he felt a lump in his throat as Bethany woke her little brother and pulled him into a massive hug.

'What are you doing here?' Jake gasped, as Bethany pulled another ration pack out of her backpack. 'Oh my god, is that a Snickers bar?'

While Jake alternated between grinning at his sister, sobbing and cramming chocolate down his neck, Lauren gave Rat a shorter embrace before going around waking the other trainees and handing out the provisions.

Within a minute, all nine trainees sat up on their beds, excitedly eating chocolate and sucking orange juice out of cartons. They seemed happier than their bruised and weary bodies gave them any right to be.

A couple of lads who James had given maths tuition to came up and asked him for an update on all the latest campus gossip, while Lauren gathered up the cartons and wrappers so that no signs of their visit got picked up by the instructors who would inspect the room at sun-up.

A snore came from the lounge a couple of metres from where James was standing. As he glanced around, he forgot the jubilant atmosphere and remembered how dodgy their situation was.

'Come on,' he whispered. 'It's not a tea party.'

As Bethany and Jake exchanged a final hug, Lauren zipped up the pack full of litter and headed towards James. But when she turned back for a final glance at Rat, Lauren paused for a second then ran to his bed to give him a kiss.

It was meant to be on the cheek, but Rat turned his head at the wrong moment and they ended up face to face. After a millisecond's hesitation, staring into Rat's sleepy brown eyes, she thought what the hell and kissed him on the lips. It didn't last long enough to be a proper snog, but it was a lot more than kissing your auntie on the cheek.

In fact, Lauren didn't know exactly what it was, only that

her mind was doing somersaults as she backed out of the room.

'You're gonna make a fantastic CHERUB agent, Rat,' Lauren choked, struggling to keep the tears back. She looked at the rest of the room, trying to hide her emotional state from James as she reached the doorway. 'And all of you are gonna make it through training,' she added.

James raised his hand in a wave as all the trainees thanked them for putting their necks out.

'Don't let the bastards grind you down,' James grinned. 'Good luck.'

After a glance into the lounge to make sure Mr Large was still asleep, James, Lauren and Bethany headed outside, exchanging a quick goodbye with Natasha before setting off at a run towards the main gate.

'That was *so* cool,' James grinned. 'Large won't get the CCTV working any time soon. How often do you get a chance to make people happy like that?'

Bethany sounded really sad. 'I hope Jake gets through training.'

'He'll be OK, Bethany,' James said, sympathising with her for the first time ever.

'He's still so little, James.'

'Tough as old boots though,' James said.

The emotional scene in the dormitory had caused a weird role reversal. James was now in charge, while Bethany was in a state and Lauren had apparently taken leave of planet earth.

'I just kissed a *boy* – on the mouth,' Lauren gawped, as if she could hardly believe it herself.

James beamed at her. 'It had to happen sooner or later.'

Lauren tipped her head back and looked up at the stars. 'A boy,' she repeated, not sure whether to grin or screw up her face in disgust.

It was only a short walk down a concrete path from the accommodation block to the front gate. James hesitated before pushing it open.

'Earth to Lauren,' he said, waving a hand in front of her face. 'Get it together, girl. When I push this gate, the alarm goes off. Mr Large will wake up from the land of fishfingers and we'd better be well out of it.'

'Mmm,' Lauren said airily.

The instant James rattled the gate, a klaxon sounded and floodlights lit up the perimeter of the compound. Deciding to put speed before stealth, he led the trio into the middle of the football fields, instead of the winding route through the trees they'd taken on the way out.

It was a six-minute run back to the main building, flat out and more or less in a straight line. They cut around to the fire door at the rear, which Lauren had propped open with a wedge to stop it from closing on itself.

Their trainers were sodden and they pulled them off in the stairwell before hurrying upstairs in their damp socks, with trainers hooked over their fingers. James said goodnight to the girls on the sixth-floor landing, leaving them four more flights to reach their rooms on the eighth.

James had a weird mixture of feelings as he walked into his room. He was really annoyed about Lauren blackmailing him, even though he now realised it had all been for a good cause.

He flung off his outer layer of clothing and crashed on to the beanbag in front of his TV, totally knackered. It was 3:06 a.m., he hadn't slept a wink and his legs killed from all the running and wading. He had a fitness training session in less than four hours and still had to shower and put his muddy clothes in soak before he could get into bed.

But before any of that, James needed a drink. As he crouched in front of his miniature fridge, trying to decide between Pepsi and Sprite, the phone beside his bed rang.

Phones don't ring at 3:06. James picked up gingerly, guessing it was Lauren or Bethany with a query about something that had happened, but the voice was much older. Soft and with a slight Scottish accent.

'Hello there.'

James' heart warped to a million beats per minute. It was Mac, the chairman of CHERUB and most senior staff member on campus.

'Oh,' James said, faking a yawn. 'You woke me up.'

'Did I indeed?' Dr McAfferty laughed. 'I take it you sleepwalked the entire journey through the trees, across the training compound, into the trainees' dormitory and back up the stairs to your room.'

'You . . .' James said, pounding his fist against the carpet as he realised that the shit had hit the fan.

'. . . sat here watching the whole thing on our backup CCTV system,' Mac said, finishing James' sentence. 'So I'll be seeing you, your sister Lauren and Bethany Parker in my office at nine-thirty tomorrow morning. Is that clear?'

'Yes, sir,' James said gloomily, cursing his luck as the phone went dead in his ear.

5. RETIREMENT

If you were in trouble, Dr McAfferty prolonged your suffering by making you wait in suspense outside his office. Nine-thirty rolled on to ten as James, Lauren and Bethany sat on a line of leatherette chairs, anxiously drumming and twitching a variety of body parts. Mac's assistant sat at the desk in the middle of the outer office, typing letters, taking calls and scowling at the KEEP SILENT sign if they dared make any noise.

The kids wanted to make a good impression and all three wore pristine CHERUB uniform: freshly waxed combat boots, olive cargo pants and the T-shirts that denoted their rank. Grey for Bethany, navy for James and black for Lauren.

The longer James sat there thinking about his situation, the angrier he got with his sister for dragging him into this mess.

It was almost eleven when they got called in. Mac's office was a stately affair, with a giant oak desk and floor to ceiling bookshelves. Many of the shelves had been emptied and the books stacked into cardboard boxes, ready for shipping out.

James was surprised. 'I thought you were here for another couple of months.'

Mac gave the bookshelves a sad glance from behind his desk. 'I don't retire until the end of July,' he said. 'It's just easier taking things home a few boxes at a time.'

'Is it true that you didn't want to go?' Bethany asked.

Mac smiled. 'CHERUB might be a special organisation, but I have to retire at sixty-five, the same as any other government employee. Besides, this is a young man's – or woman's – job. All the responsibilities of a headteacher, politician and spymaster rolled into one. I don't have the energy I used to have and there are plenty of souls more than capable of replacing me.'

'Like who?' Lauren asked.

As Mac's retirement drew near, the identity of the new chairman had become *the* hot topic on campus.

Mac gave the kids an odd expression, part serious, part misty eyed, before speaking in an uncharacteristically severe voice. 'Please sit down at the desk. We're here to discuss *your* futures, not mine. In particular, the consequences of last night's unauthorised mission.'

'How come you found out about it?' James asked, as he sat down between the two girls.

Mac's voice softened and he almost broke into a smile. 'One of the office staff caught Martin Newman stealing a key to the generator room.'

Lauren and Bethany both gasped.

'As you *well* know, Bethany,' Mac continued, 'young Martin has a crush on you. He was reluctant to tell on you and only admitted that he was stealing the key for you two after I threatened to ban him from undercover missions if he didn't spill the beans.

'I had your rooms searched while you were in class and found Lauren's masterplan,' Mac said, as he held up a large sheet of photocopied paper. 'Once I knew it wasn't a serious security breach, I decided to let you go ahead. It's always interesting to see what you kids are capable of.'

As Mac spoke, James studied the masterplan. It was all in Lauren's neatest writing, with diagrams, maps, details of when the raid was going to take place and what equipment they needed. But his eyes were drawn to the bottom of the paper and a section beneath an underlined title:

> PROS AND CONS OF TAKING JAMES:
> PROS:
> In love with Kerry, so easy to blackmail and will do what he's told.
> Strong – James can carry tons of stuff!
> CONS:
> Hates Bethany – they ALWAYS row.
> Bit of an idiot.

'What the fu . . .' James muttered when he finished reading, only backing away from the last word when he remembered where he was sitting.

As Lauren turned red and shrank into her chair, Mac smiled. The document had clearly had precisely the humbling effect he'd intended.

'James, you can go back to your lessons,' Mac said. 'I'm obviously *not* impressed with your role in this affair and you can consider yourself officially warned. But you were forced into this by your sister and I think it is she and Bethany who deserve to be punished.'

James ought to have been relieved at getting off, but Lauren's list of pros and cons was so clinical that it left him feeling like he'd been punched in the head. He loved his sister more than anyone in the world, including Kerry, but at that moment it didn't seem like the feelings were mutual.

'It's not what it looks like, James!' Lauren yelled, getting out of her chair and twisting around as James skulked out of the office.

'Lauren Adams, *sit* down,' Mac snapped. 'I don't often get angry, but you two are pushing all the wrong buttons.'

Lauren felt queasy as she lowered herself into the chair. She'd never seen Mac this angry before, which was weird because she thought she'd been in much more serious trouble the time she'd hit Mr Large with a spade.

'I deal with all kinds of trouble on campus,' Mac roared. 'Kids get in fights, kids don't do their homework or get lippy in class. I can live with those things, because it's a normal part of growing up. But one thing I can't abide is bullying.

'We train you to manipulate people during undercover operations, but it is *absolutely* unacceptable to use those skills to make your fellow cherubs do things they don't want to. Bethany Parker, you *knew* Martin Newman had a crush on you and you made him all kinds of promises that you had no intention of keeping. Lauren stooped even lower: blackmailing her own brother into doing something that might have landed him in serious trouble.'

'That's not fair,' Lauren gasped. 'It wasn't bullying. All the stuff we did was to *help* Jake and the other trainees.'

'Well hoorah for you,' Mac said sarcastically. 'Your tactics might have been more subtle than shoving a kid up against a wall and threatening to thump them, but anything that involves forcing people to act against their will counts as bullying in my book.'

'I didn't even know she was blackmailing James,' Bethany interrupted.

Lauren turned sharply towards her best friend. 'You came up with most of the plan in the first place.'

Bethany raised her hands apologetically to Lauren. She hadn't meant to try shifting the blame, but that's how it had sounded.

'You know what I think, Lauren?' Mac said. 'You're one of our most capable agents, as you demonstrated in your planning and execution of last night's little escapade. You're also one of the youngest black shirts in the history of CHERUB. I don't for one second believe that you're a bad person at heart. But I *do* think that the success you've had over the past year has rather gone to your head. You've started getting too big for your boots.

'I'm giving both of you four hundred punishment laps around the athletics track. As you run, perhaps you can think about your casual disregard for our rules, for campus property and – far more importantly – the utterly dreadful way you've behaved towards James and Martin.

'I'll also be cancelling your next month's pocket money to pay for the damage to the barbed wire and I'll expect you both to write carefully considered apologies to your victims.'

The girls were gobsmacked by the four-hundred-lap punishment, their usually overactive jaws getting a well earned break as their mouths dropped open.

Then Mac smiled a little. 'You don't have to run it all at once, obviously. I'll give you three weeks to fit the laps in. Twenty laps works out at eight kilometres per day and you'll even get a day's rest in the middle.'

Lauren felt tears welling up in her eyes. The running was going to be tough, but she'd survived worse. What really worried her was the gaunt look on James' face as he steamed out of the office. It was like she'd ripped out his heart.

6. ADMISSION

320 laps later

Lauren could run eight kilometres easily, but doing it every day was entirely different. Without time to recover, aches and pains didn't heal and after four days the fifty-minute run became too much. CHERUB's athletics coach, Meryl Spencer, advised Lauren to split the laps into morning and evening sessions and take it slowly, by walking or jogging most of the way.

This made the laps manageable, but also meant they took a two-hour bite out of Lauren's day, which, like all cherubs', was tightly scheduled with lessons, homework, combat training and occasional mission training exercises.

On top of everything else, the lifts in the main building were closed for annual maintenance. Lauren and Bethany looked shattered as they rounded the sixth-floor landing. They'd both showered after their evening laps. Wet hair ran down their backs and they held carrier bags stuffed with damp towels and running kit.

'Here,' Lauren said, holding her bag out to Bethany. 'Dump

this in my room, will you? I've made up my mind, I'm gonna go see if James is in.'

'Don't,' Bethany said sharply. 'Let him stew for a while. He'll come running when he wants something out of you.'

'AAAARGHHH!' Lauren said, shaking her hands at the side of her head. 'Stop speaking like that, Bethany. It's you thinking like that what got us into trouble in the first place.'

'Thinking like what?' Bethany said indignantly.

'You always plan out how everyone is gonna react.' Lauren said. 'You've always got to think five steps ahead.'

'Fine. Give us your dirty washing,' Bethany tutted. 'Just don't blame me if you make everything worse.'

Part of being best friends was being able say stuff that you'd only dare to think about your other mates. Lauren and Bethany always had little digs at each other, but it never turned into a big row.

'Wish me luck?' Lauren grinned, as Bethany snatched the rustling bag.

'Yeah,' Bethany smiled back, 'but if our pocket money hadn't been confiscated, I'd bet you every penny that James'll blank you.'

'With friends like you . . .' Lauren said, tailing off as she started down the sixth-floor corridor towards her brother's room.

As Lauren closed on James' door, she realised it was going to be awkward and kind of hoped he wasn't in. She didn't do her usual distinctive knock, because she didn't want to get marching orders before making it through the door.

'What?' James asked aggressively, as he turned away from

the homework piled on his desk and saw his sister in the doorway.

Lauren felt sad as she edged into the room. 'You don't really hate me do you, James?'

It was a difficult question and James didn't want to answer it. 'I've got a massive Russian essay to write,' he said irritably. 'I don't have time for this now.'

Lauren had been preparing a speech in her head the whole time she'd been doing her evening laps, but now she was on the spot her mind was blank and all she could do was whine.

'I've said sorry like *fifty* times, James. I even bought you that game for your Playstation. What more do you want me to do?'

'I don't want anything from you. I told you to take the game back to the shop.'

Lauren had felt really bad about the whole blackmail thing ever since the meeting in Mac's office, but she was also slightly aggrieved that James hadn't forgiven her.

'It's not like you're so perfect yourself, you know,' Lauren said. 'You've dumped me in the shit enough times, you've broken my stuff, you've even *hit* me.'

'I know I've got a stupid temper,' James barked back. 'But I've *never* sat around a table with all my friends, plotting stuff out and telling everyone that you're an idiot.'

'I swear it wasn't like that,' Lauren said desperately. 'I know it looked cold written down on that sheet of paper, but all I was thinking about was helping Jake and Rat. I was just trying to make the plan work and writing stuff down as it came into my head. Bethany never saw it until you did, in Mac's office.'

'You didn't give a damn about my feelings, or getting me into trouble.'

'I got it *wrong*, James,' Lauren gasped, 'and I'm really, really sorry. I don't think I've ever been so sorry, or so wrong in my whole life. But I'm being punished: I'm totally knackered, my legs ache, my thighs are all chafed, and I've got massive blisters on my heels.'

James smiled fleetingly. Lauren hoped she'd talked her brother round, but after an instant she realised it was a sly smile, not a forgiving one.

'I know what your game is,' James said, wagging his finger knowingly. 'Kyle put you up to this, didn't he?'

Lauren was baffled. 'How the hell does Kyle come into this? He's only been back from his mission for a week and I haven't exactly had a lot of time for socialising lately. I passed him in the corridor one time and congratulated him on getting his black T-shirt, but that's it.'

'So, you don't know anything about the mission we're going on?' James said, clearly unconvinced. 'It's pure coincidence that you *happened* to come waltzing in here tonight, after me and Kyle had a mission briefing this afternoon?'

'James, I came in here to apologise again,' Lauren groaned. 'Bethany was right, I shouldn't have bothered. I mean, I miss talking and hanging out with you James, but if you don't believe a word I say, there's not much I can do.'

'I don't hate you,' James said. 'Just . . .'

James felt angry with himself for warming to Lauren's argument. He stood up and pointed to a spot of carpet, directly in front of himself.

'Get over here,' James said.

Lauren didn't know if she was going to get a hug, a slap, or what, but she stepped forward.

'You think you know people,' James said, laying his hands heavily on Lauren's shoulders. 'I *thought* I knew you.'

Lauren felt a shiver down her back as James scowled. He didn't so much look at her, but right through her. The intensity was a nasty reminder of how badly she'd hurt his feelings.

'Can you look me in the eyes and tell me that Kyle said nothing about our briefing?'

Lauren sounded a little scared. 'I don't know anything about any mission, James. What's going on? You're freaking me out.'

James realised he was acting weird and let go.

'Sorry,' he said, running a hand through his hair. 'It's a pretty hefty coincidence that's all. You'd better *not* be lying.'

Lauren slapped a hand against her side. 'How many times do you want me to say it?'

'Me and Kyle got called down to the mission preparation building by Zara Asker this afternoon,' James explained, finally deciding to trust his sister. 'It looks like we'll be going on a mission in a week or so, but we need a third person to cover all the angles. Someone younger, preferably a girl. You were the obvious choice, but I told Zara I wasn't having it.'

Lauren shook her head. 'Thanks a bunch.'

'Zara agreed that it was no good having us both on a mission if we weren't getting along. She asked me and Kyle to think of another girl about your age who could go instead. So I thought about Bethany, and Victoria, and Melanie, and

Chloe and that whole girlie crowd of yours . . . I kind of realised that I'd much rather be on a mission with you than with any of them.'

Lauren was flattered, but tried not to let it show.

'Kyle's been going all out to persuade me to make up with you,' James continued. 'That's why I was so paranoid when you turned up in my doorway.'

'Right,' Lauren said, twisting her leg awkwardly and looking down at the floor. 'So . . .'

'So, there's another briefing at eleven tomorrow. If you want to come on the mission with us, I guess that'd be OK.'

7. UNCOMFORTABLE

Next morning, Lauren and James bumped into each other as they headed towards mission preparation after second lesson. They spoke without really saying anything, carefully measuring every word so as not to open up wounds.

As usual, the state-of-the-art retina identification system that controlled access to mission preparation was out of order. A note pinned on the door explained a more primitive enforcement system:

> ANY KID WE FIND WHO DOESN'T
> BELONG IN HERE WILL BE MADE TO RUN
> AROUND THE ASSAULT COURSE UNTIL THEY PUKE!

Zara's spacious office was fifty metres down a gently curved corridor. She was in her mid-thirties, but seemed older, with a mumsy air even when sitting behind a desk that clearly belonged to someone important.

Sixteen-year-old Kyle Blueman slouched on a suede-covered sofa off to one side, with his boots propped on a glass-topped table. He was reading from a stack of vanilla-coloured folders that contained police surveillance reports. Kyle had always been on the small side, but a recent growth spurt, bleached hair and a dusting of facial hair meant he'd finally started to look something like his age.

'Ah-ha,' Zara said, smiling as James and Lauren stepped up to her desk. 'Have the terrible twosome made up?'

Before James could answer, a little shriek came up from the floor beside the desk. Zara's three-year-old son, Joshua, scrambled away from a spread of toys and stood in front of James, begging to be picked up.

'James, James, James,' the toddler gasped excitedly, as he got raised off the ground by his hero.

'You're getting *sooooo* big, I can hardly lift you up,' James lied.

'Sorry to inflict him on you, James,' Zara grinned. 'Our child minder buggered off to Corfu with her boyfriend without giving us any notice and Ewart's had to take Tiffany to the doctor's with a temperature.'

'Nightmare,' James laughed. 'Remind me never to have kids.'

Zara nodded. 'Whoever the new chairman turns out to be, I'm gonna be straight round their office demanding employee day-care.'

Little Joshua gave James a pleading look. 'Play with me?'

James didn't know what Zara had planned and looked uncertainly at her.

Zara put on her strict mummy voice. 'James can play with you for *ten* minutes, but then he's got to work.'

Joshua shook his head as James put him down. 'No! Till bedtime.'

'James *can't* play until bedtime,' Zara said. 'He's a big boy, he has things to do.'

James realised what a big boy he was as he sat on the carpet amidst Joshua's toys, feeling like a bit of an idiot.

Kyle grinned. 'You and Joshua make a cute pair.'

Lauren almost butted in with *They've got the same mental age*, but thought better of it when she remembered that James was still sore at her.

As James helped Joshua line up a row of toy cars for a race across the carpet, he looked up at Zara. 'So is Joshua coming on the mission with us?'

Zara looked extremely anxious as she answered. 'It was OK when he was a baby, but he can't come on missions now he's able to talk.'

James realised he'd mentioned the unmentionable when he looked around and saw Joshua's face starting to screw up.

'I want a holiday!' Joshua squealed. 'I want Mummy and James.'

Zara smiled diplomatically. 'Sweetheart, I won't be away for long. You'll be here with Daddy and Tiffany . . .'

But Joshua had slipped beyond reason. 'I want to go,' he screamed, as he kicked out at a toy car and erupted into a full tantrum.

James looked awkwardly at Zara. 'Sorry . . .'

Kyle gave James a thumbs-up sign and shouted over Joshua's racket, 'Way to stick your foot in it, dude.'

'WANNNAAAAA GO WITH MUMMMY AND JAAAAAAAAAMES!'

'Why don't you sit down nicely and play cars with me?' James asked hopefully.

'You not my friend any more,' Joshua wailed, as he rolled on to his back and started kicking his light-up trainers wildly in the air.

Kyle glanced at Lauren and summoned her with a sneaky finger.

'Some people might say your brother's a bit of an idiot,' he whispered.

Lauren tried really hard not to smirk. 'Don't make me laugh, Kyle,' she answered anxiously. 'I was out of order and I'm still walking on eggshells.'

Kyle reached under the stack of folders and handed Lauren a stapled document.

'Here, have a butcher's at our mission briefing,' he said. 'That'll wipe the smile off.'

CLASSIFIED MISSION BRIEFING
FOR KYLE BLUEMAN, JAMES ADAMS,
PLUS ONE OTHER (TBC)
THIS DOCUMENT IS PROTECTED WITH A RADIO
FREQUENCY IDENTIFICATION TAG
ANY ATTEMPT TO REMOVE IT FROM THE MISSION
PREPARATION BUILDING
WILL SET OFF AN ALARM
DO NOT PHOTOCOPY OR MAKE NOTES

MISSION BACKGROUND – ANIMAL LIBERATION
It's often said that Britain is a nation of animal lovers. The first animal rights campaigners were British and in 1824 Britain's parliament passed the world's first animal protection laws.

Mainstream animal protection groups have always stayed within the law, working closely with governments, farmers, pet owners and other groups involved with animals. But in the late 1960s a new wave of radical animal rights campaigners came into being. Calling themselves Animal Liberationists, they believed that all human exploitation of animals should be stopped.

The liberationists argued that every thinking being should be treated as an equal. They claimed that there were no grounds for harming any living creature, just because it seems less intelligent than a human.

Liberationists opposed eating meat and fish, dairy production, fur farming, leather production, the wool industry, circuses, zoos, wildlife parks and the use of animals in scientific experiments. Many liberationists even believed that keeping animals as pets was an unacceptable form of exploitation.

DIRECT ACTION

With few supporters and little money, some liberationists decided that the best way to help animals and get their radical points of view noticed was by taking non-violent direct action: organising raids and freeing animals from captivity.

Most of the early liberationists were university students and professors, so it was natural that their first actions were staged on university campuses, freeing animals that were being used for scientific experiments.

These first raids by a few dozen activists were an extraordinary success. The media loved telling stories of idealistic youngsters breaking into laboratories and freeing defenceless animals from cruel scientists. The activists took photographs of the mangled and disturbed animals they had rescued and the dreadful conditions in which they frequently lived.

Newspapers printed horrific photographs taken by activists during the raids. They showed animals that had been subjected to major brain operations without anaesthetic, or had had their eyes burned out in tests on the toxicity of household chemicals.

The public was shocked by its first glimpse into the unseen world of animal experimentation and the liberationists' campaign gained significant popular support.

Over the next few years, the number of liberationists taking part in direct action grew from single figures to several hundred. Hunt saboteurs disrupted fox hunts and hare coursing events, anti-fur campaigners released tens of thousands of animals from fur farms and launched advertising campaigns that made wearing animal fur socially unacceptable.

The publicity given to these early British liberationists inspired others around the world. By 1980 animal liberation was a global movement, with activist groups taking direct action throughout mainland Europe, Australia and North America.

TROUBLES
But after their early success, things became much tougher for animal liberationists.

While the British government introduced new controls on animal experimentation, it also passed laws that made it easier to send activists to prison and asked the police to create special task forces to crack down on the liberationists' illegal activities.

Hunters, scientists and fur farmers began to defend their livelihoods vigorously. Many laboratories installed hi-tech security systems that made breaking in as hard as cracking a bank vault.

The scientists also won back a lot of public sympathy by hiring public relations experts, who emphasised advances in medicine that would not have happened if new drugs and vaccines hadn't been tested on animals. Activists who broke into laboratories, vandalised equipment and released animals now frequently stood accused of wrecking valuable research that could have saved thousands of human lives.

But most importantly, the liberationist campaign lost its shock value. Media interest waned, as people who were horrified by their first sighting of pictures of animal experiments became blasé the fourth or fifth time they saw them. And while the public was sympathetic when liberationists campaigned against activities that most of them did not take part in – animal experiments, wearing fur and fox hunting – support fell dramatically when liberationists targeted more common activities such as eating meat, drinking milk, fishing and wearing leather.

Schism

These setbacks caused a crisis within the animal liberation movement. Many of the less committed activists buckled under police pressure and gave up the fight. Some were arrested and imprisoned for up to ten years on charges of theft, arson and criminal damage. Others became radicalised by the setbacks and decided that using violence was the only way forwards.

All of the early liberationists were against violence. Their argument was simple: humans and animals are equal. Therefore, violence to humans is just as unacceptable as violence towards the animals they were campaigning to protect.

But a new band of more radical liberationists put forward a different argument: if humans and animals are equal, then is it not right to kill or threaten one human in order to save the lives of many animals?

RYAN QUINN

Ryan Quinn was one of the first animal liberationists. Born in Belfast in 1952, Quinn refused to eat meat from the age of ten when his father's car hit and killed a sheep during a family outing.

Soon after becoming a student at Bristol University he took part in what many regard as the first large-scale liberationist raid, when sixty-eight rabbits were freed from a laboratory conducting electric shock experiments on their spinal cords.

Quinn was arrested, and while the police dropped charges for lack of evidence, he was one of twelve student liberationists expelled from the university.

A quiet figure, who was happier working in the background than making grand speeches, Quinn steadily got to know almost all of the hundred or so hardcore activists within the British animal liberation movement. He gained a reputation as an expert in planning sophisticated raids and was involved in setting up camps that trained hundreds of liberationist volunteers from all around the world.

ZEBRA 84

In September 1984, Ryan Quinn was released from prison after serving a three-month sentence for stealing videotapes of animal experiments while working undercover at a Royal Navy research laboratory. Quinn had used his time inside to consider the future of animal liberation and decided that its big problem was a lack of focus and organisation.

None of the early liberationist groups had a formal structure. They allowed anyone to set up and carry out an operation against whatever target they fancied. The trouble with this approach was that large organisations were rarely put under pressure and felt no serious effect beyond the damage caused by a single attack.

Quinn decided to set up a new group called Zebra 84 with a different method of operation. Ryan explained the meaning of the name in a television documentary made several years later:

'A zebra is a basically a striped horse, but you'll never see a man riding one because they're too aggressive. If you try climbing on a zebra's back, he'll turn around and sink his teeth into your arse. What's more, the zebra's jawbone has a locking mechanism, which means that once it sinks its teeth in you're not going anywhere unless you leave a piece of your arse behind in its mouth.'

Like the animal after which it was named, Quinn's new group was going to sink its teeth into one organisation at a time and not let go until it was destroyed.

Zebra 84's first targets were Scottish fur farms. Typically, Quinn and three or four associates would enter a farm's premises, free as many animals as they could and then vandalise or set fire to the building in which they'd been kept.

Over the following weeks, Zebra 84 activists would ruthlessly harass anyone who had anything to do with the targeted farm. Strictly non-violent tactics ranged from vandalising delivery vans, stealing post, supergluing locks, sabotaging water and electricity supplies and generally making life hell for the farm's owners and anyone who did business with them.

A farm or laboratory targeted by Zebra 84 was usually driven out of business in a matter of months, as other companies stopped delivering vital supplies and insurers refused to renew policies covering fire damage.

Over the next fifteen years, Zebra 84's controversial tactics made it the most notorious and effective animal liberation group in Britain. Despite the success of Quinn's tactics, he resisted the temptation to expand, always relying on a small band of loyal activists and never targeting more than one organisation at a time.

This elitist attitude enhanced the group's standing and Zebra 84 steadily gained a reputation as the special forces of the animal liberation movement.

QUINN BITES OFF MORE THAN HE CAN CHEW

2001 saw Zebra 84's biggest success. Following twenty arson attacks, dozens of student marches and persistent vandalism of construction equipment – including the toppling of a forty-metre-high crane – Quinn's group successfully halted the construction of a £17 million animal experimentation lab being built by one of Britain's most prestigious universities with funding sourced from cancer charities and the Ministry of Defence.

Puffed up from this success, Quinn decided that Zebra's next target would be Malarek Research. With 1,100 employees at animal laboratories in Britain, Canada and the United States, Malarek is responsible for up to 10 per cent of all the animal experiments conducted in the world each year, including all of the experiments done by the world's two largest manufacturers of consumer products (washing powders, shaving foam, hair dyes, etc) and many experiments done by the world's biggest drug companies. Fourteen million animals per year die in its labs.

Quinn knew the campaign against Malarek would be the longest and most difficult of his life. But his small group did not have the resources to defeat a large multinational company, so he used his legendary status within the animal rights movement to form alliances with other liberationist groups in every country where Malarek does business.

THE STING

More than a dozen groups came together to form the Zebra Alliance. Unfortunately for Quinn, one of the American groups he'd contacted had been infiltrated by the FBI. Video recordings made by undercover FBI agents in which Quinn told an anecdote about toppling the crane were sent to the British authorities.

Just weeks into the Zebra Alliance campaign, Quinn was arrested and charged with arson, conspiracy to commit a terrorist act and possession of illegal explosives. He faced life imprisonment, but after a six-week jury trial, Quinn was only found guilty on a single charge of arson. The judge sentenced him to six years in prison.

THE AFM

Many believed that the groups aligned against Malarek would crumble without Quinn's leadership. While the American and Canadian campaign efforts were thoroughly infiltrated by the FBI and amounted to little more than a few heavily policed protest marches, the campaign against Malarek's UK experimentation facility had a significant effect on its operations.

Many suppliers withdrew services to the company after being harassed. Customers and employees were intimidated by threats of property destruction and the company was unable to renew insurance cover on its buildings.

But eighteen months into Quinn's prison sentence, the Zebra Alliance appeared to have hit a brick wall. Malarek UK had been granted special insurance cover by the British government and its parent company had just announced increased profits.

Two days after the profits were announced, Malarek's UK chairman, Fred Gibbons, was lying in bed when four masked women burst into his bedroom. The women grabbed Gibbons and beat him severely with aluminium baseball bats.

Gibbons suffered sixteen broken bones, including a fractured skull. His wife was also badly beaten as she tried to fend off the attackers with a golf club.

The Zebra Alliance was quick to distance itself from this attack. Quinn emphasised that the Alliance was a non-violent coalition and condemned the assault on Gibbons. A note left behind at the scene of the attack left a stark warning:

The Animal Freedom Militia (AFM)
Cordially invites Mr Frederick Gibbons
To stop working for Malarek Research
Because next time we'll kill you!
P.S. We know where your children live too!

Quinn Reaches Out

Fred Gibbons spent two months recovering in hospital and resigned from Malarek Research on health grounds, but the Animal Freedom Militia was only beginning its campaign.

Over the following months there were eleven more violent attacks on Malarek employees in the Avon area. A courier who made a delivery to the site had his home set on fire and a senior employee of a merchant bank that lent money to Malarek was blinded after acid was thrown in his face.

Meanwhile, Ryan Quinn was stuck in prison, watching the non-violent, high-pressure strategy he'd pioneered with Zebra 84 being undermined by ultra-extremists. Quinn's first chance for parole was coming up and he believed there were links between more extreme members of the Zebra Alliance and the Animal Freedom Militia.

Quinn wanted the AFM destroyed before it permanently tarnished the reputation of all animal liberation groups, but he was powerless while he rotted in prison. Quinn put out feelers to a contact within the intelligence service and made her an offer: if he was granted parole and released from prison, Quinn would help the intelligence services to infiltrate the Zebra Alliance and try to unearth the AFM suspects from within.

Quinn's only condition was that MI5 destroy all evidence relating to acts of sabotage carried out by members of the Zebra Alliance who opposed violence.

The offer of cooperation was a huge surprise and the security services were keen to pursue it, but the FBI sting operation that had infiltrated numerous American liberationist groups was still fresh in everyone's minds, and members of the Zebra Alliance were naturally going to be very suspicious of any newcomers. It was thought that, even with Quinn's assistance, it would be virtually impossible for an adult to infiltrate the Zebra Alliance and uncover members with links to the AFM.

Senior officials realised that cherubs would be the only intelligence agents who might stand a chance of successfully unearthing members of the Animal Freedom Militia.

THE CHERUB MISSION
In the four months since Ryan Quinn agreed to cooperate with the intelligence services, he has been visited by Zara Asker on a regular basis. She has been posing as Zara Wilson, an old schoolfriend who got back in touch with Quinn when she

learned that he was being held in a prison close to her home.

As soon as Quinn leaves prison, he will announce that he has fallen in love with Zara and is getting engaged. The couple will move into the village of Corbyn Copse, less than a mile from the Malarek Research facility, along with three CHERUB agents who will be posing as Zara Wilson's children from her previous marriage.

Kyle Blueman will play the role of Kyle Wilson. His age will be advanced by six months to seventeen so that he can carry a driving licence. James Adams will fill the role of James Wilson, a Year Nine pupil. The third member of the Wilson family will probably be younger and female, preferably in Year Seven or Eight.

In order to fit in with any animal rights activists they encounter, the cherubs will have to adhere to a vegan lifestyle. This means not eating meat, fish or dairy products, or wearing garments made from animal-based materials such as wool or leather.

The children will attend the local comprehensive school, while attempting to involve themselves with the Zebra Alliance and unearth information about the Animal Freedom Militia.

THE CHERUB ETHICS COMMITTEE UNANIMOUSLY ACCEPTED THIS MISSION BRIEFING. ALL MISSION CANDIDATES SHOULD CAREFULLY CONSIDER THE FOLLOWING FACTORS:

(1) This mission has been classified MEDIUM RISK. Although the AFM is not a top-tier terrorist group like Help Earth, they do have a reputation for infighting and violence. Any suspected AFM members should be treated with extreme caution.

(2) Agents are likely to be confronted with graphic images of animal experimentation in laboratory and factory farm environments. Agents who are squeamish may prefer not to be involved with this mission.

8. INTRODUCTIONS

The following Sunday, James, Kyle, Lauren and Zara drove to Cambridgeshire to meet Ryan Quinn. He'd kept his nose clean for three and a half years, earning himself the right to spend the last four months of his sentence in a minimum security prison.

It was a sunny afternoon as Zara drove up to a striped barrier in a small BMW. She waved visiting papers out of her window at a tubby prison officer stepping out of his kiosk.

'Shan't be seeing you again,' he said to Zara, as he gave the papers a cursory glance. 'Mr Quinn's heading out next week isn't he?'

'I certainly hope so,' Zara nodded. 'We're supposed to be getting married.'

'Oh, well done,' the guard smiled. 'Whose are all the kids?'

'All mine.'

The guard held his gut and boomed with laughter as he squinted through the back window at Lauren and James. 'A few weeks living with that lot and he'll probably be begging us to let him back in here.'

Lauren smiled at the guard, but her expression changed once Zara had driven them through the gate and out of the guard's earshot. 'There he goes,' she said caustically, 'the funniest man in the world.'

Kyle burst out laughing. 'Who rattled your cage?'

'I can't stand men who talk down at you like you're a five-year-old,' Lauren tutted.

They cruised over speed bumps towards the car park, passing flowerbeds and a couple of bare-chested inmates pushing Flymos over the grass.

'Call this a prison?' James carped, as he stepped out of the car and studied the lines of magnolia-painted dormitories where the inmates slept. 'Looks more like a holiday camp to me.'

Zara led the way past the lines of cars towards the visiting block. It was a single storey building and the mixture of plastic stacking chairs and prisoners' artwork on the walls reminded James of the classrooms at his old primary school.

Because it was a nice day, most inmates had taken their visitors outdoors to sit in the sun. The only company for the lonely-looking attendant was a couple snogging madly in a dim corner.

Ryan Quinn had been allocated one of the private rooms where inmates met their solicitors. Zara led the kids in and grabbed a seat at the table. There were only three chairs, so James and Kyle leant against the wall.

James thought Quinn looked more like a drama teacher, or someone who worked for the council, than a criminal. He wore naff looking plastic sandals, drainpipe jeans and a stonewashed rugby shirt that came straight out of the 1980s.

He was the type who must have been skinny in his prime, but middle age had granted him a gut and great tufts of hair that bristled out of each nostril when he exhaled.

'So this is the government's secret weapon,' Ryan said, smiling wryly at the kids as he spoke in his heavy Belfast accent. 'The most outrageous example of state fascism I've ever encountered, all logoed up for the benefit of Nike, Metallica and Arsenal Football Club.'

'Nice to meet you too,' Kyle said, leaning forward to shake Ryan's hand. 'That was very cutting. I do what I can to keep the multinationals grinding the jackboot of oppression down on the developing world, though I've actually got a bit of a sideline as a gay liberal.'

Quinn was surprised by Kyle's knowing response and his startled expression made Zara laugh.

'One of the reasons cherubs do so well, Ryan, is that people like you underestimate them,' she grinned. 'Kyle plans to study Law at Cambridge when he leaves CHERUB. James just aced his maths A-level four years early, after studying for less than ten months. Lauren is a second dan Karate black belt, she's practically fluent in Russian and Spanish and last year she almost killed a man four times her size with a hotel Biro. All three have received advanced espionage training and their capabilities are in line with adult special forces.'

'Or a Zebra eighty-four training camp,' Kyle smirked.

Ryan cracked up laughing. 'You've done your research, young Kyle. Maybe when you're too old for CHERUB, you can come over and work for the good guys?'

James nodded. 'Yeah, you've got a lot in common with

each other. I mean, vegetarians and homosexuals, it's all the same kind of thing isn't it?'

James only opened his mouth to prove he was paying attention, but regretted it as soon as he saw everyone turn and scowl at him.

'James, why don't you go dig a great big hole and jump in it?' Kyle asked.

'I was just . . . Jesus, Kyle, there's no need to get all touchy.'

Kyle tutted. 'Here's a tip, James: from now on, have a go at using your brain *before* you open your mouth.'

'Cool it you two,' Zara interrupted stiffly, as she burrowed into her handbag and pulled out a purse. 'I'm sure our young ambassador for political correctness didn't actually mean it. James, there's some vending machines out in the hallway. Take my change and sort out what everyone wants to eat and drink.'

There was a queue at the machine that dispensed depressingly small cups of instant coffee, so it was nearly ten minutes before James came back and plonked a tray of drinks, crisps and Jaffa Cakes on the table. Meantime, Kyle had been out into the hallway and grabbed a couple of extra chairs.

As James sat down, Lauren opened up a packet of crisps. But as she dipped her hand in, Ryan snatched the bag out of her hand and began reading from the label.

'Tyler's Thick-sliced Tasty Chicken Flavour. Ingredients: potatoes, vegetable oil, chicken stock powder, monosodium glutamate, colour, salt.'

Ryan leaned across the table and stared intensely at Lauren. 'Have you ever seen the inside of a chicken farm?'

Lauren shook her head.

'The birds are stacked in mesh cages, eight or ten levels high, with ten or twelve birds crammed into each tiny cage. Chickens get extremely frustrated being huddled together like that, so the farmers cut their beaks off as soon as they're born to stop them pecking each other.

'Unfortunately, the beak isn't dead tissue like a horse's hoof, it contains hundreds of thousands of nerve endings and it feels about as painful as having your nose chopped off without being given any anaesthetic.

'After six weeks crammed inside mesh cages, without ever standing on a blade of grass, or seeing a glimmer of sunlight, the birds are ready for slaughter. This whole time they've been crapping through the mesh down on to the birds below them. Right at the bottom, the sticky white chicken shit is so deep that some birds' feet are torn out of their sockets as they're pulled out of it for the ride to the slaughterhouse.

'Once they arrive, the chickens are hooked upside down on to a conveyor belt. A rotating blade is *supposed* to slit the chicken's throat. But chickens have a tendency to wriggle and the knife misses every seventh or eighth bird. Now, you might think that not getting your throat cut is a lucky break, but it's not. Because all the dangling, bloody, chickens keep rolling along until they're lowered down into a tank of boiling water to loosen off their feathers. And instead of having its throat cut, the poor bird gets boiled alive.'

Ryan pushed the *Tasty Chicken* crisps back across the table towards Lauren. 'Tuck in,' he grinned.

Lauren stared into the packet the way she might have

stared if she'd found a bloody axe in her lap. 'Well . . .' she said uncertainly.

'I'm in here because I believe that exploiting animals is wrong,' Ryan continued forcefully. 'I'll probably catch a long sentence some time and end up dying in prison. I'll never own a car or have a nice house. I'll never have kids and I doubt there'll be anyone at my funeral besides the priest and the undertaker. But, if I've made a few girls like you think about what they put in their mouths and persuade them to stop eating meat and wearing bits of dead animals on their feet, maybe it will have been worth it, eh?'

James saw that Lauren had been spooked by the lanky Irishman and it riled up his instinct to defend his little sister. 'Cut it out, eh? She's only eleven.'

Lauren shot a *don't patronise me* glance at her brother, then looked up at Ryan and smiled respectfully at him. 'It's really cool that you fight for stuff you believe in so strongly. I know it's kind of gross eating animals. We can't eat meat on the mission anyway, so I'll stop now and see how it goes.'

Ryan smiled triumphantly. 'And maybe you'll not be in any hurry to start again when your mission's over?'

Lauren shrugged. 'Maybe. There's tons of veggie girls on campus, actually.'

Zara cleared her throat. 'Anyhow Ryan,' she interrupted, 'you'll have plenty of time to indoctrinate this lot over the coming weeks. Right now, we desperately need to discuss details: names, dates, faces, and pick-up times. You're out of here in less than a week and there's a lot of things to be done to get our little show on the road.'

James reached in front of Zara and grabbed Lauren's crisps. 'Seeing as you're not eating them.'

Zara swatted James' arm with the back of her hand. Unfortunately one of her rings rapped painfully against his knuckles.

'Bloody hell,' James howled.

Lauren giggled. 'Serves you right.'

'I didn't mean to hurt you, James,' Zara said brusquely. 'But can't you at least *try* showing a little sensitivity towards other people's feelings?'

9. CORBYN

Five days later, Zara and the kids got up early and packed all their stuff into a seven-seat people carrier. A tearful Joshua had to be pacified with the promise of presents before they set off towards Bristol in the south west of England.

Ten miles shy of the city itself, the sat-nav told Zara to pull off the motorway at the next junction and take the second exit from the roundabout. After drifting past a line of superstores and a housing estate that had spawned around the motorway, the land opened out into fields, with tall hedgerows blocking in the sides of the twisting A-road.

Kyle wound down his window to feel the benefit of the country air, only to close it seconds later as the car filled with a pungent blast of manure.

'Phew,' Lauren gasped, as she wafted her hand in front of her face. 'My eyes are watering. That's worse than having to use the bog after James.'

'I think,' Zara said, as she ignored the sat-nav's instruction to take a left, 'if we take the next road in, we'll still reach the village, but we'll get a glimpse of the Malarek laboratory on the way.'

'It won't take much longer will it?' James asked. 'I'm busting for a piss.'

'Two or three minutes,' Zara said. 'I can pull over if you're really desperate.'

James shook his head. 'It'll hold for another ten minutes.'

'*Take the first safe opportunity and make a U-turn*,' the sat-nav said in its politely synthesised voice.

Zara leaned across the dashboard and switched the navigation screen off. She'd visited the area while preparing for the mission and knew her way around.

'This is the one,' she said, as she slowed up for a tight turn. The direction sign pointed towards the village of *Corbyn Copse, ½ mile*, but as soon as they were around the bend a very uncountrylike sight came into view.

All the hedges had been replaced by tall concrete sections, topped with barbed wire and video cameras. Reflective yellow signs had been placed along the roadside by Avon police: *No Stopping or Loitering, 10MPH SLOW* and *Drivers entering Malarek Research premises lock windows and doors NOW*.

Zara obeyed the order to slow down, giving the kids a chance to view the carnage along the grass verge: tonnes of litter and sodden placards abandoned by protestors, who'd also daubed thousands of slogans on the concrete walls.

As the car rounded a slight bend and approached the entrance, the road turned into abstract art, thickly layered with streaks of red, blue and yellow paint that protestors had aimed at vehicles entering or leaving the research facility.

James recognised the location from an archived Sky News report he'd watched in Zara's office. It had shown a battle between police, Malarek security guards and more than a hundred protestors, chanting, hurling objects at cars and trying to batter down the front gates. A few protesters did manage to force their way inside the laboratory compound and smashed more than a hundred windows before they were arrested.

But there wasn't much action on this particular Friday lunchtime. The scene outside the corrugated metal gate was subdued. Two police officers in yellow bibs stood guard and more sat around in a Portacabin across the road.

The protest was confined to an area marked out with crowd barriers fifty metres from the entrance. It consisted of three middle-aged women and an elderly man. They sat in deck chairs, eating sandwiches and sharing a flask of coffee, while their placards rested against the wall behind them. A banner painted on bed sheets had been tied to the police's metal barriers: *HOOT TO STOP THE SUFFERING!*

These protestors were some of the people Zara and the kids would be getting to know over the coming weeks, so she waved out of her window and gave a good blast on the horn. The four protestors smiled and waved back.

Zara picked up speed once they were past the entrance and another few hundred metres brought them to a miniature roundabout, with the white cottages at the edge of Corbyn Copse facing towards them.

As they pulled up, a Land Rover that had been following close behind cut on to the opposite carriageway and squealed to an aggressive halt alongside them. The driver looked twentyish and wore dirty blue overalls, suggesting a morning spent working on one of the surrounding farms.

'Why don't you *piss* off back where you came from?' he shouted.

Zara was startled by the outburst. 'Pardon me?'

'You heard,' he shouted. 'Bloody grockles, coming up here to gawp. You've seen it now, so turn around and sling your hook.'

James opened the electric window beside his head and gave the young driver a two-fingered salute as he sped off, 'Up yours, you hick.'

'What was that in aid of?' Lauren asked.

Zara explained as she cut over the centre of the roundabout, turning right into the village. 'The locals don't like protestors. I mean, living out here in the middle of nowhere and suddenly finding that you've got hundreds of demonstrators and the TV news turning up on your doorstep twice a week.'

The car headed up a steep hill, through a main street that consisted of a pub set in a large garden and a strip of shops. Except for a convenience store on the corner, the shops had all been converted into homes.

Beyond Main Street lay two modern housing developments where most villagers actually lived, but Zara pulled on to the driveway of a detached cottage without leaving what the locals called the Old Village.

The tiny front garden was overgrown and the exterior was shabby, but it would only have taken some pruning and a lick of paint to make it fit the picture-postcard image of an English cottage.

'Man, what a hole,' James said as he stepped through the front door and caught a lungful of musty air, before bolting upstairs to find the toilet.

'Must have been built by hobbits,' Kyle said, lowering his head to avoid ceiling rafters, as he dumped his suitcase on the carpeted floor of the pokey living-room.

'The owner wasn't keen on renting to a family with kids,' Zara said. 'We ended up buying her out, because this location is *just* perfect. You can cut through the fields at the back and be at Malarek's front gate within five minutes and some of the protestors drink in the pub down the road. The downside is that we've only got three bedrooms.'

'Bags not sharing,' Kyle and Lauren both shouted, as James came back from the toilet with wet hands.

'No towel,' he explained, as he wiped them on his tracksuit bottoms.

'Two of us have got to share,' Kyle said.

'Great,' James said sourly. He realised he had no chance of getting a room to himself because he could share with his sister or he could share with another boy, but Lauren and Kyle couldn't share with each other.

'I don't know what you lot are complaining about,' Zara said. 'I've got to share a bed with Ryan Quinn.'

James burst out laughing. 'And he's gonna be *horny* after three years in prison.'

'*Not* funny, James,' Zara said stiffly. 'I've had a king-size bed put in that room and I've made it clear to Ryan that if so much as a finger crosses the middle I'll have his nuts in a jamjar.'

10. RELEASE

They flipped a coin and for the third time in his life James ended up sharing a bedroom with Kyle. Another flip earned Kyle the top bunk. It wasn't the end of the world, but James was used to the comfy double bed in his room on campus and hated having his feet dangling over the sides and the way the springs creaked whenever Kyle changed position. At least it was better than sharing with Lauren, who snored like a pig.

It was Saturday morning. James was still buried under the covers at ten o'clock when he got woken up by Kyle jumping off his bunk and heading down the hall to take a shower. Deciding it was time to haul himself up, James threw off his duvet and gave himself a good scratch as he pottered across to the window in his boxers. He pulled back the curtain.

'Holy crap . . .' James spluttered, as he looked down and saw half a dozen people standing on the tiny square of lawn at the front of the house. They all held polystyrene cups and a few had cameras strung around their necks.

'Kyle, get out here,' James yelled.

'What?' Kyle yelled back. 'I'm getting in the shower.'

James leaned out into the hallway. 'Screw that Kyle, there's millions of journalists standing on our front lawn. What are we supposed to do?'

Wearing a hand towel around his waist and covered in beads of water, Kyle disbelievingly hopped up to the leaded window and peeked between the curtains.

'Someone must have told them Ryan's coming out today.'

'Well *duh*,' James said. 'What are we gonna do about it?'

'Don't panic,' Kyle answered. 'I've been on missions where the press are involved before.'

'Aren't we supposed to keep our faces out of the media though?' James asked. 'I mean, what was the name of that kid who got his face on the front page of all the papers? His CHERUB career was burned. There was no way they could send him undercover after that.'

Kyle nodded. 'Jacob Rich, but that was years before my time. Apparently, he was working on some threat to blow up one of the young royals. The fourteen-year-old princess falls off her horse in front of two hundred photographers and the idiot runs across to pick her up off the ground. She pecks him on the cheek as a thank you, next day his face is on the front page of all the papers claiming that he's her first love.'

'So what if that happens to us?'

'Wear a baseball cap and point your head down. If anyone's taking pictures stay in the background. But I wouldn't sweat it: Quinn's a long way short of royalty. He'll be lucky if he can get his mug on page sixteen.'

'Guess you're right,' James nodded. 'Have you seen Lauren around?'

Kyle shook his head. 'She must have gone into Bristol with Zara. They're meeting Ryan at the station.'

'You fancy a fry-up?' James asked.

Kyle nodded. 'We haven't got any eggs, but I think there's veggie sausages and tofu in the fridge.'

'*Bloody* hell,' James moaned, screwing up his face in disgust. 'I can't hack this vegetarian muck.'

'You know, someone like you, who's a bit on the porky side, would probably benefit from being a veggie. Besides, you scoffed enough of Zara's vegetable lasagne last night.'

James shrugged. 'Yeah, Zara's cooking's really improved since we were in Luton. But it still could have done with a garnish, like a nice twelve-ounce steak or something.'

*

Kyle cooked a late breakfast of veggie sausages, mushrooms and fried bread, while James took his shower. The boys were mopping their plates when Zara pulled up, blasting her horn to clear the reporters off the driveway.

As Lauren and Zara moved furtively around the far side of the car and grabbed a box of books and a large sports bag out of the back, Ryan Quinn emerged triumphantly through the sliding door on the passenger side. He raised both arms and gave victory signs; an exuberant gesture that was rewarded with a salute from half a dozen flashguns.

A haggard-looking reporter stuck a tape recorder in his face. 'Ryan, are you happy to be out of prison?'

'Very happy indeed,' Ryan said with a slight shake of the head, indicating that he thought it was a stupid question.

'In the light of Malarek's robust financial statement to the

American stock markets last month, do you really think that the Zebra Alliance campaign can be successful?'

'Absolutely.'

A female journalist took up the questioning. 'Does your coming straight out of prison and moving into Corbyn Copse mean that you want to be right back at the heart of the campaign?'

Ryan nodded. 'I hope my presence will re-energise the campaign.'

'As leader of the Zebra Alliance?'

This question knocked Ryan out of his exuberant stride. 'Well . . .' he mumbled uncertainly. 'The campaign has been ably managed by others while I was detained at Her Majesty's hostelry. I'll be meeting with the Alliance committee over the coming days, with a view to deciding my future role. Now I'm going inside for lunch, but I'll be visiting the protest site later and I hope you'll all be there to see it happen.'

'One last question,' the female journalist continued. 'What are your feelings on the activities of the Animal Freedom Militia?'

'I condemn all acts of violence towards any species, including humans.'

'Do you think the AFM has damaged your campaign?'

'If there's been any setback it will be a short-term one. A hundred years ago, most people believed that it was right for a father or teacher to beat a child who misbehaved. A hundred years from now, I believe that people will feel equally repulsed about the idea of enslaving, torturing and brutally killing animals for food, clothing or scientific experiments.'

Quinn had a childish grin across his face as he stepped into the hallway and pushed open the front door.

'Hello boys,' he said, looking at James and Kyle. 'It sure feels good being back in the heart of things.'

*

Despite Ryan's plea for the journalists to stay, they'd got the photo and quotes they'd come for and had no intention of spending any more time than they had to hanging around Corbyn Copse.

'Expected nowt else,' Ryan said bitterly, as he peered through the living-room nets at the deserted driveway. 'The lazy buggers, can't even hang around an extra half hour.'

'We should still head up to the protest site,' Zara said. 'I called my contact with the local cops. There's always a fair crowd up there on the weekends and I want the kids getting stuck in amongst the protestors as soon as possible.'

'Sure we're going up there,' Ryan nodded as he pushed home the last piece of a sandwich Lauren had made for him. 'I've already arranged to meet Madeline Laing.'

'She's the one who's running the Alliance now, isn't she?' Lauren asked.

Ryan nodded. 'Young, fiery and utterly bloody hopeless.'

The kids had read a ton of flattering press reports on Laing and were surprised to hear that Ryan held her in contempt.

'I didn't realise you had a problem with her,' Zara said.

'Nice hair, looks good in a photograph,' Ryan sneered. 'That's why the press is in love with her. But she doesn't understand how to focus a campaign, or keep the momentum going. I've spoken to a few people and it looks like we'll have to go root and branch and rebuild this whole fight against Malarek from scratch.'

'You've got to get back on the Zebra Alliance committee before you can take over,' Kyle reminded him.

Ryan wagged his finger confidently. 'Don't you worry, laddie. I was playing politics when you weren't even a glint in your mother's eye. I'll be back running the show before you know it.'

As Ryan said this, he grabbed his army surplus jacket off the sofa and headed for the front door. 'Are yous all coming or not?' he asked excitedly.

The shortcut to the Malarek laboratory took Ryan, Zara and the three youngsters across a field of long grass. They crossed the deserted road near the roundabout on the edge of the village, then walked a couple of hundred metres along the verge beside the graffiti-strewn wall. Along the way they passed a gang of protestors' little kids chasing around and screaming at each other.

The group behind the police barriers was more impressive than it had been the previous afternoon, but it was still barely thirty strong.

Dressed in smart black leggings and sporting a figure to die for, Madeline Laing stood out amidst the drab bodies in walking boots and fleeces.

'Hello there,' Quinn said brightly.

A weak round of applause broke out when the protestors realised that Ryan Quinn was on the scene. Madeline and Ryan exchanged a brief hug and cooed as they kissed on opposite cheeks.

'Still going strong,' Ryan grinned. 'I'm told you've been doing a *fantastic* job.'

Madeline was flattered by the lie. 'It's been a tough few years,' she smiled, 'but we're still fighting. And I see you've come out to a ready-made family.'

While Ryan, Zara and Madeline exchanged pleasantries, James, Kyle and Lauren's espionage training kicked in. They didn't expect a member of the Animal Freedom Militia to leap out and announce themselves from the gaggle of protestors and their bored kids, but this was the perfect time and place to start chumming up with the Zebra Alliance activists.

11. HELPER

Sunday always drew the largest number of protestors to the barricades around Malarek Research, and the combo of fine weather and articles about Ryan Quinn in the morning papers had brought the crowd up to more than a hundred. Zara wanted the kids in the centre of the action, but kept out of the way herself because a new adult – even one with three kids – would be treated with suspicion.

Lauren played the role of a helpful and slightly overexcited kid. She wasn't naturally the keen type, but running errands was a great way of putting names to faces. It was two in the afternoon and she'd spent most of the day going back and forth between the protest site and the cottage. Her many good deeds included refilling Thermos flasks with tea and coffee, donating a packet of tissues to a man suffering from hayfever and buying sticky tape and a stapler in the village shop to help fix a broken placard.

'You're a godsend,' a chubby woman in a lumberjack shirt said, as Lauren held out two vegetable pasties she'd microwaved back at the house.

'Be careful, they're probably pretty hot in the middle.'

The woman smiled down at her. 'Thank you *very* much for doing that.'

'That's OK.' Lauren smiled back brightly.

But her smile dimmed as she turned away. Lauren was supposed to be on the lookout for the Zebra Alliance's hardcore members, but she'd realised that these weekend warriors with their wellies and 4×4s parked up on the grass verges of the surrounding fields were about as far from hardcore as you got. This crowd opposed animal experimentation, but didn't have a clue about the liberationist ideas of people like Ryan Quinn. She'd even seen a couple of them tucking into ham sandwiches and Scotch eggs.

The trouble was, although Lauren had become increasingly convinced that she was wasting her time, she wasn't sure what else to do. In the end she decided to see how the boys were getting on.

'You haven't seen my brothers around have you?' Lauren asked, interrupting the woman she'd heated the pasties for, who was now having a conversation with a bearded man about the nightmare she was having getting her new kitchen fitted.

The woman sounded rather irritated. 'Yes, *thank you* darling, it's delicious.'

Lauren realised that the woman was actually saying something different. She was saying, *The grown-ups are having a conversation now, could you please go away*, which made her feel like she was a millimetre tall.

'I *asked* if you'd seen my brothers,' Lauren said, obviously narked.

'Oh,' the woman said, finally turning away from her

friend. 'No I haven't, but you could try the field across the road. A lot of the teenagers hang around over there.'

'Cheers,' Lauren said half heartedly. 'I'll go look.'

She checked there was no traffic – there almost never was around here – before springing athletically over the metal barrier and crouching through a gap in the hedge on the opposite side of the road.

The sunlit field was waist-high with bright yellow rapeseed plants whose pollen tickled the inside of Lauren's nose. She couldn't see bodies, but noticed cigarette smoke rising out of a fallow area fifty metres away.

A dozen sunbathing teens came into view as she got near the long grass. They were mostly sixteen to eighteen, plus a couple of student types who might have reached twenty.

James was at least a year younger than anyone else, but that hadn't stopped him enjoying himself. He lay in the grass, bare-chested, with his trainers off and a polo shirt rolled under his head as a pillow. His female companion looked about a year older. She was a chunky thing with enormous boobs who sat on her haunches, stripping the yellow petals off the rapeseed plants and grinning as she sprinkled them over James' head.

'Hey,' James said, sitting up with a start and guiltily flicking the bright yellow dandruff out of his hair. 'This is Robyn. Robyn, this is my sister Lauren.'

The way James flirted with anything even vaguely female and conveniently forgot about his girlfriend stuck in Lauren's throat. But after the whole blackmail thing, she was on weak ground and knew she'd start a massive row if she passed comment.

Lauren consoled herself with the knowledge that Kerry wasn't stupid: sooner or later she'd find out what James got up to behind her back and reward him with the punch in the mouth he so richly deserved.

'What's occurring?' Lauren asked.

James grinned at Robyn, then shrugged. 'Hanging out, you know . . .'

'Is Kyle around?'

'Over there,' James pointed, 'sitting behind the two rugby shirts.'

Lauren glanced at the two chunky lads blocking her view of Kyle. The threesome was having an animated conversation. 'Those dudes are *fit*,' she grinned.

Robyn nodded as she made eye contact with Lauren for the first time. 'Rugby players are *totally* fine. I don't know their names, but they're here quite a bit and I wouldn't mind finding out.'

'I've played tons of rugby,' James lied, put out by the way Robyn's attention had drifted towards the two older teens.

Lauren wanted to take James down a peg and call him a liar, but you always have to invent some elements of your fictional background on the fly and one absolute rule of working undercover is never to contradict a fellow agent in case you mess up their story.

'You are muscly, James,' Robyn purred, as she sprinkled more yellow petals over his head.

If James hadn't snogged Robyn already it was probably only a matter of time and Lauren reckoned she'd spew if she had to witness that. She thought about going over to Kyle, but his new friends were much older and she reckoned her presence would make things awkward.

'Doesn't look like much is going on,' Lauren said, tilting her head back and letting the sun warm her face. 'I'm gonna wander back up to the cottage and watch TV or something.'

'I saw you making sandwiches earlier,' James said. 'Don't suppose there's any chance of fetching one down here for us is there?'

'You're right, there isn't,' Lauren said sourly. 'Later, dudes.'

She felt a bit down as she turned tail and started the gentle stroll towards home. It seemed James and Kyle had made genuine connections with people, while all she'd done was aggravate the blisters on her feet.

*

Kyle reckoned he was on to something with Tom and Viv Carter. The brothers were seventeen and nineteen, dark hair, plenty of stubble and built like brick shithouses. They looked and spoke like a couple of loutish public schoolboys, but you didn't have to scratch far below the surface to get a far more eccentric picture.

He'd literally bumped into the pair an hour earlier as they clambered out of a rusty MGB sports car near the village pub. They were immediately recognised as protestors and heckled by a bunch of locals drinking in the beer garden. Viv's response was to bend over, pull down the back of his shorts and repeatedly slap his hairy arse. Kyle's laughter broke the ice and by the time they'd reached the protest site down the hill, their conversation was flowing.

Or at least, conversation with Viv was in full flow. Tom was the sensible brother, seventeen years old; he'd just taken his A-levels at a Bristol sixth-form college. He dressed and acted conventionally and didn't say much, although when he did it was usually something worth listening to. Viv was the total opposite, a student at Avon University with a blond streak in his hair and a pierced tongue. His mannerisms were over the top and he loved saying stuff to shock people.

As the three lads sat in the grass surrounded by rapeseed, Kyle mixed a few probing questions amongst Viv's ramblings, which bounced hysterically from Scott Walker CDs, to Barcelona, to a story about a Green Day concert where he'd ended up slipping into a urinal.

Kyle needed to know where the Carter brothers stood on animal liberation and found out that they were on the bitter edge. Both brothers reckoned it was fine to kill someone if it saved lots of animals, though Tom seemed less than convinced that it was a good idea to go round attacking employees of Malarek Research because of the bad publicity it created.

Ten minutes after Kyle saw Lauren disappearing back through the hedge, the teenagers were joined by a geeky dude in an army jacket. His name was George. He was in his mid-twenties and he gave Kyle the evil eye before demanding to know who he was.

'Kyle's kosher,' Viv said. 'He's just moved into the village with Ryan Quinn.'

George looked surprised. 'I didn't think Quinn had kids.'

'He's not my dad,' Kyle said. 'My mum got off with him when he was inside.'

Viv broke out in a machine-gun laugh. 'Your mum must be some nut, shacking up with a dude she met in the nick.'

'Whatever,' Kyle shrugged. 'Who gets to pick their parents?'

'Quinn's an admirable character,' George said, a touch pompously. 'He practically wrote the book on undercover operations and Zebra eighty-four were legends.'

'Everybody loves the mighty Quinn,' Viv said noisily. 'He should have kept it tight though. Zebra Alliance is a joke. Bunch of la-di-dah *Guardian*-reader mango heads scared of their own goddamned *snot*.'

Kyle smiled as Viv contemptuously spat at the ground, but George didn't look pleased.

'We'd be nowhere without those la-di-dah *Guardian* readers and their monthly contributions,' George snapped back.

'So, is all the equipment sorted?' Tom asked, changing the subject before George and Viv started a full-blown row.

'Mel brought it all up in her dad's Volvo,' George said, before turning to look at Kyle. 'Listen stranger, no offence, but we've got business here. Would you mind butting out?'

'I understand,' Kyle said as he backed off. 'I've got your mobile number, Tom. I'll call you about the meeting at the uni.'

'Don't leave,' Viv yelled. 'George man, Kyle's a diamond and you've spent half the last week running around campus trying to drum up extra bodies for this thing. He might just want to come with us if you tell him what's going down.'

'Look Kyle,' George said, 'no offence, but I only operate with people I know.'

Kyle obviously wanted to know what they were up to, but realised it could blow up in his face if he seemed too eager.

'Don't sweat it,' Kyle said, waving his hands to make it

clear that he wasn't offended. 'Good luck, whatever you're up to.'

As he turned away, Kyle noticed James running towards them. His voice sounded a touch anxious.

'Something's going on up by the entrance,' James explained. 'Robyn's mum came and dragged her off. The straight types are leaving 'cos two coachloads of pissed-up students just arrived, all chanting and going bananas.'

George looked at his watch. 'That'll be Madeline Laing's crack troops, right on time.'

'What are they doing?' Kyle asked.

'Information leaked out that Malarek is having a vanload of monkeys delivered today,' Viv explained.

James was mystified. 'Why not do that in the week, when there's hardly any protestors around?'

Tom and Viv had met James briefly, but George didn't have a clue who he was. 'How old are you, kid?' he asked.

'Fourteen.'

George laughed. 'And *you* saw through the police's clever ruse.'

'Hey,' Viv said, closing in on George, subtly using his physique to intimidate him. 'Why not tell these dudes what's happening and invite them along, Georgie boy? They're sound. I mean, their mum's bunked up with Ryan Quinn for *god's* sake.'

'No, *Viv*,' George said furiously as he glanced at his watch, 'you don't pick up a couple of strays ten minutes before a professionally planned operation. That's how we all end up getting nicked.'

'You're so full of your big man cloak and dagger mumbo-jumbo dog crap,' Viv sneered. '*Professional operation!* My knob is more professional than you.'

George looked at his watch again. 'We don't have time for this,' he said furiously. 'Go on then, tell your new chums. But this is the *last* time I'm hooking up with you, Viv. You've got no discipline. You're a ruddy joke.'

'Suck my arse,' Viv sneered back, before he put Kyle and James in the picture:

'Ten days back, information *miraculously* leaked out that a vanload of monkeys is being delivered to Malarek in an unmarked van at around four this afternoon. The Zebra Alliance committee took one look and decided that the information was bogus.

'The police want to get us all angry, pack the area with manpower and then steam in and nick as many of us as they can in one swoop. What the police don't know is that the drunks up by the gate are under orders to let that van drive through without making a squeak.'

'Just to make the cops look stupid.' Kyle nodded, smiling because he thought he understood.

'I guess that would make the cops look a *little* bit stupid,' Viv laughed. 'But you see, the roads are narrow round here and the cops have to park their cars and vans a fair way away. So while they're up by the entrance facing off three vanloads of frightfully well-behaved students, we're gonna jump out of the bushes and do a bit of remodelling on their cars.'

Kyle nodded in appreciation of the scheme, while James burst out laughing.

'*Sweet,*' James said. 'Let me at the buggers – I'll trash a cop car.'

'That's the spirit, kid,' Viv said, enthusiastically swiping James across the back.

George screwed up his face like he knew this was a bad idea, but nodded reluctantly.

Tom turned and looked at Kyle. 'So, are you in, or what?'

'Sounds kind of insane,' Kyle grinned, 'but I'll try anything once.'

'OK,' George said wearily. 'We are *so* bloody late, we'd better run.'

12. REMODELLING

James found it hard not to laugh as George sprinted gracelessly through the rapeseed, scrawny limbs flailing about and his camouflage jacket billowing behind like a superhero's cape.

They cut across two fields, clambered over a metal gate and ended up on the verge of the main road that led from the motorway. There were empty cop cars, minibuses and vans parked up every few metres. In places they blocked the traffic down to a single lane, creating mini jams for the fleeing protestors.

'How many do you reckon there are?' James asked, awed by the scale of the police presence as he ran alongside Tom.

'Couple of hundred cops and seventy or eighty vehicles, I'd guess. You need at least two officers for every arrest you plan to make.'

'You ever been nicked?' James asked.

Tom smiled. 'Six times. On marches, direct actions and stuff. You?'

This was one of those moments in an undercover mission

where you have to make something up on the fly. 'Nah,' James said. 'You been up in court?'

'Been fined a couple of times for criminal damage. Nothing massive, but Viv got a six-month suspended for trashing a butcher's shop.'

'Cool,' James grinned, making a mental note to mention Tom and Viv's criminal history to Zara when they got back to the cottage.

They'd reached a break in the hedgerows and a gravel path leading towards a dilapidated barn. George led them inside, passing through a large entrance whose decrepit doors had rotted off their hinges.

About fifteen Alliance members milled around, illuminated by sunbeams penetrating missing sections of the roof. They were mostly young, two-thirds male and dressed in dark clothes and hoodies. Some were pierced and tattooed, but the majority were people you'd pass in the street without batting an eye.

George hurried anxiously towards a woman holding a walkie-talkie and earned a tongue-lashing for being late. James, Kyle, Tom and Viv mooched towards a man handing out Balaclavas and disposable gloves.

'Now we're *finally* all here,' the walkie-talkie woman shouted to the crowd, glowering at George, 'put on your gloves and take one hammer and one spray canister. I don't want any heroics, so attack one or two police vehicles each and then disperse into the fields. Bear in mind that some police cars have video cameras installed and recording at all times, so wear your headgear until you're clear of the action.

'You can then abandon your mallets and sprayers, provided

you're not dopey enough to get fingerprints on them, but gloves and Balaclavas will pick up traces of DNA, so take them home and destroy them.

'Lastly, if any of you are arrested, do *not* speak to the police. Be civil, even if they provoke you, and ask to speak to a solicitor from Parker, Lane and Figgis. The Zebra Alliance will cover your legal costs, provided you don't cooperate with the police. Now, what's the name of your solicitors?'

'Parker, Lane and Figgis,' the crowd murmured back.

'And don't forget it,' walkie-talkie woman shouted.

The crowd pulled on gloves and Balaclavas before going outside and picking out hammers and pressurised bug sprayers from the rear compartment of a Volvo estate car. Fortunately for James and Kyle, quite a few activists had chickened out and there was equipment going spare.

'What's in here?' Kyle asked Viv, as he hooked a cylinder of pale blue liquid over his shoulder.

'Industrial strength paint stripper,' Viv said. 'Highly corrosive, highly flammable. Strips paint off metal in a flash. Also melts certain plastics and synthetic fabrics, including the ones they make car seat covers out of. Just make sure you don't get it on your skin.'

'OK people,' walkie-talkie woman shouted. 'I just received the go signal. The cops are all lined up in their riot gear and our scout just spotted the monkey van turning off the motorway. Good luck and remember the golden rule: when in doubt, run like hell.'

A couple of activists cheered and Viv made a typically flamboyant warbling sound as activists headed away from the barn in all directions. James and Kyle jogged off behind Tom and Viv, but found George blocking their path.

'I'll be speaking to the committee about you on Wednesday night,' he said angrily, looking up at Viv. 'You're a renegade and I can only see your attitude leading to serious problems for the Alliance.'

Viv raised his hand, as if he was going to swat George around the head. 'George, you're a tedious, gutless, pen-pushing little twit. I don't really care what you do, or what you say, so long as you stay out of my face.'

'We'll see if the committee feels the same way,' George said arrogantly, before bolting out of Viv's way and tripping over himself in the process.

'You want to watch out,' Tom said to his brother, as they set off again. 'The committee love Georgie boy. You're gonna get kicked out of the Alliance if you're not careful.'

'I'm an anarchist,' Viv said dismissively. 'I never should have joined anything with a committee in the first place.'

The four lads ran half a kilometre, staying behind the hedgerows until they reached a muddy farm entrance with three police vans and two cars parked up side by side. They'd cased it on the way over, so they knew there were no cops about.

James felt a rush of excitement as they broke cover.

'Vive la révolution,' Viv shouted, as he swung madly at a police van with his hammer.

James raced across to a BMW motorway cruiser and took off a door mirror with the first swipe, then ran around knocking out the side windows. He took three swings at the windscreen, but failed to shatter the toughened glass.

'Do the inside with your spray,' Tom shouted, as he and Kyle trashed the next car along.

James took the canister off his shoulder, poked the sprayer nozzle through a broken window and soaked the interior before squirting the corrosive liquid all over the white bodywork. He could hear more activists smashing cars up and down the road as he watched the paint on his target car bubbling up into thousands of tiny blisters.

He was planning a final squirt into the luggage compartment, but some kind of weird chemical reaction forced him back, as the melting interior plastics sent choking grey fumes spewing out through the broken windows.

As he backed off from the stench, a metallic boom erupted inside a van parked directly behind him and a ball of flame blasted open the back doors.

'Jesus,' James gasped, wrapping his arms over his face as he backed into Viv.

'Isn't this heavenly?' Viv grinned.

'What the *hell* was that?' James yelled back, as he wafted his hand in front of his face, trying to clear the smoke closing him down from all directions.

Viv held out the answer in the form of a small cardboard tube. 'Firecrackers,' he explained, as he handed one to James. 'Thought they might liven things up a bit.'

As James struggled with the acrid smoke in his eyes and tried to stem a coughing fit, he spotted a lone cop running down the grass verge towards them.

'Get rid of it, James,' Viv ordered.

The truth dawned on James almost too late: amidst the smoke and noise, he hadn't realised that the firecracker in his hand was alight. James flung it hard and it sailed over the cars, exploding in midair a few metres in front of the cop.

'You nutter,' Viv screamed happily. 'You threw it at the piggy!'

'I just got rid of it,' James said, squinting anxiously through the smoke and relieved to see that only the cop's pride – and possibly his Y-fronts – had been damaged. James had had a few run-ins with the police and wasn't exactly their biggest fan, but he drew the line at blowing them up.

'Better get out of here, kid,' Viv said, grabbing James' shirt and tugging him towards the fields. 'They'll murder us if they catch us now.'

Kyle and Tom had already set off into the fields, after demolishing a custody van and two cars and abandoning their sprayers and mallets the instant they'd heard the explosion inside the van.

'Lose the gloves and headgear,' Viv ordered, removing his own as they jogged across the open field. 'You're the man, James. A bona fide crazy cracker after my own heart – a cop-killing *lunatic*.'

James managed to half smile at Viv, but he'd just come within a few seconds of getting his fingers blown off and was seriously shaken up.

Viv Carter was the kind of nutcase who was going to end up killing someone.

13. UNIFORM

... two senior Zebra Alliance officials were arrested following the attacks, but released without charge. In total thirty-three cars were damaged and twenty-five of these declared total write-offs. Police sources estimate that the bill for damages could exceed half a million pounds.

Avon Chief Constable Derek Miller admitted that he now faced a shortage of vehicles, but denied that it would seriously undermine police operations in the area. Miller refused to comment upon rumours that an attempt to feed misleading information to the animal rights activists had dramatically backfired. But he did admit that three senior officers have been suspended from duty pending a full enquiry ...

BBC Radio Bristol

Lauren had always enjoyed tearing into the cellophane-wrapped perfection of something she'd never worn before. Stripping off the tissue paper, peeling the stickers and snapping the plastic label tags. But not this time.

It was Monday morning and the packets contained a grey skirt, knee socks and a white blouse. She could hear James and Kyle fighting over the bathroom upstairs and Ryan was on the phone in the kitchen, raving to someone about *bloody Madeline Laing* this and *bloody Madeline Laing* that.

As Lauren pulled the adult sized Gorillaz T-shirt she'd slept in over her head and started getting dressed, she tried consoling herself with the fact that the summer holidays were only a month away and so she wouldn't have to keep going to school if the mission dragged on. But that wasn't much of a relief because it still left her facing the thing she hated most: settling in.

Cherubs are supposed to act like ordinary kids, so they have to go to school. And while Lauren could run ten kilometres with a heavy pack, speak three languages and cook a squirrel in five different ways, she still dreaded being the new kid in Year Seven.

She hated the boys who took the mickey and told you that their mate fancied you, the girls who snubbed you because you weren't part of their clique and the teachers who didn't give a damn so long as nothing bothered them.

As Lauren pulled up her knee socks, she tried cheering herself up by imagining that it might all be OK this time. She'd arrive in class, her form teacher would be friendly and she'd find one or two girls who were a good laugh and easy to get on with.

Then she looked down at the weird shoes she had to wear and realised that it wasn't going to happen. Zara had ordered them out of a vegan shoe catalogue and they'd looked OK in the picture, but the reality wasn't quite right. The uppers were made from thick, shiny plastic and the soles were made from . . .

Lauren held one of the shoes up for inspection, poked the bottom and decided that the only thing it resembled was one of the crispbreads that her mum used to eat when she was on a diet. And there was no way around the fact that wearing shiny plastic shoes that resembled a high-fibre snack was going to mark her out as a freak.

But she slid them on, gritted her teeth and stepped out of her room to go get breakfast. She told herself that there were people with no arms and legs and starving babies in the world, and that compared to them a pair of crap shoes really wasn't much to complain about. Then she saw James rounding the bottom of the stairs in his school uniform and a pair of black leather trainers.

'Where's your vegan school shoes?' Lauren asked.

James burst out laughing. 'Me and Kyle both took them out of their boxes and decided that it wasn't gonna happen. If anyone asks, we'll say we only went vegan when we moved in with Ryan and our mum couldn't afford new shoes for all of us.'

'What if you're not allowed to wear trainers?' Lauren asked.

James shrugged. 'Most schools let you, as long as they're black. If not, the worst they'll do is tell us to wear something else tomorrow.'

Suddenly feeling a lot happier, Lauren spun back into her room. She dived under her bed to grab her black trainers, but only saw her white canvas Nikes and a pair of dark blue Converse. She realised that she'd left her black trainers at campus, as well as a pair of black canvas slip-ons that would have been absolutely perfect . . .

Lauren pounded wrathfully on her mattress as she stood

up, then jumped out of her skin as the leaded window behind her shattered. A half brick bounced energetically across the carpet before hitting the radiator with a clang.

'Scum,' a boy's shrill voice yelled from the field out back, less than twenty metres away. 'Get out of our village.'

Lauren caught a brief glance of the boy's grey uniform as Zara burst through the door and stared in shock at the shards of glass covering the carpet.

'Are you OK?'

'Fine,' Lauren gasped, as she ducked under Zara's arm and opened the door leading out to the back garden. 'I saw him. He looks about my age.'

The crispbread soles made running uncomfortable, but Lauren spotted the lad belting through the overgrown field and set off at full pelt.

'You're *so* dead,' she shouted, as the long grass flicked against her legs.

Lauren didn't gain any ground over the first couple of hundred metres, but she was fitter than her target, who began tiring after he'd vaulted over a metal gate and turned on to a straight road that led towards the modern houses on the northern outskirts of the village. By the time she'd finally closed the young lad down, he'd cut into an expanse of lawn sandwiched between two houses.

'Gotcha,' Lauren yelled triumphantly, as she wrapped her arm around the boy's chest and bundled him into the side wall of a house.

But she didn't get her grip right and he spun out and threw a wild punch. Lauren ducked it, hooked her foot around his right ankle and swept his feet from under him. She dived on top, rolled the lad on to his back and pinned his arms under her knees. The boy was taller than Lauren and visibly shocked at how easily he'd been taken down.

'You could have had my eye out with that glass,' Lauren growled.

The boy jerked his head and spat in her face. 'Good. That's what you'd deserve.'

Lauren was furious at being spat on, but fought off the urge to punch him out. 'What did I ever do to you?' she asked.

'When you let me up you'll be sorry.'

Lauren grabbed the boy's nose between her thumb and finger and gave it an almighty twist. 'So I'm gonna be sorry am I?'

'Let go, *bitch*,' the kid yelled.

The chase had happened so quickly, Lauren hadn't had a chance to consider what she'd do when she caught up. She could drag the boy back to the house and call the police, but that would turn into a whole massive thing and Ryan wouldn't appreciate having the cops sniffing around. Her combat training gave her a range of abilities, from knocking the lad out to breaking his arms or even killing him. They were all too extreme, but he'd thrown a brick through her bedroom window and spat in her face, so there was no way she was just going to let him go with a warning.

'Get up, turd,' Lauren ordered as she released the boy from the pin.

He had no way of knowing that Lauren had done two years of advanced combat training and thought his opponent was nothing more than a girl, who was smaller than him and had got lucky. So as Lauren stood up, he lashed out again and his Timberland boot thumped painfully against her shin.

Lauren countered ruthlessly, snatching the boy's wrist, jamming her heel between his shoulder blades and twisting his arm into an agonising lock.

'Think you're tough, do you?' Lauren asked, as she glowered down at her opponent. 'One more twist and you'll have to explain to all your mates how your arm got broken by a girl.'

'Please,' the boy begged, as Lauren notched up the pain until the shoulder was close to popping out of its socket.

'No funny business when I let go this time, OK?'

'*Yeah,*' the boy gasped.

The instant Lauren let go, he rolled on to his back and glanced up submissively as he rubbed his painful shoulder.

'Nice boots,' Lauren said, looking at the almost new Timberlands on her opponent's feet. 'What size are you?'

'Two and a half.'

'Close enough. Pass 'em over, and your trousers.'

The boy hesitated for a moment and Lauren broke into a confident smile.

'Look dude, the choice is yours: take them off, or I beat the living crap out of you and pull them off myself.'

The boy leaned forwards and began to unlace his boots. Once they were off, he unbuckled his belt and stood up to wriggle out of his trousers.

'Give us,' Lauren said, snatching the black trousers and beginning to inspect the pockets.

She threw his door keys to the ground and used one of his

clean tissues to wipe the spit off her face. Then she unbuttoned the back pocket and slid out a nylon wallet.

'Well, well, well,' Lauren said, ripping the Velcro apart and studying the sports centre membership and bus pass inside. 'Stuart Pierce, born eighth of May 1994, number twenty-one Nicholson Villas, Corbyn Copse, Avon. Picture doesn't flatter you, does it?'

Lauren flung the wallet at Stuart's head. He looked close to blubbing as he stood helplessly in his socks and underpants. She scrunched the trousers into a ball and lobbed them high into the nearest tree. They snagged on a branch and unravelled, leaving the legs flapping in the wind several metres out of reach.

'If you or any of your mates come near my house again, I'll smash every bone in your body,' Lauren snarled, as she bent down and picked up the boots. 'And thanks for these, kid. They're exactly what I was looking for.'

*

Lauren gave the boots a good blast of deodorant and wore two pairs of socks because they were a bit big. They had to get a bus to school and James was still giggling as they headed for the stop with Kyle.

'Imagine having to run home in your undies,' James smirked. 'You're *so* bad, Lauren.'

'Yeah, well he could have done me an injury throwing that brick in my window – *and* the dirty git spat in my face. Mind you, I reckon I enjoyed myself a bit *too* much. It's true what they say about power going to your head.'

'Might be trouble if he grasses,' James said.

Lauren tutted. 'It won't happen, James. If he grasses me

up for nicking his boots, he'll get done for bricking the window which is ten times worse.'

'I know who he is,' Kyle said triumphantly.

'Who?' Lauren asked.

'That name, Stuart Pierce,' Kyle said. 'It was bugging me all through breakfast. I read a report about the AFM attacking a woman named Christine Pierce. She lived in Corbyn Copse and had two sons, Stuart and Andy. I bet that's why he bricked us.'

'I read that,' James nodded. 'They threw enamel paint in her face and blinded her.'

Lauren stopped walking and looked guiltily down at her boots. 'Poor kid,' she gasped. 'I can't wear these, everyone's gonna hate me. I'd better dive home and put the veggie shoes on.'

James looked at his watch. 'Not if you want to catch the school bus you won't.'

The stop was on the road between the old and new parts of the village, not far from the alleyway where Lauren had humiliated Stuart. There were about a dozen secondary-school kids waiting at the stop. Three of the bigger ones steamed forward, blocking James, Kyle and Lauren's path.

'We're not looking for trouble,' Kyle said. 'Just the bus.'

Lauren caught a glimpse of Stuart sitting on a wall about twenty metres away. He'd sneaked home for another pair of shoes and trousers, but held his shoulder like it was still hurting and his eyes had red rings that suggested tears.

'You don't want trouble?' a tough-looking lad smirked, as he squared up to Kyle.

He was a bigger version of Stuart with zits and Lauren realised it had to be his older brother, Andy.

'Well you're getting trouble,' another lad said, facing off James.

'Start then,' James said cockily, giving the boy a shove. 'See where it gets you.'

Kyle knew James had a temper and pulled him back.

'Peace, man,' Kyle said, raising his hands. 'I know you're Andy Pierce. I read what happened to your mum in the paper and I'm sorry. But we've all gotta live here together and—'

'Don't you talk about my mum,' Andy Pierce spat. 'She's blind. She's lost her job and we're gonna lose our house 'cos of scum like you.'

A few other boys, including some chunky-looking sixth formers, murmured their support for Andy.

'Our mum's shacked up with some guy and we got dragged down here to live,' Kyle said. 'It's not our fight.'

While Kyle and Andy argued, the lad James pushed had closed in again and silently mouthed, *Your mum*.

'What was that, penis head?' James asked.

'I said, *your mum*.'

James stepped back and held out his arms. 'Come on then, big man. Take a shot; show me what you've got.'

'*Don't* start, James,' Lauren said uneasily.

The lad took a swing. James ducked out of the way, before bobbing up and planting a right jab square in his opponent's mouth. It was a nasty punch, but not the jawbreaker James could have thrown if he'd really wanted to.

'Leave it out!' Kyle yelled.

'Anyone else wanna try?' James shouted, as the kid he'd punched stumbled back against the bus shelter and spat blood on the pavement.

The punch had cranked the tension up to number eleven and the local kids were shouting and yelling advice ranging from *calm down* to *kick their heads in*.

Lauren got the feeling that a mass brawl was about to break out, so it was a huge relief to see the school bus coming round the corner. There was a fair bit of shoving and cursing as everyone piled on board, but Kyle made sure he and James sat away from the youths they'd been facing off and most of the sting had gone out of the situation by the time the bus got underway.

'You dick,' Kyle whispered, scowling at James. 'You're too aggressive.'

James shrugged unrepentantly. 'I wanted them to know that we're best not messed with. They're miles bigger than Lauren and I don't want them getting any ideas about starting on her when we're not around.'

Meanwhile, Lauren had noticed Stuart sitting across the aisle one row in front of her and slid across to the empty seat behind him.

'I didn't know what happened to your mum until Kyle told me,' she whispered. 'I can't go round barefoot all day, but I'll fetch the boots back to your house this evening, OK?'

Stuart looked around with a sour face. 'Keep 'em,' he said. 'I don't want 'em now they've been on your stinking feet.'

14. BUNS

Lauren didn't make any good friends in her first three days at school, but the kids in her class were OK and nobody dared give her any hassle. The only stressful scenes had been daily slanging matches between James and Andy Pierce at the bus stop. It had only been verbals, but Lauren had a nasty feeling that it would kick off into something bigger.

The mission was progressing, although nothing sensational had happened since the weekend. While the kids were at school, Ryan tapped out e-mails and made endless phone calls to his contacts. Zara spent a lot of time dealing with all the domestic stuff that goes with keeping a family going and the rest catching up with the paperwork that formed a major part of a senior mission controller's job.

She also made sure that the kids went down the hill and showed their faces at the protest site every day. Lauren would visit straight after school and put on her good girl act, dishing out drinks and hot cross buns to the pensioners who stood loyally by their placards for up to ten hours a day. They were generally decent sorts, who always made a big fuss of Lauren and raved about her tea-making skills.

Most of the oldies had dead spouses and grown-up kids and Lauren got the impression that the daily vigil behind the police barriers filled a big hole in some empty lives. And hanging out with them wasn't a total waste of time. Even though they were about as softcore as Zebra Alliance members got, they'd overheard a million conversations and their gossip let you know whether an approaching activist was considered a sweetheart, a psycho, or someone rumoured to be an undercover cop.

None of it was hard evidence, but Lauren noted the names of anyone the pensioners didn't like and scored a surprisingly high hit rate when she checked them against the criminal intelligence database back at the cottage. They also turned out to be right about the undercover policewoman.

Kyle and James usually visited after homework and dinner, when the sky was beginning to turn dark. The oldies had packed up their folding chairs and newspapers by then and given way to a livelier crowd of students, young couples and the odd kid. They were a friendly bunch, but every so often an eager young buck – usually drunk, trying to impress a girl, or both – would unleash paint, eggs, or bags of flour at the staff driving in or out of the Malarek compound.

It was fifty-fifty whether the thrower escaped or got nabbed by one of the police officers who concealed themselves behind the hedgerows whenever the crowd looked boisterous. The arrests were good-natured and the suspects always got cheered as they were handcuffed and loaded into a van for the twelve-kilometre ride to the police station.

*

It was Wednesday, coming up to 4:50 p.m. Lauren was cutting across the field behind the cottage holding a tray of empty picnic cups and the remains of a packet of biscuits when she spotted Stuart Pierce standing thirty metres away, up to his knees in thistles and grass.

'Hey,' he said, using the least threatening voice he could manage and wearing a *please don't kick my arse again* look on his face. 'I know you told me not to come over here, but is it OK if we talk?'

Stuart was in Lauren's year at school and they'd even been on the same basketball team in a PE lesson, but this was the first time they'd spoken since Monday.

'Guess it won't kill me,' Lauren shrugged, feeling an odd mix of emotions for a kid whose mum had been blinded by the AFM, but who'd also spat in her face.

Stuart smiled uneasily as he wandered over. 'I know we got off to a bad start.'

'I take it you're referring to the brick that you threw through my bedroom window?'

'I'm sorry, Lauren . . . Is it OK to call you Lauren?'

Lauren had come to realise that Stuart was a quiet kid. He only had one mate around school, a skinny Asian dude who didn't live in Corbyn Copse. 'Well, what else are you gonna call me?' she smirked.

Stuart realised he'd said something dumb and started going red. 'I'm not a yob or nothing, you know? I never did anything like that before. Did they fix the window? I've got money saved up. I can probably pay for it.'

'They've put a board in, but it's leaded glass so they've got to make all the little squares into a new piece.'

'Oh,' Stuart said weakly.

'It's OK,' Lauren said. 'I didn't tell my mum your name and she's claiming the money on insurance.'

'Cool,' he said, looking down at the black plastic shoes on Lauren's feet. 'You know on the bus, when you said I could have my boots back?'

Lauren nodded. 'They're in my room. I thought about leaving them on your doorstep, but I didn't want to bump into your brother and his mates.'

Stuart tutted. 'My brother's such a dick, going round acting like he's sticking up for me. He used to batter me all the time when my mum was out working.'

Lauren set off towards the house. 'It's sad what happened to your mum. But Ryan and my mum are nothing to do with the AFM. They're totally anti-violence.'

'You really kicked my arse. Where'd you learn to fight so good?'

Lauren used the standard CHERUB excuse. 'My dad was a Karate instructor.'

'*Sweet*. So you must be at least a black belt, or something.'

Lauren nodded. 'Second dan black belt. My brothers – James and Kyle – are both third dan.'

'I wish I was tough,' Stuart said. 'Not that I'm a weed or anything, but I've never had proper lessons. One time Andy had me pinned. I grabbed this *massive* book and knocked him spark out. He puked about eight times.'

'Must have been funny,' Lauren giggled, as they passed through a wooden gate into the back garden of the cottage.

Lauren's room was just down the hall from the back door and even though she'd lived here for less than a week, she'd managed to turn it into a bomb-site, with tangled clothes, schoolbooks and fizzy drink cans everywhere.

Stuart looked guiltily at the boarded-up window as Lauren grabbed the boots from under a jacket and some dirty jeans.

'My feet aren't that bad and I only wore them one day.'

'Cheers,' Stuart grinned. 'I told my aunt that I'd lost them when I changed for games. She was doing her nut 'cos she paid eighty quid and I've only had them for a month.'

'Your aunt?' Lauren said curiously.

Stuart nodded. 'She moved in with us after the attack, to help look after us and that. She feels bad, 'cos she got my mum the job at Malarek in the first place.'

'Does your aunt still work there?'

'Nah, she got scared and quit not long after the AFM started attacking people. My mum hated working there as well.'

'So why didn't she get another job?'

'My dad went off with another woman and left a big mortgage behind. Malarek has to pay danger money. It's three times what you can make working on a farm or in one of the superstores and they're always short staffed so you can do all the overtime you like.

'My mum didn't like what they do to the animals. I even heard her crying a few times. All she did was feed the animals and hose out cages and stuff. They offered to give her training so that she could do injections and eye drops and that. It would have been more money, but she used to get upset just watching other people doing it.'

'That's sad,' Lauren said, glancing at her watch. 'Listen, it's not that I want to kick you out, but my family's going to some Zebra Alliance meeting at the university tonight and I've got to change out of uniform and stuff.'

'Right,' Stuart said. 'Thanks for the boots.'

Lauren smiled. 'I haven't got any mates around here, so if you want to come over for dinner one night or just hang out, that's cool.'

'Yeah,' Stuart said. 'My mum's been totally down since the attack and it's not nice being stuck at home when she's in a mood. Sometimes I end up wandering around the village thinking dark thoughts, like *Maybe I'll throw a brick through that window.*'

Lauren burst out laughing. 'Next time just ring the doorbell, eh? See you at the bus stop in the morning.'

15. UNIVERSITY

Ryan's deep, Northern Irish accent seemed to pass effortlessly through ceilings and walls. His endless phone calls had driven the entire household nuts and it was even worse when you were trapped inside the people carrier with him. Zara drove, while Ryan sat in the middle row of seats, blaring into a Nokia:

'Susan . . . Susan it's me, Ryan. Hi . . . Yes, I'm on the way to the meeting now. I know you said you were considering your options, but I was just ringing again to see if I could count on your vote this evening . . . ? Well, I understand what you're saying. I know Madeline is a great little fundraiser, but frankly, the whole Zebra Alliance campaign is a shambles.

'There's no bloody focus. I keep seeing bits of campaigns. Great ideas, fantastic people, but precious little sign of the strategy we really need to bring down a giant. We've got to put a squeeze on all the little companies that supply Malarek, whether it's half a million quid's worth of laboratory equipment, or the dude that comes in and refills the coffee machine.'

After listening to the voice on the other end for a few

seconds, Ryan spoke with the wounded tone of scolded kid. 'Well . . . OK Susan, I guess I've said all that I can. You and I go back a long way and I feel very let down hearing you say that.'

Ryan pressed the end call button and stared vacantly out of the window. 'That's another one'll be voting Madeline Laing for chairman.'

'Perhaps you should settle for a spot on the Alliance committee until you find your feet,' Zara suggested gently. 'You've been in prison for three years. Madeline has brought in a lot of her own people. You can't expect them to hand everything back to you on a platter.'

Ryan tutted. 'There wouldn't even *be* a Zebra Alliance without me.' He looked away from Zara and started dialling a number into his phone. 'Hello, Sebastian. How's tricks . . . ? Excellent. Listen, I don't mean to keep pestering you, but it sure would be good to know if I can count on your vote at the meeting this evening?'

*

It was thirty minutes' drive from Corbyn Copse to the shabby, brutalist campus of Avon University. It was beginning to turn dark when they arrived and James ogled student girls through the glare, while Zara wound the people carrier through a tortuous one-way system. They passed accommodation blocks and the glass and concrete bunkers where students attended lectures.

'I nearly did my degree here,' Zara said, as she pulled up at a zebra crossing to let two hockey teams cross in front of them. 'At least, I would have done if I hadn't got my scholarship to Yale.'

'Look at *that*,' James gasped, rubbing his hands as his eyes followed a cute, mini-skirted Goth with a pierced lip. 'I can't wait to get to uni.'

Lauren tutted. 'Don't drool over the upholstery, will you.'

James didn't answer back, because Kyle's mobile gave out a triumphant blast, indicating that he'd received a text.

'Is it Tom?' James asked.

'Yeah, *finally*,' Kyle said, before bursting out laughing. 'He said he'll meet us by the bar at the Zebra fundraiser. Apparently Viv's up before the committee for setting off the firecrackers.'

'What's funny about that?' James asked. 'They *should* kick Viv out. That basket case nearly got me blown up.'

'I know,' Kyle said, still giggling. 'That's not what I'm laughing at.'

James reached over to grab Kyle's phone, but Kyle snatched it out of his reach.

'Private,' Kyle said firmly. 'Hands off.'

James looked upset. 'You'd better not be taking the piss out of me.'

'Oh listen to that ego,' Kyle tutted, as he typed out his reply to Tom. 'The entire world doesn't revolve around you, you know.'

It took another couple of minutes to reach the car park at the rear of the refectory building. This large structure was the social hub of the university, with five restaurants, several bars, a nightclub and more than a dozen meeting rooms spread over five floors.

Ryan led the way through the main entrance into a bland concrete atrium enlivened by clusters of students standing in circles, or lounging on the aged leather sofas that rested against the floor-to-ceiling windows. One wall carried a noticeboard. It was twenty metres long and every centimetre was plastered several layers deep with notices. They advertised everything from second-hand bicycles to meetings of the Young Conservative Association.

It took half a minute to pick out a Zebra Alliance poster, promoting the regular Wednesday fundraiser and directing guests to the Purcell Room on the second floor. In big letters at the bottom it said: *Admission £1, All Drinks Buy One Get One FREE until 9 p.m.!*

'How can they raise money if they're giving drinks away?' Lauren asked, as they set off up the stairs.

Ryan burst out laughing. 'Ahh, to be so young and innocent! Once you get a few drinks down a student's neck, they'll keep coming back for more.'

The Purcell Room was big enough for several hundred people. Lauren waved to a few familiar faces from the protest site as they entered. They cut across an empty dance floor, dodging a bunch of little kids doing skids on the polished wood. The real action seemed to be taking place in a carpeted bar area at the far end of the room.

There were forty odd people there, a mix of students and Zebra Alliance members. They sat at hexagonal tables, with empty glasses stacked in front of them and cigarette smoke lurking over their heads.

Ryan headed up to the bar with Zara and Lauren. He broke into a big smile as he shook hands and hugged old friends.

James and Kyle branched off when they spotted Tom and

Viv sitting in an alcove by the window. Viv wore a T-shirt with a drawing of a policeman with his head cut off and a slogan underneath: *Hip, hip Hooray!* He had a muscular arm around a leggy girl who could have come straight off the fashion pages.

'Hey guys,' Viv smiled. 'This is my girlfriend, Sophie.'

Kyle reached out and shook her hand before sitting down next to Tom.

'This little psycho is James,' Viv said proudly. 'The one I told you about.'

Sophie broke into a big smile and gave James a smoky peck on the cheek as he grabbed the chair next to her.

'The cop killer,' she grinned. 'You made Viv's day lobbing that firework.'

James had told Kyle and Zara that he hadn't aimed the firecracker at anything, but it worked in his favour if Viv thought he had so he wasn't about to contradict him.

'What are you all doing here?' Sophie asked.

James shrugged. 'Just tagging along. Kyle was meeting Tom, and Ryan wanted to bring my mum up to see everyone. I figured anything's better than sitting around the cottage on my own watching bloody *EastEnders*.'

'So, tight wad,' Sophie said, looking across at Viv. 'Are you gonna get the drinks in or what?'

'Skint,' Viv said.

'My arse,' Sophie grinned. 'Your bloody dad owns half of Lincolnshire.'

'Yeah, but I ain't got none of that yet. Not unless I drive up there and shoot the old git.'

As Viv said this, he went into his wallet, peeled out a twenty-pound note and waved it under Sophie's nose.

'Oh, I'm getting them am I?'

'You're nearest,' Viv smirked.

Kyle and Tom had started their own conversation and both burst out laughing at something James hadn't heard.

'What's your poison, Kyle?' Sophie asked.

'Pint of Fosters,' Kyle said.

Sophie looked at James. 'Same as,' he said.

Sophie gave him a *you must be joking* look. 'Coke or orange juice?' she asked pointedly.

He felt his face boil up with embarrassment. 'Coke, I guess.'

James tried not to be too blatant as he watched Sophie's stunning figure slink off to the bar.

Kyle looked over at Viv. 'So what's going on with you and the committee?'

'Spineless tits,' Viv sneered. 'They're gonna kick me out, but I'm not losing any sleep. The only reason I'm going to the meeting is so I can personally tell them where they can shove their pathetic bloody alliance.'

'So what will you do?' Kyle asked. 'Give up campaigning for animal rights?'

Viv smirked. 'No *way*, man. My dad owns half a million pigs and I've seen the way they're treated. I went veggie when I was thirteen.'

James was shocked. 'Your dad's a farmer?'

'He doesn't get up at 4 a.m. and muck them out personally, but his estate is one of the biggest pork producers in the country. Dad's seventy now though, so it's run by our half-brother, Clyde.'

Tom made a dickhead gesture with his hand.

119

'Precisely,' Viv nodded. 'Twenty-eight years old and he struts around in a Range Rover, wearing green wellies, cloth cap and a walking stick like he's lord of the manor.'

'Doesn't speak to us since Viv nutted him two Christmases ago.'

James burst out laughing.

'It's true,' Tom giggled. 'Permanently flattened the bridge of his nose. I saw him a couple of months back when I was visiting our mum and he looked like a retired boxer.'

Viv slammed his massive fist into his palm. 'When I hit someone, they *stay* hit.'

James suddenly stopped laughing. Viv was easy to get along with, but you couldn't allow yourself to forget that he was a nutter.

'So, what will you do?' Kyle repeated.

Viv shrugged. 'There's other groups out there that are doing rather than talking.'

'Some of them kick arse,' Tom added. 'The Zebra Alliance isn't worth shit. All they're interested in is getting their faces in the paper. They're scared of doing anything radical in case the moderates cancel their direct debit payments.'

Viv nodded. 'They're hardly a liberationist group at all any more.'

Kyle decided that the social situation made it safe to probe a little deeper. 'So, is there a particular group you've got your eye on?'

'One or two,' Viv shrugged.

Kyle phrased his next question as a joke, but he wanted to see how Tom and Viv would react. 'Maybe we should go all out and join the AFM. You know any of that lot?'

'Might do,' Viv laughed. Then he raised his voice so that the whole bar could overhear. 'The AFM are better than these do-nothing Zebra Alliance pussies.'

Viv got the attention he sought, as occupants of the surrounding tables turned to scowl at him.

Meantime, Sophie was back with a tray of drinks. She sat in her chair, before plonking a pint of Fosters in front of James.

'I thought the little cop killer deserved his beer,' she grinned. 'But drink it here; don't go wandering around where everyone can see you with it.'

James couldn't help smiling as he brought the pint up to his lips and drank five mouthfuls, but put down the glass abruptly as Zara, Ryan and George came up to the table.

George wore an ill-fitting brown suit that made him look particularly geeky. 'I'm taking Ryan and Zara across to the committee meeting,' he said, pompous as ever, as he looked at Viv. 'Would you like to come, or shall I just tell them you've tendered your resignation?'

'You kidding me?' Viv asked. 'When have I ever turned down a chance to run off with my big mouth? *Nice* suit by the way, Georgie boy. How many toasters did you sell today?'

'Some of us have to work for a living,' George said. 'We can't all live off money inherited from our grandmothers.'

James looked slightly confused as George led Ryan, Zara and Viv across the hall and out the door. 'Isn't the meeting held here?' he asked.

Tom shook his head. 'Nah, the committee always meets in a secret location. It's not wise for some members to show their faces and they're totally paranoid that they're under police surveillance. It's usually held in someone's room over in the halls of residence.'

As James drained his pint down to the halfway mark, Sophie gave him a nudge and gently grabbed the scruff of his T-shirt. 'Come over here, with me.'

James didn't know what was going on, as Sophie grabbed a pint in each hand and led him towards another table to join a couple of her girlfriends.

'Why'd we move?' James asked.

Sophie gave her two friends a look. 'I think Tom and your brother would appreciate a little privacy.'

'Why?' James asked.

The three nineteen-year-old girls sitting around the table all laughed.

'Kyle *is* gay, isn't he?' Sophie asked.

'Yeah,' James admitted grudgingly.

The coin dropped as James sneaked a glance over his shoulder at Kyle and Tom: the text messages, the laughing, the way they'd been sitting there in a world of their own – it all suddenly made sense.

16. SLAB

Things livened up as the evening wore on. The number of students swelled and once the bar ran out of seating, they began propping themselves along the walls of the dance-floor area. Down by the entrance, two folding tables had been brought in. One did a brisk trade giving away leaflets and selling liberationist books and STOP *Malarek* posters. Lauren volunteered to help out on the other table, which hosted a free vegan buffet.

Quite a few students looked like they needed a good meal and she happily ladled out guacamole, bean dip, corn chips, marinaded mushrooms and fruit salad. Every so often a bunch of hotheads would swagger in from another bar or meeting looking for trouble, or at the least to try winding up some veggies. One red-faced drunk in a Fred Perry shirt asked Lauren if she had any chicken drumsticks stashed under the counter.

She was prepared to go along with the joke, until the dude tried dunking a grubby finger in the bean dip. She grabbed his thumb, twisted it into a lock and brandished a fork with her free hand before doing her best little-girl grin.

'Leave,' she growled. 'Otherwise, you'll find out which orifice I plan to insert this fork into.'

The humiliated student staggered out of the Purcell Room as Lauren received bows and applause from his mates.

The food had been prepared by a middle-aged woman called Anna Kent. 'You're quite a little firebrand,' she said, as the drunks shuffled out of the room.

Anna tousled Lauren's hair, a gesture Lauren found oddly upsetting because it was exactly what her real mum used to do when she was proud of her.

*

James felt out of his depth sitting with Sophie and her two mates. They asked him if he had a girlfriend and he said no, which set the trio of girls off in a conversation about their first boyfriends.

Their stories about first kisses and getting caught in compromising positions by angry parents made him laugh and the girls bought him pints – or more often half pints – until he felt drunk and giggly. But he was also a touch sad, because the trio of beautiful, intelligent girls were all five years older and no matter how much he liked them, he was just a kid as far as they were concerned.

'What took so long?' Sophie asked, when a red-faced Viv finally sidled up alongside her.

'It's pistols at dawn in there,' Viv said. 'There's this whole massive bun fight going on over who gets to run the Alliance.'

James had heard so much of Ryan's rambling over the past days that he couldn't help being curious about how it was panning out. 'Have they had the vote yet?'

'They had the first vote straight away, unanimously reelecting Ryan on to the committee, but he's made it clear that he wants to take over from Madeline. They were also pretty pissed off that he'd brought Zara along to a secret meeting.'

'So what about you?' James asked. 'Did they kick you out?'

'Actually, they said I was a valuable activist and just wanted to suspend me for three months. But I told them exactly where they could stick that idea. And as I was heading out, I pointed at Georgie Boy and I goes *If I ever see you again, I'm gonna pin you down and shit on your head.* You should have seen the look on his mug.'

Fuelled by the beer, James started laughing out of control at the image of weedy little George getting crapped on.

'That's *very* mature,' Sophie said, smiling wryly at her girlfriends.

'So what do you reckon?' Viv asked. 'I can't stand this stuffy hole. Who's up for driving out somewhere and howling at the moon? I've got Jack Daniel's and vodka in the car.'

Sophie shrugged. 'Yeah, what the hell.'

Viv looked at Kyle and Tom, who were now snuggled up with their arms around each other's backs.

'Oy, poofters,' Viv shouted. 'Gonna take a spin. You coming?'

Tom and Kyle both nodded as Viv looked at James. 'What about you, cop killer? You up for a ride, or has Mummy gotta tuck you up early on a school night?'

James didn't fancy being the odd man out amidst two couples, but he had a mission and Zara would expect him to go.

'She likes me home by eleven,' James grinned. 'But she's not around to stop me, so I'm in.'

As James stood up, Kyle passed by, heading for the toilets, and gave him a nudge that clearly meant *come with me*.

The toilets were nasty, with a smell that made your eyes water and an overflowing urinal that had turned the entire floor into a puddle.

'OK,' Kyle said, looking over his shoulder to make sure nobody was around as he stood at the urinal beside James. 'I've been working on Tom. He reckons Viv is planning to get in with another group. It's apparently something to do with a mate of Sophie's.'

'Is it the AFM?' James said, as he started peeing.

'He says they're extremists,' Kyle said. 'I doubt it's the AFM itself, but all the intelligence reports say that the number of radicals out there is small, so there's a strong possibility that they're linked.'

'What's our plan?'

'All we can do is hang around Tom and Viv. Keep ourselves in the picture and gradually put the idea across that we want to get involved with an extremist group too.'

'Might be tricky for me though,' James said. 'I mean, you and Tom are practically ripping each other's kit off in there, but there's a big age gap between me and Viv. That thing with the firecracker might have been a perverse stroke of luck, but I can't see him hanging around with my fourteen-year-old butt once the novelty wears off.'

Kyle nodded as he zipped up his jeans. 'Well, you know what Viv likes about you. You'll just have to play it to the max and act even crazier than he does.'

It was gone eleven when Ryan and Zara arrived home in Corbyn Copse. Lauren had dozed off in the back, but woke up as Ryan tried carrying her into the cottage.

'Better have a shower before I get into bed,' Lauren yawned. 'I stink like an ashtray.'

As she headed dozily up to the bathroom, Ryan slumped in an armchair and buried his face in his hands.

'That was a total bloody betrayal,' he said listlessly. 'Three years in prison. Five votes out of twenty-four. They can stuff their bloody committee. I'm setting up my own thing.'

'Not while this mission's going on you're not,' Zara said firmly.

Ryan looked up, surprised. 'Pardon me?'

'We need you inside the Zebra Alliance,' Zara explained.

'That wasn't our deal,' Ryan said indignantly. 'I wanted the AFM out of the Zebra Alliance, but if I'm not even part of the Alliance, there's no point.'

'No point for *you*,' Zara said. 'But our mission is to unearth the AFM. I want you inside that committee room feeding us information.'

'How can I go back in there?' Ryan said. 'They utterly humiliated me.'

'Swallow your pride and do your job.'

'Or what?' Ryan sneered.

'Don't try my patience,' Zara snapped. 'I'm dead tired and I've been listening to your voice since half-six this morning. Your parole states that you can't leave the county of Avon. If you want to pick a fight with me, I'll see you wake up in a

London police cell and serve the other three years of your sentence.'

'Now we're seeing your teeth,' Ryan yelled. 'The British government and its crack teams of underage fascists.'

'Ryan, the AFM is out there and people are getting killed,' Zara yelled back. 'I've put six months' work into this mission. We've got three agents in place, we've spent two hundred and fifty grand on a house and a car and I'm missing out on my own kids growing up. Once we've got solid information on the AFM, you can set up your own group with no one but your parole officer to worry about. Until then you *will* stick to our deal.'

Ryan twisted uncomfortably in his chair, knowing he was beaten. 'I'll speak to Madeline tomorrow. I'll apologise and tell her that I hope we can work well together in future.'

Zara hadn't enjoyed laying down the law, but the kids might be in danger if Ryan stepped out of line so she had to be absolutely certain that he knew who was boss.

'I'm going to heat up some cocoa in the microwave,' Zara said. 'Would you like a mug?'

'Soya milk?' he asked.

'That's the only kind we have,' Zara nodded.

'I'm sorry,' Ryan said, rubbing his eyes. 'I came out expecting a hero's welcome, but I guess people forget about you faster than you'd expect.'

*

Viv's car was an ancient Mercedes saloon. He was too drunk to drive so he let Sophie sit behind the wheel. She pulled up sharply at the end of a pedestrian alleyway between two metal-sided superstores.

'Is this it?' Sophie asked, peering into the darkness.

'It'll do,' Viv said, as he flung open the front passenger door. James did the same with the door behind him.

'Keep the engine running,' Viv said, leaning into the car and looking at Sophie. 'Give us a shot of that JD.'

Tom reached around the front passenger seat and his older brother grabbed a bottle of Jack Daniels and began tipping it down his neck.

'Have a drop for courage,' Viv said, holding the bottle out to James.

The whisky burned as it passed down James' throat and he almost doubled over coughing.

'Jesus,' James croaked, clutching at his throat.

While the trio inside the car giggled at James' discomfort, Viv opened up the boot. It struck James how reckless Viv was as he looked inside at spray cans, tools, bolt croppers, Balaclavas, gloves, Zebra Alliance pamphlets and a video camera. If the police ever searched Viv's car, they'd have a field day.

'Right,' Viv said, grabbing a can of spray paint and a cardboard stencil, before pointing at a large triangular lump that had been broken off the edge of a paving slab. 'You got the strength to carry that, James?'

'I'll manage,' James slurred, feeling his muscles tighten as he reached into the boot and grabbed the chunk of stone.

Viv ran off down the alleyway and promptly tumbled over a pile of black rubbish bags that were made invisible by the darkness. James cracked up laughing, despite the weight straining his arms.

'Goat shaggers,' Viv screamed, kicking out wildly at the bags and sending one on an arc several metres into the air. It crashed down to the echo of empty tin cans.

The pair ambled down the rest of the alleyway, and found themselves at the entrance to a supermarket. The sliding doors were locked for the night, but all the lights were on inside. The aisles were blocked up with giant metal trolleys and sour-faced staff stacking the shelves.

'Right,' Viv said. 'You ready?'

James nodded, as a Jack Daniel's fuelled burp seared up his throat.

Viv's stencil was about half a metre across. He checked there were no supermarket staff looking his way, before pressing it up against the glass doors of the main entrance, and spraying paint through the gaps. This technique was much faster than writing graffiti and when he pulled the stencil away the slogan was written immaculately: MEAT IS MURDER.

'Righty ho,' Viv said. 'Your turn, cop killer.'

James took a three-step run-up and lobbed the chunk of paving through a plate-glass window. The shatterproof sheet broke into a million greenish pebbles as the stone sailed on, demolishing a display stand filled with credit card application forms.

Viv was heading back towards his car even before the glass broke and James only took a brief glance at the astonished shelf stackers before going after him.

Sophie hit the accelerator as James bundled on to the back seat, squeezing alongside Kyle and Tom. The car was already in second gear by the time he'd slammed the door.

'*Yee-haa,*' Viv shouted, giving a two-fingered salute out of the window as his ancient Merc squealed out of the deserted parking lot and on to a main road.

17. BREAKFAST

Lauren grinned at her brother across the breakfast table. 'You look *so* rough.'

'I feel it,' James moaned, as he limply stirred the Weetabix floating in his soy milk.

'What time did you get home?'

'About quarter to three.'

'How much did you have to drink?'

'It was mostly halves. Three or four pints altogether I s'pose and we were slugging back bourbon in the car.'

Kyle staggered through the door in his boxers. His hair was sticking up everywhere and he had dried blood on his earlobe.

'I don't remember that happening,' James said.

'Me neither,' Kyle said. 'There's blood all over my pillow. I must have caught my earring on something and been too smashed to notice.'

'Some night,' James grinned, struggling not to gag as he swallowed a mouthful of cereal.

'I saw you getting off with Tom in the bar,' Lauren said. 'Is it just for the mission, or do you really fancy him?'

Kyle smiled. 'What do you think?'

'He's bloody good looking,' Lauren giggled. 'Everyone says it's about time you had a boyfriend.'

'Who's everyone? Kyle asked, as he poured a huge heap of instant coffee powder into a mug, hoping the caffeine would give his brain the kick-start it desperately needed.

Lauren didn't want to name names. 'You know, Kyle, just campus gossip.'

'Well, well, well,' Zara said cheerfully as she stepped into the kitchen. 'This isn't a pretty sight. You boys had better get your uniforms on sharpish if you expect to catch the bus.'

She wore heels and a smart brown business suit. James had never seen her with her hair up before.

'You look nice,' Lauren said, before breaking into an open-mouthed yawn.

'Yeah,' James nodded. 'What are you all done up like a dog's dinner for?'

Lauren gave him a kick under the table. *Don't be rude*, she mouthed silently.

'I've got to attend a senior staff meeting back at campus,' Zara explained, as she caught her reflection in the window and pushed her hair into shape.

'What about Ryan?' Kyle asked.

'He's sulking up in bed. I had to give him a piece of my mind last night. He was talking about quitting the Alliance. I want you three to be extra nice to him for the next couple of days – he needs a boost.'

'I feel sorry for him,' Lauren said. 'Coming out of prison and finding that everyone's stabbed him in the back.'

'You've had a few close chats with Ryan, haven't you?' Zara smiled.

'He's not a bad guy,' Lauren said. 'The world's full of people who are all talk. Ryan might be a bit odd, but he's devoted his whole life to doing what he thinks is right. You've got to admire him for that.'

'Pity it's all a bunch of veggie crap,' James sneered.

'It's not crap, James,' Lauren said bitterly. 'Maybe if you'd done the background reading you were supposed to do for this mission, instead of playing your Playstation and lusting after anything in a skirt, you'd understand how cruel people are to animals.'

'I understand the issues.' James smirked. 'Animals are dumb and they taste delicious.'

'Grow up, James,' Lauren said, springing out of her chair. 'Millions of animals suffer in factory farms and experiments every single day and idiots like you don't even care.'

'OK, OK,' Zara interrupted. 'Calm down, you two. James and Kyle, you've got less than ten minutes to get ready for school.'

'Actually,' Kyle said, 'I was wondering if me and James could stay home today. We've only had four hours' sleep.'

'I'm really tired as well,' Lauren added.

'She can go to school,' James tutted. 'She's not hung over and she's always sitting up half the night nattering to Bethany when she's on campus.'

'Get stuffed, James.'

Zara glanced anxiously at her watch. 'I've got an important meeting,' she repeated. 'And I don't want to spend my day worrying about you three hanging around the house fighting. You're going to school, OK?'

'Hey,' Kyle said indignantly. 'James and Lauren are arguing, not me.'

'*All* three of you,' Zara said. 'Now I'm running late. I'll be back this evening and if I find out that any of you didn't make it to school, there's going to be trouble.'

Zara steamed out towards the car, then came running back and grabbed her handbag off the counter top.

'You're both idiots,' Kyle said, as he headed out of the room to get dressed. 'We probably would have got out of school if you two had stopped picking at each other for five minutes.'

*

James' morning was a nightmare. If you're feeling queasy and you want peace and quiet, Year Nine double art class isn't the place to be. Kids yelled across the classroom, the teacher yelled at the kids for trashing the still life and there was a game of *throw an eraser at another kid's head as hard as you can* going on. The English period before lunch was quieter, but James was horrified when he looked at his timetable and discovered that the whole afternoon was games.

He'd forgotten his kit, which meant he'd either have to run around in unhygienic rags handed out by the PE teachers, or try and get off by saying he was ill. James hadn't encountered the PE teachers at this school, but based upon past experience the only way of persuading PE teachers into letting you out of games was if you had a note, or some obvious problem like a missing limb or a pickaxe handle sticking out the back of your head.

James decided that his only option was to bunk off. As soon as the bell went for lunch, he headed out the main gate towards the small parade of shops with hundreds of other kids and just kept on going. James didn't know the area well, but the school bus passed through a village with a decent-sized shopping street a couple of kilometres from the school and that's where he headed.

It was a narrow road without a pavement. The traffic was light, but it didn't hang around and you had to keep your wits about you when you walked around a bend. The sun was out and the combo of country air and brisk walking cleared James' head. He'd only managed a few mouthfuls of cereal at breakfast and by the time he arrived at the shops he'd started to feel properly hungry.

James' first thought was to wonder where he could buy vegan food. But as he passed a travel agent's and a baker's with gingerbread men and massive cream cakes stacked in the window, he realised that nobody was around and that he could eat whatever he liked. He felt inside his blazer pockets and was relieved to discover a fiver and a couple of quid in change.

Even better, he spotted a burger bar across the road. It was old school, with laminated menus standing on the Formica tables and ketchup dispensers shaped like giant tomatoes. It was busy, but not packed and the waitress told James to sit wherever he liked.

Ten minutes later she slid a Coke and an oval plate in front of him. It was stacked up with fries and a massive dual patty cheeseburger filled with cooked mushrooms and grated onion.

James was still dehydrated from the booze the night before and downed half of his Coke before grabbing the burger and tearing out an enormous bite.

It was easily the tastiest thing he'd eaten in days and he loved the hot trickle of fat running out of the meat and the sharp, crunchy onions. But as he moved in to take the second bite, he looked at the two slices of ground-up beef and started to wonder.

He remembered reading that hamburger is made from the tough old meat that comes from dairy cows once they get too old to produce milk. Milk machines, one book called them: kept crammed in tiny metal stalls for most of their lives, pumped with hormones and antibiotics, constantly impregnated to keep the milk flowing. As James looked at his melting cheese, he remembered a picture in a book of a cow with an infected udder, and stories of how the bacteria-filled pus leaks into the milk.

'How's your food, young man?' the waitress asked.

'Mmm, good,' James nodded, finally taking his second bite.

It was as good as any burger James had ever eaten, but the background reading for the mission and the talk amongst the activists made it hard to separate the images of cruelty from the food he was putting in his mouth.

James had no intention of going vegetarian, but as he tucked into his lunch he had the uncomfortable realisation that his conscience was going to nag him every time he ate a piece of meat from now on.

18. DINNER

James didn't want to get nabbed sneaking back on to the school bus, but that left him at the mercy of a local bus service that ran once an hour and only got within four kilometres of Corbyn Copse. He walked a couple of kilometres from the adjacent village before he got lucky and was picked up by one of the elderly protestors.

Even so, it was nearly six when James came through the door and he expected a blasting from Zara. But she wasn't back from campus and instead he found Ryan and Lauren working on the evening meal in the kitchen. Ryan was telling some of his old Zebra 84 anecdotes and Lauren lapped them up as she chopped onions and dropped them into sizzling oil.

'I called your mobile about six times,' Lauren said. 'Miss Hunter came to my class and asked if I knew why you weren't in PE.'

The truth was obvious, so James didn't even attempt a lie. 'My head was killing me so I bunked it.'

'Zara's gonna *love* you. You're getting a letter home and you've got to go to the head of year's office tomorrow.'

'Fabulous,' James said wearily, as he slumped at the dining table. 'Mind you, with a bit of luck I'll get suspended for a few days.'

'What about your mobile?' Lauren asked.

'It was panic stations getting ready this morning,' James said. 'I think it's still upstairs in my jeans from last night.'

'We need to talk to Zara but we can't get through,' Lauren explained.

'What's up?'

Ryan took over. 'I got a call from one of my few sympathisers in the Alliance. Anna and I go way back, even before Zebra eighty-four.'

'She's the one I was helping out with the buffet at the university last night,' Lauren explained.

James nodded. 'I remember – nice friendly lady.'

'So, Anna called me this morning,' Ryan continued. 'The vast majority of experiments at Malarek are on mice, rats and rabbits, but they're still using a couple of hundred dogs per month and the Alliance has spent years looking for where they're bred. Anna received a tip-off about a kennel down in Trowbridge, thirty miles south of here.'

'Is the information solid?' James asked.

Ryan nodded. 'She's sent people down there to sniff around and it looks real enough. They have cages and sheds where they breed dogs for pets, but there's a special kennel where pups are grown in isolation for experimentation.'

'Why in isolation?' James asked.

'Scientists don't want puppies that have been rolling around on the grass picking up diseases and parasites that might spoil their experiments. They want dogs that are separated from their mothers at birth and kept in single cages.'

'Anna is leading a mission to rescue as many of the dogs as possible and it's on for tonight,' Lauren explained, as she added chopped courgettes to the pan of onions.

'Turn the heat down or they'll burn,' Ryan said urgently. 'The thing is, I've been invited along. But I really need Zara's say-so before I can go along with something like this.'

'Why?' James asked.

Ryan suddenly sounded narked. 'Zara and I had a chat last night and she made it clear that I'd find myself back in prison if I stepped out of line.'

'When did you last ring Zara?' James asked.

'Just before you got in the door,' Lauren said. 'I've left her loads of voicemails.'

'Did you try speaking to someone on the switchboard in mission preparation?'

'Yes,' Lauren sighed. 'They said Zara couldn't be disturbed unless we had an emergency. I asked if there was anyone other than Zara who knew about our mission. The dude asked around, but nobody knew a thing.'

'Well it's down to us then,' James said. 'What does Kyle say?'

'He's not here,' Lauren said. 'Tom came over in his MG after school and they've gone into town for a curry.'

'Great,' James tutted, realising that he couldn't ring Kyle to discuss the mission while he was with Tom. 'The decision's down to us then. And if you ask me, Ryan, we want you as involved in the Alliance as possible.'

'That's what I said,' Lauren nodded, as she grabbed three dinner plates out of the cupboard.

Meanwhile, Ryan was pulling a nut roast out of the oven.

'But one of us should go with you,' James said. 'You might meet some interesting activists.'

Ryan and Lauren both looked surprised at this suggestion. 'I can't just turn up with a kid in tow,' he said.

'Suppose you're right,' James said, feeling a little stupid. 'Just thinking out loud.'

'It would be good though,' Lauren said. 'Anna's a really nice person and she's got four daughters. Maybe you could say that Zara's away and I'm too young to be left on my own. Then I could sleep in the car or something.'

Ryan thought for a second as he split the nut roast between three plates. 'Or,' he said, waggling his finger excitedly, 'do you like dogs, Lauren?'

Lauren smiled. 'I love dogs. I always wanted one when I was little but you weren't allowed them round our flats.'

'Not that it stopped all the local villains from owning Rottweilers and pit bulls,' James added.

'Right,' Ryan grinned. 'Then I've got a way for Lauren to come along and help out. Are you both *sure* this is going to be OK with Zara?'

'I'll take responsibility,' James said. 'It's bloody ridiculous Zara disappearing like this in the middle of a mission. What's she playing it?'

'Don't knock her until you know why,' Lauren said sharply. 'For all we know there's an emergency on another mission or something.'

Meanwhile, Ryan had grabbed his mobile. 'Anna, I've got good news and bad news. The good news is that I'm in for tonight if you still want me. The bad news is that Zara's not around and I've got a little childcare problem. How would you feel about having young Lauren as an extra pair of hands at the stables?'

*

Zara had the only car, so Ryan called a mini-cab which took them on the fifteen-kilometre trip to a multi-storey car park in the centre of Bristol.

They headed up to the fifth floor, using a concrete staircase that reeked of urine, then along a corridor where Ryan knocked on a door with SANITATION written on it. It was opened by a dreadlocked man called Lou and they joined him in a gloomy room, with mops standing in metal buckets along one wall and shelves stacked with cleaning solutions.

'You know the rules,' Lou said. 'Everyone has to be checked for bugs.'

'I *made* the rules,' Ryan grinned, as he was padded down. Next, he pulled his T-shirt off, stepped out of his trainers and dropped his trousers down to his ankles. Once Lou finished inspecting Ryan's trainers, he looked uneasily at Lauren.

'I have to do the same for the little lady,' he said, clearly uncomfortable at the idea of asking an eleven-year-old to strip off in front of him.

'It's OK,' Lauren smiled, as she pulled her T-shirt over her head. Ryan had told her not to bring her mobile phone and all she had in her pockets were door keys and a few pounds in change.

Once the formalities were over, Ryan and Lou pulled each other into a hug.

'Long time no see,' Lou grinned. 'Sorry I didn't visit you inside, but I've never been one for showing my face.'

'Don't worry about that,' Ryan said. 'I appreciated people making the effort, but to be honest the company only made me feel worse.'

Lauren was intrigued by Lou as she slid her trainers back on. She thought she'd seen surveillance pictures of all Ryan's close associates, but this distinctive black man would have stuck out and she'd definitely never seen a picture of him.

They headed back out into the car park and found a shabby Vauxhall Astra. Ryan joined Lou in the front and Lauren slid in the back.

'Cars are a problem nowadays,' Lou explained, as he backed out of the parking spot. 'There's speed cameras everywhere that can read your number plate. We never go anywhere near a raid in our own cars. I pick up cheap, nondescript motors at auctions and put false plates on them.'

Ryan nodded. 'Sounds expensive.'

'It is that. I know you're no fan of Madeline Laing, but we're never left wanting for money. And as the police get their hands on better surveillance technology, our operations get more expensive.'

'We're slowly turning into a police state,' Ryan said.

'You said it,' Lou nodded, as the car pulled out of the multi-storey and into daylight.

'So, you and Anna keep it tight?'

'Very tight,' Lou said. 'It's basically us two and a few others from the old days. We're part of the Alliance, but we keep out of anything that takes place within five clicks of Malarek and stick to special operations. The only people we use regularly who you might not know are Anna's eldest two daughters.'

'I'm their godfather, as a matter of fact,' Ryan grinned. 'If I had two pennies to rub together, I'd have bought them an eighteenth birthday present.'

'I'm told you've got a nice cottage back at Corbyn Copse.'

'That's Zara's money talking: her husband was something in the oil industry and she got a juicy divorce settlement.'

'Funny,' Lou smiled, 'I never saw you settling into a house with kids and that.'

'Me neither,' Ryan said, as Lauren caught a glimpse of his face in the mirror. She could see how uncomfortable Ryan felt lying to his friend.

19. GIRLS

It was turning dark when the Astra pulled into a lay-by close to the junction of two busy A-roads. Lauren stepped out of the car as Lou gave her directions.

'I'd take you up there, but we're running late. Just walk straight for about a kilometre. It's safe, there's a grass verge all the way. The first building you'll come to is a modern house: red brick, plastic windows and a stable block out back. They know you're coming.'

'What time should you be back?'

'Hard to say,' Lou shrugged. 'Depending on the breaks it could be any time between midnight and three in the morning.'

'Or not at all if we get nicked,' Ryan added.

'Right,' Lauren said, as she leaned into the car and gave Ryan a kiss on the cheek. 'Good luck, guys. I hope everything goes to plan.'

'Thank you,' Ryan grinned, startled by Lauren's apparently genuine burst of affection.

Once the car set off, Lauren began a slow trek towards the house. As she walked, she realised that she wanted Ryan,

Lou and Anna to succeed in rescuing the dogs. She wished she'd been able to go with them, because her espionage training might have come in useful.

'You must be Lauren,' a young woman dressed in wellies and jeans said a few minutes later, as Lauren stepped through the front gate. The woman moved awkwardly because she had a large drum of disinfectant hanging off each arm.

'You must be Anna's daughter,' Lauren smiled. 'You look just like her.'

The twenty-year-old nodded. 'I'm Miranda. My sister Adelaide is in the house, putting the two little ones to bed.'

'Little ones?' Lauren asked.

'Our half sisters, Polly and Cat. They're three and five.'

'You don't live here, do you?' Lauren asked.

Miranda shook her head. 'The house belongs to a supporter. It's usually let out, but the location is perfect for tonight. Do you want to come around to the stables and see what we're setting up?'

'Sure,' Lauren said. 'Do you want a hand with one of those drums?'

'I can just about manage,' Miranda said as she waddled awkwardly around the side of the house.

The stable block had berths for ten horses and was in pristine condition. It came complete with a grass paddock, enclosed by a neat wooden fence, but there were no horses to be seen anywhere. Most of the stable doors had been swung open and inside each one was a trestle table with several plastic bowls lined up on it.

'What's all this in aid of?' Lauren asked. 'I thought the dogs were already kept in isolation.'

'None of our people has been inside the isolation unit, but our source reckons the dogs are kept in filthy conditions. Young dogs are extremely playful and if you separate them from their siblings and put them in a tiny cage without any toys, the only thing they're left to play with is their own filth.'

'You mean wee and poo,' Lauren gawped, screwing up her nose at the thought.

'Afraid so. Our tip-off claimed that the cages are hosed out a couple of times a week, but the dogs themselves only get disinfected immediately before they're shipped off to Malarek.'

'That's so disgusting,' Lauren said. 'How can anyone let an animal live like that?'

'I know – it's beyond belief, isn't it? I'd really appreciate it if you could help out. I've dealt with similar situations before and cleaning the animals takes a strong stomach, but you can make yourself useful even if you just run back and forth with the hot water.'

'I'll do whatever I can to help,' Lauren said. 'What will happen to the puppies afterwards?'

'We can't keep them here for long. But over the years we've built up a network of unofficial sanctuaries for animals we've rescued, so they'll all go to good homes.'

*

By the time everything was set up inside the stables, Anna's youngest daughters were asleep. The house wasn't huge, but seemed so to Lauren after the pokey cottage in Corbyn Copse. She ended up in the living-room, sandwiched between Adelaide and Miranda, with her socked feet resting on a coffee table and communal bowls of tortilla chips and salsa in her lap.

The TV was going, but they weren't really watching. Mostly, Lauren listened to stories told by the two sisters. It sounded like they'd had an amazing childhood. Their dad had left home when they were toddlers and Anna's full-time commitment to animal liberation meant that she survived on donations and state benefits. The sisters had even spent eighteen months in foster care while their mother was in prison.

But the girls didn't seem to resent any of the hardships. They clearly adored their mother, even if they weren't so keen on their stepfather, and they told fantastic adventure stories. As ten-year-olds, they'd run into the woods in the middle of the night in their dressing gowns, holding rabbit cages while the police searched their home. As teenagers they'd been smuggled out of Romania in the boot of a car after taking part in a protest against blood sports and they'd each spent three months in a young offenders' institution following an arson attack on a meat market.

Lauren was a natural born cynic, but she was impressed by these two resourceful and intelligent young women. As interesting as their stories were, however, she'd been up past midnight the evening before and eventually lost the battle with her eyelids.

*

Lauren woke with a start from a dream she instantly forgot. The TV was off, Miranda and Adelaide had left the room, but she could hear conversation down the hallway.

She hoped she hadn't slept through all the excitement as

she slipped her trainers on and rushed through to the kitchen. There were six people sat or standing around the dining table, keeping themselves awake with mugs of coffee.

The new arrivals were a middle-aged couple called Phyllis and Ken, a student called Jay who was Adelaide's boyfriend, and an elderly man whose leather bag made him instantly recognisable as a medic, in this case a vet.

'Ahh, here she is,' Miranda said.

'What did I miss?' Lauren asked anxiously. 'You didn't let me sleep through anything did you?'

'Don't worry,' Miranda smiled. 'Lou made a call about half an hour ago. Security was featherweight; they managed to get in and out of the kennels without any trouble. They should be here in ten to fifteen minutes. The only thing is, we've got seventy-three beagle pups to deal with.'

'How many were we expecting?' Lauren asked.

'Thirty or forty,' Miranda replied. 'It's a good job you came. We're really going to have our work cut out getting that number of dogs cleaned up and shipped off to the sanctuaries by sun-up.'

'Lou's wife and sister are coming over to lend a hand,' Adelaide added. 'But they won't get here for at least another hour.'

20. DOGS

All hell broke loose when the two vehicles arrived – Ryan and Anna in a seven-ton truck and Lou in the Vauxhall Astra. It was pitch black, so Lou pointed his car towards the truck and left the headlamps burning so that they had light to work in.

Lauren and the others donned breathing masks and thick rubber gloves, as Anna pushed up the steel shutter at the rear of the truck. The wave of putrid air was beyond anything Lauren imagined possible. She ripped off her mask and staggered forwards to vomit at the edge of the driveway. Phyllis had exactly the same reaction, and several others were gagging.

'Are you OK?' Miranda asked gently, as she rubbed Lauren's back. 'Do you want me to get you some water?'

'Help the dogs,' Lauren gasped as she staggered towards the house. 'I'll be OK.'

She ran into the kitchen and quickly swished her mouth out with water. She felt queasy, but was determined to get back out there and show that she could be of some use.

The puppies had been placed on the floor of the truck in

cardboard pet carriers. Each was designed for one small dog, but the haul of pups had been beyond expectations and the rescuers had resorted to putting two dogs into some of them.

Braving the appalling smell, Lauren grabbed two boxes that Anna handed down from inside the truck. As she ran around to the stables behind the house, one box was alive with the sound of two frightened pups scratching at their enclosure, while a single pup cowered at the rear of the other.

Each stable had a tap rigged up with its own supply of cold water. The only source of hot ran down a long hose from the kitchen and Adelaide had asked everyone to use it sparingly because the tank wouldn't last for ever.

Lauren walked into an empty stable. She put the two dog carriers on the stone floor and flipped on the light, revealing a trestle table with three bowls on it. She'd been concerned about the quiet pup and wanted to deal with it first, but as soon as she put the boxes down a riot broke out between the other two and Lauren could see the dogs scrapping through the air holes.

She wasn't used to dealing with animals, so her heart raced as she popped the cardboard box open and – taking pains not to inhale the smell in case it made her sick again – pulled out a skinny, wriggling object no bigger than a guinea pig. The little dog twisted and yapped as her gloves tightened around its waist.

Lauren wanted to cry when she saw the state of the little thing. Its eyes were bright, but its brown and white coat was stained yellow and its fur was matted with dried out smears of excrement.

'Poor baby,' Lauren choked, but then she almost dropped the frightened dog as it blasted a warm jet of pee down her arm. She hurried forwards and plonked it in the first empty bowl, as Phyllis came into the room holding the hot-water hose.

'Do you need a squirt?'

'I guess I do,' Lauren said, smiling uneasily.

Phyllis had vomited at the same time as Lauren, but apparently didn't possess the same determination to get over it and still looked green. She held her breath as she ran warm water into the second and third bowls.

Meanwhile, Lauren grabbed the cold hose off the floor and turned on the tap. She felt really mean as she began dribbling the cold water into the first bowl and the little dog yipped as it lapped against its paws.

It reared up on the side of the bowl and tried scrambling over the side, forcing Lauren to pin the animal gently in the middle of the bowl before spraying its coat with the cold water. The little dog squealed miserably as Lauren hosed the filth out of its coat.

'I know it's not nice,' she said soothingly. 'But you'll feel better when we've finished and we'll find you a nice new home.'

'Brilliant, you've started already,' Ryan said, pulling on his gloves as he stepped inside behind her. 'I tell you what, I'll take over at the dirty end and you can deal with the disinfectant and the final rinse.'

Lauren handed Ryan the hose and watched as he demonstrated a technique based upon years of rescuing laboratory animals.

'Start at the head and move your hands down the body in smooth strokes,' he explained. 'Always move from head to tail; that way you're less likely to get something unpleasant in its eyes or mouth.'

While Ryan expertly massaged out the filth and snipped out clumps of hopelessly matted fur with a pair of scissors, Lauren poured a mixture of disinfectant and dog shampoo into the second bowl.

'Little dogs *always* drink the bath-water and go potty when they get the taste on their tongue,' Ryan said. 'So prepare to get wet.'

Sure enough, as soon as Lauren plopped the shivering dog into the warm, foamy water it started going berserk. She squirted shampoo directly on to the dog's coat and worked it into a lather. After a minute or so, the poor thing had yapped itself into a state of complete exhaustion and by the time she lifted it into the third bowl to rinse the shampoo out of its coat, the panting dog had resigned itself to being washed.

After a squirt of deodorant, a blast of flea powder and a quick towelling off, Lauren held the bundle out for Ryan, who was already hosing the next pup in line.

'It actually looks like a dog now,' she said, grinning helplessly at the sour-faced lump in her hands.

'OK,' Ryan nodded. 'Well done. Take him through to the vet in stable number two, and then get back here.'

'Come on doggy,' Lauren smiled, as she headed out of the stable and past the cleaning operations going on next door. 'The big man's probably going to stick a needle in your bum, but after that, we've got a stable laid out with water and nice bowls of vegetarian dog food. And you'll be able to make friends with the other puppies.'

*

Ninety minutes later, Lauren delivered her eleventh damp puppy to the vet. He seemed like a nice old chap, but he had beagle pups coming at him from four different cleaning stations and no time for chit-chat.

As Lauren headed back towards Ryan in the other stable, Miranda stepped in front of her.

'You look worn out,' she said. 'Phyllis is making hot drinks in the kitchen. Why don't you take a ten-minute break?'

'What about Ryan?' Lauren asked.

'I'll help him out, then he can go for a break when you come back.'

Lauren became acutely aware of the mess she was in as she stepped into the kitchen. Her jeans and T-shirt were spattered with soap suds, filthy brown water and the residue from several dogs peeing and one throwing up. She'd gradually got used to the foul odours, but guessed that she smelled worse than she'd ever done in her whole life, easily surpassing the five-day wilderness training exercise during CHERUB basic training.

The previously immaculate kitchen floor swam with brown water.

'Sit yourself down,' Phyllis said. 'Don't worry about the state of the place; I'll nuke it with bleach once all the dogs are cleaned. What would you like to drink? Tea, coffee, soy-milk cocoa?'

'Cocoa,' Lauren smiled, as she sat at the table and got the horrible itchy feeling of wet knickers sticking to her bum.

By the time the microwave heating the cocoa pinged, Lauren had pulled off her breathing mask and gloves, revealing a set of shrivelled fingertips. At the opposite end of the eight-seat dining table, Adelaide worked frantically at a beefy laptop which had two camcorders and a jog-shuttle controller plugged into its rear ports.

'Want to see yourself at work?' Adelaide asked.

Lauren carried her steaming mug around the table and looked at the biggest laptop screen she'd ever seen. It was divided into a row of video feeds at the top, with a mass of timelines, sound waves and buttons beneath.

'What is that?' Lauren asked.

'Adobe Premiere, video editing software,' Adelaide explained. 'I'm putting together a press pack. We've already e-mailed the BBC and all the other big media organisations with a batch of still photographs we took inside the kennels. Now I'm editing together a ten-minute film that we can upload to the Zebra Alliance website.'

While Miranda spoke, she'd flipped the screen to some video footage taken inside the stable. It showed Lauren from the back, frantically scrubbing one of the pups before transferring it from the disinfectant bowl into the final rinse.

'Cool,' Lauren said. 'I didn't see you filming.'

Miranda smiled. 'You were so into it that you didn't hear me coming up to the stable doors and I didn't want to disturb you because the image of a young girl helping to scrub the dogs is just *perfect*.'

'Ryan's on parole you know, if someone recognises him . . .'

'Don't worry about that,' Miranda smiled. 'I take every bit of footage and pixelate the faces. Then I destroy the original tapes and wipe the hard drives of the laptop. Just to be extra safe, the Alliance has a media lawyer who watches every video and photograph. Then he gets one of his assistants to send it to the media from a twenty-four-hour internet café, which makes it impossible to track down our location.'

'So when will pixelated me be uploaded to the Zebra Alliance website?'

'Less than three hours, hopefully. We've got magnificent footage of the filth inside the kennels. Lou even videoed a couple of puppies that had died from infected wounds in their enclosures.'

'Poor little things,' Lauren said sadly.

'It's sad that the animals were so badly treated,' Miranda nodded. 'But the upside is that we can notify the RSPCA and the local council as soon as their offices open. Those kennels will have their dog-breeding licence removed and be forced to shut down.'

'Cool,' Lauren said. 'And I bet no other kennel will want to supply Malarek with dogs.'

Adelaide nodded. 'If they do, they'd better keep it secret from us.'

Lauren drained her cocoa and clonked the empty mug on the table. 'Well,' she said. 'I'd better get back out there so Ryan can take his coffee break. I think there's less than a dozen dogs left to clean now.'

As she stepped outside, Lauren could see the sun rising behind a line of trees. She glanced back inside at the kitchen clock and was stunned to see that it was quarter to five in the morning.

21. MEATBALL

'Hey,' Ryan said, as he gently brushed his fingertips against Lauren's cheek to wake her up. His hairy chest was bare and he wore a set of Lou's jeans that were several sizes too big for him.

Lauren opened her eyes and realised that she was on a sofa, squeezed up inside a Bob the Builder sleeping bag. Sunlight blazed through the curtains.

'Anna's making you lunch,' Ryan said.

'*Lunch*,' Lauren gasped. 'What time is it?'

'Ten past one.'

'Blimey. Does Zara know where we are?'

'I've spoken to her,' Ryan nodded. 'She's fine about last night and everything. She's on her way down in the car to pick us up.'

As Lauren unzipped the sleeping bag and sat up, the events of the night before came flooding back. Once the last batch of dogs had been dealt with, everyone had headed into the house to clean themselves, but the hot water had run out. After a freezing cold shower, Lauren had towelled off and changed into an oversized T-shirt and shorts that belonged to Miranda.

As Lauren wandered through to the kitchen, her arms and shoulders ached from the effort of scrubbing the dogs.

'Hello,' Anna said brightly, moving across to the dining table and pouring Lauren a glass of orange juice. 'How does vegan French toast sound?'

'Sounds great,' Lauren grinned, hitching up her massive shorts as she sat down. She looked around and noticed that everything was spotless, with no trace of the paraphernalia they'd used the night before. 'Are all the dogs gone?'

Ryan nodded as he sat next to Lauren. 'Lou took some, Adelaide and Miranda left with the rest.'

'Oh,' Lauren said, feeling sad because she would have liked a chance to see them all cleaned up and happy.

Anna's French toast came dusted with icing sugar, strawberries and slices of melon on the side. The hot, sweet bread was exactly what Lauren felt like after the exertion of the night before.

'I'd better be going, Ryan,' Anna said, once she'd switched off the oven and rinsed the baking tray under the tap. 'I've got to pick Cat and Polly up from school at three. Would you mind washing Lauren's dishes and locking up? You can hand the keys back to Phyllis; she's always up at the protest site on the weekend.'

'No problem at all,' Ryan nodded. 'Don't wait around here on our account. Zara should be here in half an hour or so.'

After eating and waving goodbye to Anna on the doorstep, Lauren found her trainers and wandered outside for some air and a final look at the stables. She felt a lump in her throat as she imagined the excited puppies sitting in the backs of cars and vans, smelling of disinfectant as they headed for sanctuary.

She also felt proud. She'd worked hard, she'd been part of a great team and there were no doubts in her mind that rescuing the dogs was the right thing to do. Even if stealing animals was against the law, and even if some animal experiments were for important medical research, there was never an excuse for forcing animals to live in their own filth.

As she headed back towards the house, Lauren heard a high-pitched noise. She stood still for a couple of seconds while she convinced herself that it was one of the stable doors creaking in the wind. But as she headed away, she heard it again and this time it sounded uncannily like a whimpering puppy.

'Hello?' Lauren said loudly, then realised she was being daft. It wasn't as if the dog was going to start a conversation.

She considered running back to the house and fetching Ryan, but the dog was close by and she didn't want to lose it. In fact she could see thirty metres clear in all directions, so the dog had to be inside one of the stables.

The stable doors were split into two halves so that horses could poke their heads out. Lauren opened the top part of one door and leaned inside to flip on the light switch.

'Look at you,' Lauren giggled, as she saw a tiny dog cowering on the bare concrete floor near the back wall. 'Did they leave you behind?'

She pushed the bottom part of the door open and stepped inside. The brown-faced pup's only previous human encounters had been with kennel hands, vets and people intent on dunking its head in a bowl of disinfectant, so it was less than delighted to see Lauren and made this clear by baring its teeth.

'I won't hurt you,' Lauren said softly, as the dog backed into the corner.

As Lauren bent to grab the growling dog, her giant shorts slid down her legs and the pup dashed for the stable door, which she'd carelessly left ajar.

By the time she'd yanked up her shorts, the pup was out on the stable yard.

'Ryan,' Lauren screamed frantically, as the dog belted along the gravel path leading to the paddock.

She was desperate to get hold of the pup before it reached the trees, because she'd never find it once it got tangled up in the undergrowth. Fortunately, the dog had spent its entire life in a cage and hadn't got the knack of running. As Lauren closed in, with one hand holding up her shorts and the other ready to scoop up the dog, it stumbled over its own front legs and flipped head over heels on to its back.

But the little thing rolled out of Lauren's grasp and headed back along the courtyard towards Ryan, who'd raced away from the washing-up to investigate the yelping. He stood in the middle of the path, spreading himself out wide to grab the puppy belting towards him as Lauren charged after it.

Ryan got his hand on fur, but the dog turned its body around and wriggled free.

'*Sod*,' Ryan yelled, as Lauren carried on the chase.

The pup was tiring and she'd almost caught up by the time it cut down the side of the house towards the road. It was barely two metres ahead of Lauren when it reached the gravel driveway at the front of the house. She heard a noise and looked up, taking her eyes off the dog just in time to see Zara's giant blue people carrier bearing down on her.

Lauren experienced blind terror as the vehicle closed her down. Time froze and her eyes fixed on Zara's sunglasses and gaping mouth inside the car. She was running flat out and had too much momentum to stop. All she could do was put her arms in front of her face to cushion the inevitable blow.

Fortunately, Zara already had her foot over the brake and by the time Lauren clattered into the front of the vehicle it had stopped moving. Her elbow made a hollow thud on the windscreen, catching a nerve and sending a painful spasm towards her hand.

But Lauren had survived worse and she was determined to get her hands on the little dog before it disappeared. Too proud to let the pain show on her face, she rolled off the bonnet, gritted her teeth and crouched down to see where the animal had gone after it disappeared between the front wheels.

'Did you see it?' Lauren yelled desperately, as Zara jumped out of the car.

'See what?' Zara steamed. 'Are you off your rocker, running out without looking like that? I nearly flattened you.'

'I'm chasing after a puppy,' Lauren explained, as she stood back up.

'It's in the bloody road,' Ryan yelled, as he raced around the passenger side of the car.

Zara and Lauren both looked around to see the small brown and white dog standing in the middle of the road, panting and turning its head around as if it couldn't decide which way to go. A second later, a small Nissan rounded the gently curved road and skimmed over the pup at more than fifty miles an hour.

'No!' Lauren squealed, covering her eyes and expecting the worst. But Ryan kept his head and dashed on to the tarmac. The dog had been swept off its feet by the turbulent air beneath the car and Ryan grabbed the confused animal before it knew what had almost hit it.

Ryan's momentum carried him on to the other side of the carriageway and a truck holding a loaded skip blasted its horn and swerved as he reached the verge and skidded down a slight embankment, crashing into a tangle of wild flowers.

Lauren and Zara let a couple more cars pass before running through a break in the traffic. Lauren was massively relieved to see that Ryan had managed to keep the wriggling dog clutched firmly between his hands.

'Are you hurt?' she asked.

'I'll live,' Ryan puffed, as Zara gave him a hand up. 'But that truck aged me a few years.'

'You know what?' Lauren grinned. 'I recognise that dog: the brown face and the one eye slightly lower than the other. It's the first one we cleaned last night.'

Ryan smiled as he turned the dog towards himself and looked into its eyes. 'The poor fella needs a good drink to cool down. I feel like I'm holding a hot water bottle.'

'What are we gonna do with him?' Lauren asked.

'Can't leave him here on his tod,' Ryan said. 'We'll have to take him back to the cottage.'

'He can share my room,' Lauren grinned. 'I think this is fate – I've always wanted a dog.'

'Only for a few days, until we can find somewhere else for him to go,' Zara said tautly. 'Only red shirts are allowed pets, so don't let yourself get too fond of him.'

'And it's pretty dodgy,' Ryan added. 'Me living in a house with a beagle pup when the Alliance just rescued seventy-three of them.'

'Meatball,' Lauren smiled, ignoring all the warnings. 'I'm gonna call him Meatball.'

22. JULY

Three weeks later

It was a beautiful July day and James came in from school with his shirtsleeves rolled up and sweat glistening on his forehead.

'I'm home,' he shouted.

Zara yelled something back from the kitchen as James cut into the living-room. Meatball stood up and padded over with his tail wagging. He'd almost doubled in size since Lauren had chased him around the stables and while there were various sound reasons for getting rid of the puppy, in the end nobody had the heart to do it.

'Hey dude,' James grinned, as he crouched down and swept his hand through the dog's brown and white coat. 'You're hot aren't you? Never mind, you've had both your injections now. You'll be safe to go outside for walkies in another week.'

Meatball rolled on to his back and let James tickle his belly.

'Aren't you a cutie pie?' James smiled. 'Where's your ball?'

He reached under an armchair and grabbed a pink rubber ball. Meatball knew what this meant and sprang up excitedly as James lobbed the ball behind the sofa. The dog spun around and raced behind the furniture, emerging at the other end with the ball in his mouth.

'Aren't *you* a clever boy?'

While Meatball had grasped the idea of fetching a ball, he was less keen on letting go once he had it. As James tried prising the ball from Meatball's mouth, the little dog narrowed his eyes and growled for all he was worth.

'Good boy,' James grinned, when Meatball finally let go.

James leaned in close and stroked the dog, then let him lick his cheek. He couldn't help but love the puppy as he looked into his docile brown eyes. After another lick, James picked Meatball off the carpet and kissed the top of his head.

'You're the cutest dog in the world, aren't you?' James said, as he stroked Meatball. 'Who's a cute doggy?'

'He always gets like this with animals when he doesn't have a girlfriend,' Lauren said acidly.

James glanced up from the floor and saw Stuart Pierce and Lauren standing in the doorway, giggling.

'Hey Stu,' James said. 'At least some of us have got girlfriends, eh?'

Lauren tutted. 'We're just doing homework together.'

'If you say so, lovebirds,' James smirked.

Meatball had spent most of the day snoozing in the warm room on his own and couldn't cope with suddenly having three people to play with. His tail was in overdrive and he raced back and forth, unable to decide whose attention he wanted.

'Are you coming to my room?' Lauren asked, as Meatball reared up and rested his front paws against the bottom of her school skirt. 'You don't mind do you, James?'

James shrugged. 'Nah, I'm going upstairs for a shower. I'm sweating like a pig.'

'Come on then, Meatball,' Lauren said, as she leaned across the hallway and opened the door of her bedroom.

Meatball belted across the hallway and jumped on to Lauren's bed.

'You know you shouldn't lick James' face,' Lauren said as she stroked the little dog. 'You don't want to go catching all his germs.'

'Hey,' James gasped, as he grabbed his pack and headed for the stairs. 'I heard that.'

'Later, James,' Lauren grinned as she closed her bedroom door.

'You'd better keep those trousers on, Stuart, 'cos I'll kick your arse if you get my little sister pregnant.'

Lauren stuck her head out of the door and gave her brother the finger. 'You just get funnier every day, don't you, James?'

*

After his shower, James trundled down the hallway, wrapped in a towel, and walked into his bedroom. Kyle was on the top bunk reading a copy of Catch 22, dressed only in a set of beach shorts.

'Thank god it's Friday,' James huffed, as he sat on his bed and grabbed a cleanish pair of cargo shorts off the floor. 'How was study leave?'

'Not bad,' Kyle grinned. 'I got up at ten, sunbathed in the

garden until noon and then Tom came over for a couple of hours.'

James tutted. 'Doesn't he have to go to school either? Sixth form is such a doss.'

'Tom's finished his A-levels and starts uni at the end of September. Provided he gets his grades, of course.'

The hot weather was getting to James and he broke into a full-on rant. 'I bloody hate going to *stupid* lessons at *stupid* schools where you don't learn *anything*. It's a gorgeous day and I had to spend two hours sitting in a classroom doing maths. I've done A-level maths and this wasn't even GCSE. I felt like twanging my idiot classmates around the head and going *Why are you all so thick?*'

Kyle laughed. 'We can't all be mathematical geniuses, James. I worked my balls off to get A-level maths last year and still only scraped a C.'

'So, what did Tom say?'

'No news, really. Sophie and Viv are still putting out feelers to try getting involved with one of the radical groups, but they're all so wary of infiltration that nothing is happening fast.'

'You know what's gonna happen, don't you? Me, Kerry and Lauren are scheduled to go on summer holiday at the CHERUB hostel *together* for the first time ever. What's the betting this mission ends up dragging on for months and we miss out?'

'You're a golden beam of sunshine today, aren't you?' Kyle grinned. 'I missed out on summer hostel a few years back, and all for some crummy mission based on a false tip-off about a heroin smuggler. You've been lucky so far, James –

all your missions have panned out. Sooner or later you're gonna get one that goes tits up.'

'You reckon this could be it?'

Kyle shook his head. 'I'm optimistic, but they reckon the AFM could have as few as a dozen members. We were never likely to unearth a small group like that quickly. I reckon we did well hooking up with Tom and Viv as fast as we did.'

'Guess you're right,' James said, feeling slightly happier as he leaned back and put his feet up on his bed. 'And school finishes next week. This mission's gonna be a real doss once summer holidays start.'

James felt a lump under his back. He reached beneath his covers and pulled a red and green rugby sock out of the folds in his duvet. It certainly wasn't his and Kyle wouldn't be seen dead in sportswear.

James leapt off his bunk. 'Kyle, why the hell is your boyfriend's sock inside *my* bed?'

'Oh, that's where it got to,' Kyle said casually. 'We looked everywhere.'

'Were you and Tom using my bed for . . . you know, *gay* stuff?'

'Where else can you sit in this cupboard?'

'You could have used your own bunk,' James said indignantly.

Kyle moved his hand between the top of his bed and the ceiling. 'There's less than half a metre between my mattress and the ceiling. Besides, Tom's a big guy; the bunk would probably collapse with both of us up here.'

'So what *exactly* did you two get up to on my bed?'

'Nothing,' Kyle said. 'We just snuggled up and kissed for a while.'

'After taking your clothes off,' James added.

'*Some* of our clothes,' Kyle said, as he pointed at the sunlight streaming through the window. 'It's eighty degrees out there. Do you expect us to make out in our overcoats?'

'Look, you and Tom are both over sixteen. I've got nothing against you being gay and doing whatever the hell you like with each other. Just not on my bed, OK?'

Kyle jumped down off his bunk and faced James off. 'You're a total homophobe,' he said angrily.

'No,' James said. 'I've known you're gay for yonks. It's not made the slightest bit of difference between us.'

'You know what?' Kyle spluttered. 'You're the worst kind of homophobe, too. I'd prefer it if you just came out and said you didn't like me being gay. Instead of being all *it's OK, it's OK*, but secretly turning your nose up behind my back.'

'You're putting words in my mouth,' James gasped. 'All I said was that I didn't want you two romping around half naked on my bed. What's wrong with that?'

'*Batman Begins*,' Kyle said, jabbing his finger against James' chest. 'We watched it on DVD in your room back at campus. I sat on the floor while everyone else sat on your bed. You were making out with Kerry, Gabrielle was making out with Daniel Satter and Callum was attempting to make out with god knows who. You didn't bat an eyelid, even when Gabrielle and Daniel were practically humping each other.'

'Well . . .' James said weakly.

'It's a total double standard,' Kyle said bitterly. 'If I'd

snogged a girl on your bed you wouldn't have said a word, would you?'

James realised Kyle was right, but he wasn't prepared to admit it. 'Just keep your boyfriend off my bed, Kyle.'

'Get stuffed,' Kyle said, giving James a shove and heading for the door. 'Some bloody friend you are.'

But he didn't get out because Zara was on her way in. Her voice was quiet, but furious. 'I don't know what you two are arguing about,' she hissed, 'but I can overhear you talking about campus downstairs in the kitchen and in case you haven't noticed, we have a guest in the house. Fortunately, Lauren has had the sense to turn her music on.'

James gasped. He'd totally forgotten about Stuart.

'I'm going out for a walk,' Kyle said sourly, grabbing a pair of trainers and a T-shirt before heading out of the room.

'Care to explain what all that was about?' Zara asked James, once Kyle was downstairs.

'I found out Kyle and Tom were making out on my bed earlier. I told Kyle I didn't want them doing it again.'

'Did they leave a mess or something?'

'No, just . . .'

Zara smiled knowingly. 'You're uncomfortable because they're gay.'

James nodded as he remembered why he liked Zara so much: she always understood where you were coming from.

'I know you're not supposed to have anything against gay people,' James explained. 'I mean, I really like Kyle, but whenever I think about the idea of two guys wanting to shag each other, it just makes me go *EUGHHHH!*'

Zara smiled. 'It's a common reaction, especially amongst

teenage boys. Have you ever tried explaining to Kyle how his sexuality makes you feel?'

James shook his head. 'No way, he'd freak at me.'

'I'll have a word with him when he comes back,' Zara said. 'Hopefully it'll sound better coming from me. You two are such good mates; it'd be a shame if you fell out.'

'Cheers,' James grinned.

23. WOMEN

James was always amazed at the way an entire weekend whizzed by faster than a fifty-minute History lesson on a Monday morning. He had his head resting on his desk and watched the seconds count down on the Fossil watch Lauren had bought him for Christmas. The teacher was called Miss Choke – James' late mother's surname – and he wondered if she was some distant cousin of his as she babbled on about the 38th parallel, General Walker and the Korean War.

As James stared intently, looking forward to the momentous instant when his watch would display 11:11:11, the mobile phone in his pocket played its little *message received* sound. He sneaked the Samsung out of his pocket and flipped it open.

'Mr Wilson,' the teacher said sharply.

It took half a second for James to register that this was his current surname and look up.

'I know you're new at this school, James, but I shouldn't have to remind you that mobile telephones are to be switched off during all lessons.'

'Sorry, Miss,' James said, but he was more interested in the message he'd received from Kyle:

AM AT FRONT GATES. MEET NOW. MEGA URGENT!!!

Things had been awkward between James and Kyle since their row on Friday afternoon, so it had to be something to do with the mission.

'Erm . . .' James said, standing up and grabbing his backpack. 'Family crisis. Sorry Miss, but I've got to run.'

The teacher looked startled and James' classmates were staring at him with looks that clearly said *pull the other one it's got bells on.*

'Just because it's the last week of term does *not* give you the right to come and go as you please,' Miss Choke said angrily, as James stuffed his history books into his pack.

'Yeah,' James gasped as he headed for the classroom door and set off at a run down a short corridor. 'Sorry.'

He bolted down two flights of stairs and out of the main school entrance, ignoring the woman at reception demanding to know exactly what he thought he was playing at. Kyle was across the road outside the school, dressed in jeans and polo shirt with a backpack slung over his shoulder.

'What's going on?' James asked, looking around anxiously. 'We'd better get moving. The school secretary was doing her nut and they're bound to send someone out after me.'

Kyle pointed at an old Mondeo parked less than twenty metres away. 'Don't worry, I've got a cab. We've had the call.'

'What call?'

'The feelers Viv put out,' Kyle explained. 'Apparently him

and Tom met up with some dude on the university campus late last night. I got a call from Tom this morning and another from the activists about an hour later. They want to meet us, soon as poss.'

'Sweet,' James said, as they headed towards the cab. 'So are we back on speaking terms now or what?'

Kyle shrugged as he opened the front passenger door of the car. 'You're not exactly my favourite person in the world, but Zara had words and we have a job to do.'

As James climbed in the back of the cab, he could see the school's deputy head on the other side of the road, waiting for a break in the traffic.

'Where to, boss?' the driver asked, in an East European accent.

'Take us into Bristol,' Kyle said. 'Some shopping centre called King Street Parade. Do you know where that is?'

*

The driver got lost going through the tangle of one-way streets in the centre of Bristol and the fare ended up being over twenty quid.

'So what are we supposed to do now?' James asked, as they headed up an escalator towards a food court that had once been the top floor of a department store.

'They told us to sit at a table and await instructions,' Kyle explained. 'We've got no idea how sophisticated these groups are, so we'd better assume that we're being listened to. Stay in character at all times.'

'Right,' James said, almost tripping at the top of the escalator because he was concentrating on ripping off his school tie.

The food court was a standard deal, with a dozen deserted kiosks and twenty people queuing up at the McDonalds. It wasn't quite lunchtime, so there was plenty of space to sit.

'Shall we get something to eat?' James asked, as they sat down at a small table.

Kyle's phone rang the split second his bum touched his plastic chair. 'Hello.'

A female voice came back at him. Kyle thought it sounded sinister, although that probably had more to do with the realisation that he was being watched.

'I see you made it,' she said. 'Took you long enough, didn't it?'

'I told you I had to get James out of school,' Kyle said, craning his neck around in an attempt to spot the woman on the other end of the phone.

'Don't bother looking, Kyle, you'll meet me soon enough. What equipment have you got on you?'

Kyle was baffled. 'Equipment?'

'Telephones, wrist watches, pens, pencils, tape recorders, pocket knives, wallets. You must have some of that stuff on you.'

'Sure, a couple of bits.'

'OK, I can see you've both got backpacks. I want both of you to take everything off, including your telephones, and place them inside the packs. It that clear?'

'Crystal,' Kyle said.

'Once you've done that, wait at your table for ninety seconds. Then head to the lift and take it down to parking basement three. When you step out of the lift, you'll see our van. Climb in the back, hand us your packs without making eye contact and then lie face down on the floor.'

The phone went dead in Kyle's ear.

'And?' James asked.

Kyle allowed himself to smile a little. 'Looks like we're in.'

Two minutes later, a set of elevator doors broke apart and James and Kyle stepped out, surveying the lines of parked cars, looking for their ride. While the other passengers headed towards their vehicles, Kyle stood by the doors looking confused.

'Are you sure you got the right floor?' James asked.

'She definitely said basement three.'

Kyle was beginning to wonder if it was one of Viv's crazy jokes, when a red Volkswagen Transporter turned off the entrance ramp and started coming towards them. The woman in the driving seat had made herself unrecognisable with a baseball cap and dark glasses. She pulled up gently as the rear doors swung open.

As instructed, James and Kyle clambered into the rear compartment and lay face down on the ridged metal floor.

'Packs,' a woman shouted, as someone else closed the rear doors, plunging everything into darkness.

As the van pulled away, James tried glancing up.

'Face down, kid,' the woman shouted, clanging her boot on the metal floor in front of his head to emphasise the point. As the van twisted its way around a series of ramps to leave the car park, one of the women in the back flipped on a roof-mounted interior light, before both of them squatted down on cinema style fold-out seats and began rummaging through the backpacks.

'Homework diary,' the woman with James' backpack

smiled. 'That takes me back a few years. Pens, books, mobile telephone . . .'

The woman flipped James' mobile open and began looking through the stored numbers. As always, James had a special SIM card fitted just for the mission, so none of his friends or contacts on campus were listed. Once Kyle and James' phones had been checked out, the women switched them off to prevent their signals from being tracked.

'I suppose you're a bit young to be an undercover cop,' the woman grinned, as she zipped up James' backpack. 'Both of you sit up, face towards the rear doors and take off everything except your underpants. Don't try looking at us unless you want my boot up your arse.'

Stripping down was an awkward experience because the van kept stopping and starting as it moved through some heavy traffic. The women checked the pockets and turned each item of clothing inside out before throwing it aside. The boys couldn't see out of the van, but by the time they were told to get dressed again, they'd clearly made it out of the city centre and were doing a good speed on a stretch of open road.

A quarter of an hour later, the van pulled off the fast road and after some twists, turns and the squelch of mud under the tyres, came to a halt.

One woman threw blindfolds at James and Kyle. Once they were tightly knotted, the boys were led across a muddy path and into a space that echoed to their footsteps.

The blindfolds were ripped off and it took James and Kyle's eyes half a minute to adjust to the brilliantly lit space. The building seemed modern and was built from breeze blocks. It had a concrete floor, giant skylights cut into the roof and James guessed that it had been built as a small factory.

The three women were bigger than average, but hardly imposing. They wore trousers and boots and all three had slipped into Balaclavas before removing the boys' blindfolds. James was stunned to realise that the tall one standing in the centre had a handgun pointing at his chest.

'James, Kyle,' she said, in an accent with a touch of American to it. 'Thanks for coming. I'm sorry that we have to treat you this way, but the police and intelligence services are extremely keen to uncover groups like ours, so we take every possible precaution to protect our identities. For the purposes of this meeting, you can call me Jo, although that isn't my real name.'

James and Kyle each took a small bottle of mineral water from one of the other women. It had been stifling inside the van and both lads unscrewed the caps and drank greedily, keeping one eye on the gun.

'So you're the AFM?' James asked.

'Some of us have undertaken actions in that name in the past,' Jo nodded. 'But we've moved on. We're setting up a new organisation, the Animal Freedom Army. If you really believe in animal liberation, this is probably the best opportunity you'll ever have to make a difference.'

'Is it really necessary to point that gun at us?' Kyle asked edgily. 'Maybe I've watched too many movies where people get shot accidentally, but you're freaking me out.'

'Please don't take offence. Your sister was overheard mentioning that you're both third dan Karate black belts,' Jo explained. 'Think of it as a compliment: I'm only holding this gun because you two could overpower us in a straight fight.'

'Can't you at least point it at the ground?' Kyle grinned.

James thought he could see a hint of a smile through Jo's Balaclava as she lowered the gun. 'Your stepfather, Ryan Quinn, devised a wise strategy and always kept Zebra eighty-four as a small group. Recruiting members is the riskiest thing any anti-government organisation has to do. The less recruiting you do, the longer you're likely to stay in operation. But of course, there's a downside to that way of working.'

James butted in, 'You can't do much if you don't have any members.'

'Precisely,' Jo nodded. 'We're part of a new organisation that aims to raise the bar for the animal liberation movement. We're putting together a spectacular: probably the most sophisticated liberationist raid ever. We'll need some fit young lads like you to pull it off and if we succeed, you'll be helping to generate unprecedented global publicity for our cause.'

'So what is this masterplan?' James asked cheekily, fully aware that he wouldn't get an answer.

'I'm afraid I can't reveal details until immediately before the operation, but I'll be frank with both of you. The operation we're planning is a huge gamble. I'm confident that my plan will work, but I'm not going to sugar-coat the risks: if either of you are caught, the chances are that you'll be charged under anti-terrorism laws and go to prison for many years. You're both extremely young – are you *really* comfortable with that possibility?'

Kyle shrugged uneasily. 'No smoke without fire, I guess.'

'Are Tom and Viv going to be involved?' James asked.

Jo nodded. 'They've both agreed to work with us.'

'I'm in if Tom and Viv are,' Kyle said.

Jo smiled. 'It's good that you're both enthusiastic. But when you're planning a complex operation, every member of the team must show absolute commitment. The only way I can be confident that you won't back out under stress is if your abilities are put to the test.'

'Tested how?' James asked.

'If you accept the invitation to join our group, we'll assign you an operation to carry out with Tom and Viv. The task we set will be risky, but straightforward. If you perform it successfully, you'll be considered a paid-up member of our group and you might even get to see our faces.'

'Sounds fair,' James said.

'So, do you tell us about our operation now, or what?' Kyle asked.

Jo shook her head. 'My colleagues will drive you back into town and you can expect to hear from us at some time within the next couple of weeks. I want you both to think seriously about what we're asking you to do.

'If you have any doubts, just say the word and you can walk. But once you've made a commitment to our group, I expect it to be absolute. If one of you chickens out and ruins a major operation, we might have no option but to kill you in order to maintain security. Is that understood?'

James and Kyle both nodded.

'Shall we take 'em back to the van?' one of the other women asked.

Jo nodded, but suddenly changed her mind. She stepped

forwards and pointed the gun at James' black school trainers. 'Are they leather?' she asked accusingly.

'Yeah, my mum's always been veggie, but we only went vegan when we moved in with Ryan.'

Jo shook her head with contempt. 'If I see you walking around with bits of dead cow on your feet again, I'll shoot your bloody toes off.'

24. DEBRIEF

Zara phoned Lauren on the bus from school and told her not to bring Stuart home that afternoon. Meatball greeted Lauren in the hallway, barking and wagging his tail, but the little dog found himself shunned as she rushed through to the kitchen to find the cause of all the excitement.

'Unbelievable,' Lauren grinned, once the day's events had been explained. Then her face dropped. 'Pity I'm not involved in any of this.'

James, Kyle and Zara were leaning over the kitchen table. They'd spread out a *40 Miles Around Bristol* map and the boys had made some educated guesses about where they might have been driven to, based upon the turns they'd taken, the types of road and the amount of time they'd been inside the van.

The trouble was, Bristol is the intersection point of the M4 and M5 and a network of minor motorways that lead traffic across the bridges into Wales. They'd realised that the van could easily have branched off on a slip road and doubled back without the boys noticing, so the only real certainty was that they couldn't have made it much farther than thirty kilometres from the centre of Bristol during the twenty-five-minute ride.

'Did you get the numberplate of the van?' Lauren asked.

'Course,' James said.

'Maybe some of the motorway surveillance cameras picked it up,' Lauren suggested.

Zara nodded. 'We can run the police recordings through our numberplate recognition software, but we have to put in an official request through the proper MI5 channels. It'll take two or three days to get any result and it's far from foolproof, especially in the kind of nose to tail traffic you get around here.'

'Those girls knew what they were doing,' James said. 'The numberplate is the most obvious way to track them down, so I'd bet my left nut that the van was wearing falsies and they probably changed them again as soon as they dropped me and Kyle off.'

'The building you boys described was quite distinctive,' Zara said. 'It was modern and it was out of use. I'll get one of my research assistants on campus to call up the commercial estate agents and see if they've got any buildings that fit your description on their books. If that fails, they can take a trip around the local council offices and start working through the planning applications for anything like that built in the last ten years or so.'

'How long will that take?' Lauren asked.

Zara shrugged. 'Days, maybe even weeks. I think things are going to progress too quickly for the information to be of much use, but you can never be sure.'

James looked at his sister. 'Did we tell you why Jo pointed the gun at us?'

Lauren shook her head.

'She said it was because one of their associates had overheard you telling someone that me and Kyle were Karate black belts.'

'Oooh,' Lauren said, intrigued. 'It must be someone I've spoken to up by the Malarek gates. But who out of that whole flask and sandwiches crowd is gonna be involved with radicals?'

'The more time you spend hanging around them, the more chance that you might get to find out,' Zara said. 'And it goes to show: just because your part of the mission isn't the most glamorous, it doesn't mean you should go around moaning that it's a waste of time.'

'What fun,' Lauren smirked. 'But if I hear one more story about prostate surgery, or if one more old dear tells me what a lovely little girl I am . . .'

'It's not all good news,' James said. 'I know we're making progress, but I reckon we should be worried. We've got no idea about the people we've been asked to work for. We don't know when we're gonna be asked to take this test, or what it's going to involve. I mean, for all we know they're gonna ask us to batter someone, or worse.'

Kyle nodded. 'And if Viv's with us, things could easily get out of hand.'

James looked gloomy at the prospect of working with Viv. 'That guy puts the shits up me. Even if we're asked to do something straightforward, it could end up ten times worse with that nut on the scene.'

Zara looked pensive. 'It's a sliding scale,' she said. 'I mean, if they ask you to kill someone then you've obviously got to pull the plug. If smashing windows and graffiti can get you accepted into the core of this mystery group, then you obviously do it. The trouble is, there's a grey area in between those two extremes. You'll just have to use your best judgement as the situation unfolds.'

'With luck it might even be a bluff,' Lauren said. 'Remember when James and Kerry were on that drugs mission? They got sent off to deliver cocaine, but it turned out to be harmless white powder.'

Kyle nodded. 'Let's hope so, eh?'

*

James' head of year was an Aussie-born PE teacher called Mr Snow. He bounded around the school in shorts, showing off his giant smile and hairy legs. He was the type of teacher who girls fall in love with and boys think is a git. James and Zara had an appointment to see him first thing on Tuesday morning.

'You've been at this school for barely a month,' Snow said, leaning across his desk and steepling his fingers. 'Two instances of truancy in such a short time period is wholly unacceptable.'

James didn't give a damn, because Zara was fine about everything. But they had to keep up the pretence of being a normal family to maintain their cover.

'James has had a lot of difficulty settling in around the village,' Zara explained. 'And he did get a call from his older brother yesterday, who was having a girlfriend crisis.'

Mr Snow gave an *I know better* grin. 'Mobile phones must be switched off during lessons at this school – or any other school I've ever heard of. If there's a reason for you to leave class on an urgent matter, the correct procedure is for someone to ring the school secretary, who will fetch you from your class. The secretary will then speak to a senior member of the teaching staff and obtain the necessary authorisation for you to leave school. Is that clear James?'

'Yes, sir,' James nodded.

'I know that you're new here and I appreciate that everyone encounters difficulties settling in. *But*, we have a zero tolerance policy on bunking off and I can't allow the other pupils in your class to see you behaving like this and getting away scot-free. Therefore, I'm proposing that you be suspended from lessons for the remaining three days of the summer term.'

James worked hard not to grin. He'd feared detentions, but suspension was *perfect*. Especially when the weather was so nice.

'Hopefully you'll come back in September with a better attitude. Year Ten marks the start of your GCSEs and it goes without saying that it will be a very important year for your education.'

James grinned wildly as he headed out towards the school car park with Zara. He ripped off his tie and helicoptered it around his head. There was a slight chance he'd have to go back to school if the mission dragged on for another seven weeks, but that looked unlikely.

'Lauren's got three more days of school,' James gloated. 'She'll go nuts when she finds out I'm suspended.'

'Try looking less happy and a bit more like an ordinary kid who just got in serious trouble,' Zara said wearily. She liked James, but found him irritatingly full of himself at times.

James realised Zara was right and stopped messing about, but they'd almost reached the people carrier by then anyway.

As they drove home, Zara's mobile rang. She looked for it on the centre console, before realising that it was inside the linen jacket she'd thrown into the middle row of seats.

'Grab that for us, will you,' she said to James, who sat next to her.

James reached between the seats and grabbed the phone. It had been ringing for ages by this time, so he thought he'd better answer.

'Zara's phone.'

It was her husband, Ewart.

'Hang on,' Zara said, as she grabbed the handset. 'I'm stopping the car.'

She didn't like talking and driving and pulled up at the side of the lane.

'Oh you got it,' Zara said, a quiver coming into her voice. 'So is it good news or what . . . Yes, idiot head, of *course* I want you to open the envelope.'

James was intrigued by the drama, even though he had no clue what Zara was talking about.

'My god, I don't believe it,' Zara gasped. 'Oh *yes*.'

James was shocked to see her bouncing up and down in her seat as a tear welled up in her eye. 'I never thought I stood a chance at my age and with two kids under five . . . So when is it?'

The call went on for another minute and ended with Zara and Ewart exchanging *I love yous*.

'Are you pregnant again?' James asked, as he handed Zara one of the tissues in the glovebox to dab her eyes.

Zara giggled and sniffed at the same time. 'No. Well . . . I suppose you deserve an explanation after that display, but please don't spread it around campus. Not even to Kyle and Lauren, in fact.'

James tried to look cool as he nodded, but he was bursting to know Zara's secret.

'Remember when I went up to campus, the day Meatball was rescued?'

'Yeah, for a senior staff meeting or something.'

'Well, that was a little white lie,' Zara grinned. 'It was a job interview.'

'Job interview?'

'I wasn't going to apply. There are quite a few strong applicants and I thought I was too young and having two young children would count against me. But Ewart prodded me into it and said it would be good experience, if nothing else . . .'

James got the horrible feeling that Zara would be leaving CHERUB before he made the link between Zara applying for a job and the one job he knew was about to become vacant.

'Are you the new chairman of CHERUB?' he gasped.

'Not yet,' Zara grinned. 'They interviewed eight applicants. Ewart called to tell me that I've made the final shortlist of two. I've got to go to London next Tuesday for an interview at Number Ten.'

'Downing Street?'

Zara nodded. 'The final interview takes place with a panel of three: Dr McAfferty, the Prime Minister and the intelligence services minister.'

James was happy for his favourite CHERUB staff member. 'I can't *believe* you managed to keep it under your hat for so long,' he grinned. 'I really hope you get the job. Who's the other candidate?'

Zara squirmed a little. 'Well, that's the trouble. He's called Geoff Cox. He's an outsider with no CHERUB experience, but he's much better qualified than me. He's in his fifties; he worked as an intelligence operative in the 1970s and then left to become a teacher. He's spent the last seven years as headmaster at one of London's nuttier comprehensives, turning it from a sink school into a science and technology academy with some of the best exam results in the country.'

'Sounds like an idiot,' James said, waving his hand dismissively. 'I'd vote for you.'

'Most people would probably regard me as the underdog, James. But you never know. I didn't even think I'd make it on to the final shortlist.'

'This is *so* cool, Zara. The only thing is, I'm gonna be lying awake in suspense, wondering if you're gonna get the job.'

Zara burst out laughing. '*You'll* be losing sleep, James. How the blazes do you think I feel?'

25. CALL

Lauren sat in the living-room dressed in her nightshirt. She had a bowl of cereal in her hands and wasn't paying attention to the lame Saturday morning kids' show on the TV. Meatball sat on the cushion beside her, half asleep. She didn't notice James and Kyle sneaking a glance at her through the front window, or hear them creeping in the back door and stripping off their shorts, socks and T-shirts in the hallway outside.

She flew half a metre into the air as the boys burst in and bombarded her with balled-up running kit. Her breakfast bowl tipped over as she ducked to avoid James' trainer sock and Kyle's shorts.

'Don't *do* that,' Lauren scolded, standing up and staring at the giant circle of milk soaking into her nightshirt. 'You idiots.'

James cracked up laughing. 'The look on your face was *classic*.'

Meatball thought that chasing after flying clothes was a great game and came charging across the floor. But he ran headfirst into a running vest dangling over the arm of the sofa and got his front legs caught up in the neck hole. Kyle laughed as he crouched down and untangled the dog.

'You two,' Lauren said, folding her arms angrily but smiling at the same time. 'I'm trying to have a quiet Saturday morning doss here. Now I'm soaked.'

'Ahh,' James said, putting on a baby voice. 'I know my little sister-poos can't stay angry at big brother James. Come on, giss a kiss.'

'Don't you *dare*, James,' Lauren snapped, putting her arms out to stop him. 'You stink, of BO.'

James thought his sister might really blow up if he went through with the kiss, so he backed off and started gathering up the items spread across the floor.

'How was the run?' Lauren asked.

'Good,' Kyle nodded. 'We did about seven Ks, right around the Malarek compound, out through the fields then we sprinted the last bit, back through the new part of the village.'

'Stuart's trousers are still up in that tree,' James added.

'You should have come with us,' Kyle said. 'It's amazing how fast your fitness drops off when you're on a mission and you're not training regularly.'

'Yeah,' James nodded. 'Believe me, you don't want to get put on an emergency fitness plan when you get back to campus. You know what psychos the instructors are.'

'I know,' Lauren nodded. 'But unlike you two skiving gits, *I've* been at school all week. I reckon I deserve one morning of TV and Coco Pops.'

'Next time?' Kyle asked.

'Sure,' Lauren nodded. 'Oh, Kyle,' she added, 'I could

hear your phone ringing when I was on the loo. You'd better check your messages.'

'Right, cheers,' Kyle said. 'You might as well take the first shower, James. I'll see who called.'

As James grabbed a towel out of the cupboard at the top of the stairs and locked himself in the bathroom, Kyle cut into his bedroom, stepped over James' mess and grabbed his mobile off the window ledge.

He'd missed two calls from Tom. He hoped they might be an invite to go see a film or something later on, but as his phone returned the call something dawned on him: Tom and Viv lived the bachelor lifestyle, partying into the small hours and never surfacing before noon on weekends.

'Kyle, baby,' Tom said exuberantly.

'You must have had a call from our terrorist friends,' Kyle said.

'How'd you know?'

'Your first missed call was at nine forty-three. You're not usually conscious at that hour, let alone making phone calls.'

Tom sounded worried. 'She gave me instructions, but there's an almighty spanner in the works. Viv took Sophie out to some new vegan restaurant in town. He's been up and down all night with gutache and he keeps getting the shivers.'

'Did you say that to the person who called?'

'Yeah and she chewed my ear off: *We expect results not excuses. If you can't work your way around a simple operational difficulty then our organisation has no use for you.* Then she slammed the phone down.'

Kyle was relieved that Viv was in no state to come along, but he couldn't say that to Tom. 'Well me and James just went out for a run, so we're both in good shape. What else did she say?'

'Not much, you know how cautious they are. The call lasted under a minute. She told us to head up to Rigsworth services on the M5. We've got to get there by six this evening and head into the buffet area.'

'Someone's gonna meet us?' Kyle asked.

'She didn't go into details, just told us not to be late. Rigsworth is only an hour's drive, but I reckon we'll give it an extra half hour in case there's traffic. So, I'll swing by in Viv's Merc and pick you and James up around four-thirty.'

*

Tom had only passed his driving test a few months earlier and looked edgy behind the wheel of the Mercedes, which was double the size of his MG. He kept in the slow lane and looked worried every time he had to pull out to overtake a tractor or caravan.

It was the first weekend of the school holidays, so half the country was on the move and the service station was hell on earth. Tom circled the car park for ten minutes looking for a space. Inside, they had to queue up to use the urinals, the restaurant area was jammed and every kid in the joint seemed to be bawling about something their brother had done or something they hadn't been allowed to buy in the gift shop.

In the end, Kyle bought three bottles of mineral water from a vending machine and the boys propped themselves on a tiled ledge by the windows at the back of the food court. James' phone rang at six on the dot.

'How's it going, youngster?' a female voice asked. She didn't give a name, but it sounded like Jo.

'Not bad,' James said. 'So what are we doing? Is someone meeting us here or what?'

'You'll be meeting an old friend, of sorts. Head into the car park, row G, three bays from the end. The keys are taped under the wheel arch on the driver's side. You'll find your instructions and all the equipment you need inside the vehicle.'

The phone went dead. James slid it inside his black tracksuit bottoms as he stood up and led the others outside. They headed into the early evening glare, dodging the traffic circling for a parking spot.

'Tharrr she be, mateys,' James said, inexplicably putting on a pirate voice when he spotted the red VW van.

It was the same van he'd ridden in with Kyle three days earlier, though the lower half of the bodywork had been sprayed canary yellow and logos had been stuck along both sides and on the rear doors: *Rapid Trak – Speciality Courier*. James reached under the wheel arch and threw the key at Kyle.

Tom looked a little put out. 'I thought *I* was driving.'

'No offence, gorgeous,' Kyle grinned, 'but you drive like my grandma.'

The trio piled into the front of the van – Kyle in the driver's seat, Tom in the middle and James on the passenger side. James flipped open the glovebox and a mass of papers slid out into his lap.

'Bloody hell,' James moaned, as he reached down and picked them all off the vinyl floor.

The first thing he came to was a leaflet advertising Rapid Trak: *Whether it's a human kidney, oversized artwork or a six-*

tier wedding cake, *Rapid Trak has been delivering the undeliverable for more than 30 years*. To emphasise the point, the accompanying picture was of a white-coated doctor vaccinating a baby, while a pretty nurse stood in the background holding a red and yellow Rapid Trak package.

The next document James came to was a map of Wales. It was folded, but he could see parts of a detailed route that had been marked across it with a highlighter pen. Next he came to a large envelope with *Read Me!!!* written on it.

He peeled back the gummed flap, slid out four identical sets of stapled paperwork and handed one to Kyle and Tom before he started reading:

Hello Boys!

Today marks the launch of a new animal rights group. Yours is one of three synchronised actions that will be carried out under the banner of the Animal Freedom Army. This document gives you all the details you need to carry out your operation successfully. You will find the equipment you require in the rear of the van.

Over the last three years, pressure has been put on all of the major international courier firms and all have agreed to stop delivering to Malarek Research premises within the UK. However, Rapid Trak has refused even to meet with members of the Zebra Alliance and continues to make deliveries, which include the transportation of live mice and birds to be used in experiments.

In March 2006, Rapid Trak even took delivery of a special unmarked van so that it could continue its lucrative trade with Malarek. It is the last reliable courier service available to Malarek Research and one of the core companies that enables it to continue to do business. This operation will make it clear to the Rapid Trak management that profiting from animal experiments is unacceptable.

Please read the rest of this document carefully, paying particular attention to the sections on leaving behind DNA, fingerprints and other biometric evidence at the scene, and on the safe destruction of your vehicle.
Good Luck,
The AFA Team

26. NAPALM

The VW van juddered over a bump as it cruised a badly lit section of dual carriageway. James and Tom sat in the back, sweating into Balaclavas and disposable gloves. Just to make them even less comfortable, pungent kerosene vapour seeped out of the highly explosive napalm drum welded into the rear of the vehicle.

'Ever seen *Apocalypse Now?*' Tom asked.

'Don't think so,' James said.

'They blast all these Vietnamese with massive napalm bombs, and afterwards this nutty colonel takes this giant sniff and goes, *I love the smell of napalm in the morning.*'

James smiled, though Tom couldn't see it through the Balaclava. 'Is it a good movie?'

Tom nodded. 'I've got the DVD. If we don't blow ourselves up tonight, you can borrow it.'

'Cheers,' James nodded. 'I'll have loads of time to kill now it's summer holidays.'

James felt like he was getting on well with Tom, so it seemed a good moment to ask a more probing question.

'So where do you reckon the AFA got hold of napalm?'

'DIY I expect,' Tom said. 'Viv got this recipe for napalm off the Internet one time and we looked into making a batch ourselves. It's only petrol or kerosene, with a gelling agent dissolved into the mix.'

'I didn't know that,' James lied.

'If you want to burn something down, napalm is the dogs,' Tom explained. 'Petrol combusts so fast that it burns itself out before anything else catches light. Napalm sticks to everything and it burns hot and slow.'

James had learned about napalm and a variety of other common terrorist weapons in training, but he made an effort to sound suitably impressed at the older boy's knowledge.

'So how come you and Viv never made any?'

Tom grinned. 'First off it's seriously explosive. It would only take a spark to set that whole drum off. Second, the idea of my brother running around with napalm doesn't bear thinking about.'

'Viv's a nut,' James giggled. 'No offence . . .'

'None taken. He *is* a nut, but he's also the *best* brother. Our family is a freak show, but me and Viv have stuck up for each other, right from when we were toddlers.'

James and Tom turned to look as Kyle slid back the little flap between the cab and the rear compartment.

'Time to cut the banter,' Kyle said. 'I can see the Rapid Trak depot over the hill.'

'Right,' James nodded.

'Good luck, dude,' Tom added. 'Keep calm.'

Kyle felt like he'd been driving the van for ever. The journey from the outskirts of Bristol to the Rapid Trak depot in Wrexham, North Wales, shouldn't have taken any more than three and a half hours, but the holiday traffic had been horrendous and it was now past one in the morning. His knees and ankles ached from working the pedals and only fear of what they were about to do kept him awake.

Still, he knew things could have been a lot worse: the operation they'd been assigned by the AFA involved large-scale property destruction, but no deliberate harm to humans, and Viv going sick was a blessing.

After turning into a deserted industrial estate, the van passed two illuminated Rapid Trak signs in front of a modern, brick-built sorting office. This building was open 24/7, although it ran on a skeleton staff at weekends and there were fewer than a dozen cars parked up in a lot with space for a hundred.

Kyle continued along the eerily quiet road until he came to a smaller sign on the opposite side which pointed out Rapid Trak's vehicle depot. A middle-aged woman dressed in security-guard black stepped out of a kiosk as Kyle rolled up to the metal barrier. He wound down his window as she gave him a smile.

'What happened to you?' the woman asked. 'I thought the last driver was due in at nine.'

'I was due in at *eight*,' Kyle lied, acting stressed out. 'It's the great summer getaway. Big pile up on the A49 – I've never seen traffic like it.'

'You must be new,' the woman said. 'I'm Eileen Rice; I don't think I've seen you before.'

'Just left school,' Kyle said. 'I'm Eric Cartman, good to meet you.'

'Nice meeting you, Eric,' she said, as she stepped back into the kiosk and flipped the switch to open the gate.

As the gate rose up, Kyle drove on to a lot containing over a hundred commercial vehicles. They ranged from juggernauts down to compact vans, every one decked out in Rapid Trak livery. He pulled into a space between two VW Transporters identical to his own, before jumping out of the cab and opening the sliding side door to let out James and Tom. They both grinned at him.

'What's so funny?' Kyle asked.

'Eric Cartman,' Tom grinned. '*Very* smooth.'

Kyle didn't understand, so James explained. 'Eric Cartman: the fat kid in *South Park*.'

'Oh *shit*,' Kyle gasped. 'I'm such a plum. I thought there was something odd about that name when I said it.'

'Wouldn't worry,' Tom said. 'I'd say that old girl's more into soap operas than *South Park*.'

'She sounded like a nice old stick,' James added, as he reached inside and grabbed a Stanley knife and two giant reels of carpet tape off the floor of the van.

'Don't start feeling too sorry for her,' Kyle said. 'She's got an alarm button and she'll hit it if you give her a chance.'

Before jogging off towards the kiosk with James, Kyle zipped on a black hoodie and swapped his Rapid Trak cap for a Balaclava, then leaned into the van to grab a length of rubber hose.

'Call me sexist if you like,' Tom whispered, as he sneaked up on the kiosk with James. 'But this doesn't sit too well. It's like being asked to duff up someone's granny.'

As they approached the kiosk, the boys could see the

woman sitting inside. She had a radio on and her attention focused on a puzzle magazine.

'Hands in the air,' Tom yelled, putting on a decent tough-guy act as he grabbed the door of the kiosk and bundled the woman off her stall.

She screamed as she hit the floor.

'Shut your hole, woman.'

James knelt down beside her. As Tom kept her pinned under his foot, James stuffed a rag into her mouth, before winding tape around her head so that she couldn't spit it out. He then grabbed her handbag from under the security console and found a set of keys.

'Got 'em,' James said.

'OK, old timer,' Tom yelled as he released his trainer and showed his strength, lifting the guard effortlessly to her feet with one arm. 'Time for walkies and no messing.'

'You'll be fine if you do as you're told,' James added, figuring that he'd be Mr Nice to Tom's Mr Nasty.

The woman shook with fear as the boys frogmarched her out of the compound, along the chain link perimeter fence and down an overgrown embankment at the edge of the next lot, which had apparently been abandoned by an engineering company.

'On the ground,' Tom ordered, giving the woman a shove.

Once she was face down in the grass, James taped up her wrists and ankles, then linked the two sets of bindings together, so that she was trussed and couldn't roll off some place.

'Right,' James said, passing the guard's car keys across to Tom. 'You go across to the other side and get her car, I'll help set up the fire.'

As Tom crossed the deserted road and headed for the parking lot outside the sorting office, James cut back around the gate and realised that he couldn't remember where Kyle had parked.

'Dude,' James yelled cautiously, wanting to attract Kyle's attention without alerting the whole world.

Kyle was so close his reply gave James a fright. James cut between two vans and found him at the back, with the hose connected up ready to spray the napalm.

'I've got the controls on this tank sussed,' Kyle said. 'Do you want to go up front and drive?'

'Right,' James nodded.

'Don't forget to grab the backpack with all our stuff in when you get out.'

James climbed behind the wheel and turned the keys hanging off the steering column.

'Keep it slow,' Kyle yelled, as he stepped into the back of the van. 'I don't fancy falling out into a puddle of napalm.'

James put the van in first and crept out of the parking space, unfamiliar with the biting point of the clutch and anxious not to stall. As he drove at walking pace, Kyle leaned out the back doors with the hose, spraying globs of napalm over the fronts of the parked vehicles on either side and laying the odd streak across the Tarmac to ensure that the fire passed rapidly from one vehicle to the next.

There were four lines of vehicles, but Kyle was worried by the time they got halfway down the third. He scrambled inside the van and thumped on the divider. James pulled up and glanced back through the flap.

'The pressure in the tank is down to nothing,' Kyle

explained. 'However hard I crank the pump, I'm only getting a dribble. I want to make sure this van gets everything that's left in there, because it's covered in our fingerprints.'

'Fair enough,' James nodded.

James pulled the key out of the engine and felt a twinge of sympathy for a van that had turned its last wheel with less than 3,000 kilometres on the clock. He slung the backpack with all the maps and stuff over his shoulder and jumped out, catching the full-on stench of the jellied fuel they'd spread over more than sixty trucks and vans.

His stomach somersaulted as he realised that he was one crackle of static electricity away from being turned into a stick of charcoal. Kyle pointed the hose at the van and splattered it with the last of the napalm.

'I'm shaking,' James said, grinning uneasily at his gloved hands. 'Let's get out of here. Have you got the miniature bottles?'

Kyle nodded. 'And the lighter's in my back pocket.'

The boys moved quickly towards the gate, but pulled up sharp as they glanced at their only escape route: there was no sign of Tom, or the security guard's car, but a Rapid Trak van was stopped outside the gate with its engine running and a uniformed driver stood in the kiosk using the telephone. Three more Rapid Trak employees were heading towards the scene.

'Shit,' James gasped. 'What do you reckon?'

'Where's Tom?' Kyle asked, glancing up and down the road.

'Either he got nabbed getting in the guard's car, or he chickened out when he saw the van pull up and the driver go looking for the security guard.'

'Great,' Kyle huffed.

'So what do you reckon?' James asked. 'Run for it?'

'No choice,' Kyle said. 'If we get busted our mission is down the pan, and I'm not gonna stand around here and wait to get roasted.'

James and Kyle started running and made it past the kiosk before the guy inside glimpsed their black outlines. He yelled out and the trio walking towards the scene gave chase as the boys broke into a full sprint up the middle of the deserted road. Two of the men were fat jellies, but the third was a massive black dude with a serious turn of speed.

By the time they'd run three hundred metres, he'd got close enough to James to bundle into him. From running at full pelt, James turned his ankle and clattered into the concrete, shredding his plastic gloves as he put his hands out to protect his face.

James tried scrambling up, but an expertly aimed Karate kick slammed his ribcage and sent him crashing back to the tarmac. Kyle realised his companion was in trouble and turned back. The black guy went into a fighting stance and Kyle wasn't confident: the guy was a slab, half a metre taller than him and clearly knew his stuff.

But salvation came as twin headlamps roared out of the darkness. Tom had pulled out of a side turning in the security guard's Fiesta and ploughed into the giant at thirty miles an hour. He rolled up over the bonnet and smacked into the ground with a hollow thud that didn't bear thinking about. For a second, James and Kyle froze in shock.

Then, as the car pulled up sharply, Kyle grabbed James' arm to help him up.

'You OK?' Kyle asked.

'Can't breathe,' James moaned, clutching his chest. 'My ribs are killing me.'

Kyle opened the back door and took some of James' weight as he staggered across and collapsed on to the rear seat.

'Where'd you disappear to?' Kyle asked angrily, slamming the front passenger door as Tom roared away.

'I was waiting for you in the car outside,' Tom explained. 'But that dude pulled up in the Rapid Trak van. He saw there was no one in the kiosk and he started coming towards me, so I pulled out and went for a drive around the block.'

'Idiot,' Kyle said, as he ripped off his Balaclava. 'He's smaller than you and you had surprise on your side. Why didn't you rush over and lay him out, instead of giving him a chance to call out the cavalry?'

'Didn't think,' Tom confessed, taking another left, then pulling up at the rear of the Rapid Trak depot.

'Why have you stopped?' Kyle asked.

But Kyle realised before he heard Tom's answer. In the panic to get away, he'd forgotten what they were doing in the first place. He opened the electric window while grabbing two miniature whiskey bottles out of his top. Each bottle had shredded paper poking out of the top and extra thick globs of napalm filling the bottom third.

'Keep your foot on that accelerator 'cos this is really gonna blow,' Kyle said.

He lit the paper shreds sticking out of the two miniature bottles and flung them high over the chain link fence. James and Kyle looked backwards as Tom downed the accelerator and shifted the car up through the gears.

But twenty seconds passed and nothing happened.

'Shall we go back?' Tom asked, slowing the car.

'What are the odds on that?' Kyle said furiously. 'That whole place is soaked in fuel.'

'Unbelievable,' Tom gasped, hammering on the steering wheel as the car stopped moving.

'We can't turn back now,' Kyle said. 'The cops must be on their way. It's too dan—'

The sky lit up before Kyle finished his sentence. The little Ford was several hundred metres clear of the depot, but the blast still made it wobble. Car alarms went off, windows in the surrounding buildings shattered and the blast of heat was so intense that James could feel it on his neck, magnified through the glass in the rear window.

The front tyres squealed as Tom floored the accelerator. They turned out of the industrial park and back on to the dual carriageway as a secondary explosion sent towers of flame fifty metres into the air. When the noise faded, they could hear police sirens in the distance.

27. GETAWAY

Twenty minutes later, James, Kyle and Tom arrived at a mock-Tudor house seven kilometres outside of Wrexham. The light came on in the garage as they pulled on to the driveway and by the time they'd stopped inside, a lanky man had run around the back of the car and pulled down the metal door.

'No sign of a tail?' he asked, as three car doors opened.

'Not as far as we can tell,' Tom said.

'I'm Mark,' the beanpole said, as Kyle looked around and noticed that he wore disposable gloves and had a handgun tucked into the waistband of his shorts. 'Leave your maps, dirty gloves and everything else we gave you inside the car. I'll switch plates, take it across town and burn it out in a field before sunrise.'

James had to lean against the garage wall as he hobbled around the outside of the car.

'How you doing?' Kyle asked.

'Got my wind back,' James nodded. 'But my ankle's bloody agony.'

'I've been listening to a police scanner all night,' Mark

said. 'By the sound of things you three pulled it off good. There's over two million quid's worth of wheels in that depot and I doubt there'll be a serviceable set left when the smoke clears.'

Tom looked at Mark. 'I ran a guy down with the car. Did you overhear anything about that?'

'Only that there was an ambulance called to the scene,' Mark said, as he produced three sets of disposable gloves from his shirt pocket. 'Come through to the house. Afraid you'll have to wear these, and for safety's sake, I'd strongly recommend that you burn the shoes and clothing you used in tonight's operation when you get home.'

'Our mum's gonna love having to shell out for two new pairs of trainers,' Kyle said, as he helped James limp through a connecting door into a smartly fitted kitchen.

'Money is one thing the AFA doesn't worry about,' Mark smiled. 'I'll sort you out with enough cash to replace everything before you go.'

'Is this your house?' James asked.

Mark shook his head as he leaned into the garage and flicked out the light. 'It's a holiday let. We're nicely out of the way and we've paid for two weeks' rent, so I'll have plenty of time to clear up after you've gone.' He glanced at his watch. 'You three don't want to be hanging around this area for too long, but I know you've been on the go for hours, so you're welcome to take a breather before setting off in the other car. I'll put the kettle on, there's samosas in the fridge, or I can make sandwiches if you'd prefer.'

'Samosas sound great,' Kyle said, 'but I'm worried about the state James is in. He's all grazed and bloody and he'll stand out a mile if the cops stop us at a roadblock or anything. Can he take a shower?'

'Sounds like a sensible precaution,' Mark nodded. 'The bathroom is at the top of the stairs. Clean towels are on the rail. I'll make sure everything is scrubbed down with bleach before I leave.'

'I'll help you up the stairs,' Kyle said, looking at James.

James hobbled out of the kitchen and along a short hallway. He looked back at Kyle when he reached the bottom of the stairs. 'I'll manage,' he said.

'I'll make sure Mark and Tom don't come upstairs,' Kyle whispered rapidly. 'Take the quickest shower you can, then check out the bedrooms and see if you can find any of Mark's stuff. This is gonna be our only chance to get something solid on the AFA before we're dragged into the major operation.'

'OK,' James nodded. 'But I'm not gonna be moving anywhere quickly, so you'd better kick up a fuss if anyone starts up the stairs.'

*

Mark gave them another map with a different route home. It was farther, but quicker because it involved crossing back into England and riding the whole way on the motorway.

The car was a chunky Nissan X-Trail and it was 2:30 a.m. by the time they set off, so the traffic was light. Tom dozed in the front passenger seat and James laid out in the back.

Kyle was shattered and fought to stay awake as the cat's-eyes marking out the lanes tried to hypnotise him. He played mental games to stop himself from nodding off: doing times tables and working his way through the alphabet trying to think of car brands, rock groups, or foods that started with each letter.

He knew that driving when you're sleepy is dangerous and was tempted by the signs advertising rooms from £39 a night. But he reckoned they'd all be chock full with families who'd given up on the traffic jams and even if they weren't, he wouldn't be able to check in without a credit card.

But despite drifting out of lane a couple of times and one hair-raising moment when he found himself closing up rapidly on a coach that had no business in the fast lane of a motorway, everyone was still alive when he pulled into Rigsworth services at a quarter to six in the morning.

The sky was a mix of orange and mauve as he stopped in a bay twenty metres from where he'd collected the van eleven hours earlier.

Kyle unclipped his seat-belt and gave Tom a shove. 'Wakey, wakey.'

'Tell me that wasn't all a dream,' Tom grinned, as he rubbed the sleep out of his eyes. 'We kicked some ass, didn't we?'

James glanced at his watch before sticking his head between the two front seats. 'You made good time, Kyle.'

'I'm wiped out,' Kyle said. 'How're your war wounds?'

James pulled up his T-shirt and inspected the purple and black blotches across his chest. 'Tender,' James said, prodding himself gently. 'I don't reckon anything's broken though, it doesn't hurt bad enough.'

'What about your ankle?'

'It's swollen, but I can't really tell until I get out and put some weight on it.'

All three boys needed the toilet. They gathered up their stuff before popping their doors open. James was first out, leaning against the roof as he took his first tentative steps. Each one sent a sharp pain up his leg, but he'd walked off a similar injury during basic training and at least this time he didn't have to run an assault course while an instructor screamed that he was a lazy worm who was faking the injury.

'I've got to shut the keys inside the car,' Kyle said, as he took in a refreshing lungful of morning air. 'Make sure you've got everything 'cos we'll be locked out.'

James and Tom did a final check, before slamming the doors and heading towards the service station. Kyle stuck close to James in case his ankle gave out, but Tom said he was busting and raced off towards the toilets.

Kyle excitedly mouthed the question he'd been burning to ask for five hours. 'So what info did you get in the house?'

'Got a good look at his driver's licence. His real name is Kennet Marcussen. I found a pen and jotted down all the numbers off the speed dial on his mobile and a couple of credit cards. I texted the whole lot through to campus while you were driving and Tom was asleep.'

'Great stuff,' Kyle said, stifling his grin because he knew someone from the AFA might be waiting nearby to collect the big Nissan. 'I didn't realise you were sending messages back there. MI5 might even be able to put a surveillance team on Mark before he leaves the house.'

'I expect they'll have someone here ready to take pictures of whoever comes out and collects that Nissan too.'

'Not a bad night's work,' Kyle grinned, as they stepped

through the automatic doors and on to the just mopped tiles inside the service station entrance.

'Tom ran that bloke over though,' James said. 'And the way those flames went up, what if one of the dudes hanging around near the kiosk got caught by the blast?'

'They'd have had to be seriously stupid not to have backed off once they saw us run out,' Kyle said. 'The smell of fuel was eye-watering and for all they knew we had some kind of timed detonator ticking away in there.'

'I bloody well hope you're right,' James said. 'If we've misjudged it, we'll have some awkward questions to answer when we get back to campus.'

'When you're playing with big boys' toys, it's never risk free,' said Kyle. 'I flicked the radio on a couple of times while you were asleep and they mentioned the fire and another arson attack down south. But they only said *unconfirmed reports of casualties*, nothing specific.'

As they headed into the toilets, the boys passed couples and families eating full English breakfasts and looked on enviously.

'I could murder a bacon sandwich,' Kyle said. 'Then about fifteen hours' sleep and I'll be fine.'

*

Tom dropped James and Kyle back at Corbyn Copse. It was almost 7 a.m. and they found Lauren on the living-room couch watching Sky News.

'Are you OK?' she asked. 'The Animal Freedom Army is the top story.'

James and Kyle were anxious for news. 'What are they saying?'

'In your attack: a hundred and six vehicles totalled and two guys taken to hospital with smoke inhalation,' Lauren said. 'And did you run someone over?'

'Tom did,' James nodded.

'He's in the hospital, described as serious but stable. If you keep watching for a few minutes, they'll show pictures of the flames again. The fire crews are still dousing the buildings. And there was another attack down south, too.'

James and Kyle noticed the text scrolling along the bottom of the screen: BREAKING NEWS: CLYDE WAINWRIGHT, CHAIRMAN OF MALAREK UK CRITICALLY INJURED IN CAR BOMB WHILE HOLIDAYING IN CANARY ISLANDS.

'Jesus,' James gasped.

'I thought you knew,' Lauren said. 'Didn't you have a radio in the car?'

'I clicked it on and off a few times while we were on the motorway,' Kyle said. 'But the one in Viv's car is busted.'

'When did the car bomb news come through?' James asked.

'It came up as a newsflash about half an hour ago.'

'This is bigger than we thought,' Kyle said, shaking his head. 'We thought the AFA was a splinter group of the AFM, but it looks like more than that now. It takes organisation and a lot of money to pull off three operations on this scale.'

'Mark pulled out three hundred quid for me and Kyle to replace our clothes and trainers without batting an eyelid,' James added, before gawping as Ryan appeared on the television screen.

The TV people had tamed Ryan's hair and dressed him up in a jacket and tie. James read the caption to make sure his tired eyes weren't deceiving him: *Ryan Quinn – Founder, Zebra Alliance.*

'He was a bit miffed,' Lauren grinned. 'The BBC were sending him a car, but they cancelled when they got hold of Madeline Laing and he ended up getting Sky instead.'

James smiled, as Ryan condemned the AFA actions and began explaining the background to the campaign against Malarek Research.

'Morning, boys,' Zara said brightly, as she rushed into the room and kissed both lads on the cheek. 'It's good to have you both home safely.'

'Have you heard whether anyone was hurt when the napalm went up?' James asked anxiously.

Zara shook her head. 'I just got off the phone from campus and it looks like the only serious injury was the man who got hit by the car. He has a fractured arm and pelvis, but there's no reason why he shouldn't fully recover.'

'Nice one,' Kyle said, as he exchanged relieved grins with James.

'MI5 ran a check on Kennet Marcussen,' Zara continued. 'He's a Dane. He was involved in British and European liberationist groups in the eighties and early nineties, but he fell off the radar. Everyone assumed he'd gone back to Denmark and started a family or something. He was part of a long-defunct group called EAA: Extreme Animal Action. The group was small, but always had plenty of money and most of its members originally lived in a women-only commune near Birmingham.'

James nodded. 'Sounds uncannily similar to what we've seen of the AFA. Do we know the names of any EAA members?'

'Most of them have MI5 files,' Zara nodded. 'They'll start making enquiries and they're trying to get a surveillance team on Marcussen before he leaves the house in Wrexham. But we've got to proceed gently, because if he suspects he's under investigation your cover will be blown apart.

'We'll also be making discreet inquiries amongst the local body shops. Your van had a pressurised cylinder welded in the back, a complete respray and Rapid Trak logos applied to the side. There can't be many places capable of pulling off a remodelling job like that in three days flat. We're going to start putting together a list of places that can do that kind of work in this area and see if any of them have links to known animal rights activists.'

'At least we're finally getting somewhere,' Kyle said, stretching into a yawn, 'but I'm exhausted. Is there anything you want me to do, or can I grab a few hours' sleep?'

Zara scratched her head. 'James' text messages were pretty thorough, so I think I'm up to speed on everything that happened.'

'I might turn in for a few hours as well,' James said, catching on to Kyle's yawn.

'Afraid not,' Zara said. 'You took a nasty kick to the ribs and I want it looked at properly.'

'I'm fine,' James tutted. 'I've been up half the night. I need six hours' sitting around in a casualty department like a hole in the head.'

'It's not my idea of fun either,' Zara said. 'But you could

easily have cracked a rib. I want you X-rayed and examined by a doctor.'

*

Kyle felt sorry for James, but it was a bonus being able to fall asleep without his constant fidgeting in the lower bunk and the irritating whistle made by his left nostril. He slept solid, but the hours of driving had stamped themselves on his mind and when Lauren shook him awake, he'd been dreaming about a motorway.

'Your phone,' Lauren said, reaching up on tiptoes and jiggling the mobile in front of his blurry eyes. 'Unrecognised number, *answer* it.'

'Yeah, hello,' Kyle said dozily as he flipped his phone open.

He perked up when he heard the familiar female voice. 'You did an excellent job last night. Welcome to the Animal Freedom Army.'

'Thanks,' Kyle said. 'It went pretty well, didn't it?'

'I tried calling James, but his phone is switched off.'

'Yeah, our mum saw the state of his chest and took him to casualty. You have to switch your mobiles off at the hospital.'

'Do you think she was suspicious?'

'Nah,' Kyle said. 'Don't worry, James always gets in scraps. We told her we stayed at Tom and Viv's and that James fell down the stairs.'

'So, you're ready for the big time?'

'Ready, willing and able,' Kyle said enthusiastically.

He knew he wouldn't get details of the big operation itself, but Kyle figured that the previous night's actions had earned him some respect and decided to try finding out when he'd be needed.

'There's one problem,' he explained. 'I can pretty much come and go as I please, but James is only fourteen and our mum keeps tabs on him. So, a bit of advanced notice would make our getaway a lot easier, especially if you're expecting us to stay out overnight again.'

Kyle half expected to get chewed out, but the woman paused for a moment before replying in a friendly voice. 'We'll pick you up on Wednesday afternoon. If all goes to plan you should be back home by Friday morning. Can you manage that?'

'That's great,' Kyle said. 'I'll start buttering our mum up right now. Say that we're staying in town with a mate or something.'

'I'll call you Tuesday evening and tell you what to bring and where to meet us,' the woman said.

'Look forward to it,' Kyle said. 'Bye.'

Kyle flipped his phone shut before handing it down to Lauren.

'Do us a favour, Lauren. Call campus and tell them that the AFA operation is taking place between Wednesday and Friday and that me and James are definitely both involved.'

'OK,' Lauren nodded. 'You know, I can't help wondering what they're planning. I mean, two major arson attacks and almost blowing up the chairman of Malarek, but *apparently* all this is just a warm-up . . .'

'Tell me about it,' Kyle nodded. 'We came on this mission to catch a big fish, but I think we've accidentally hooked ourselves a whale.'

28. REVEALED

One advantage of knowing that the AFA didn't need Kyle and James until Wednesday was that the kids could take a break while Zara went to her interview in Downing Street.

After the two and a half hour drive to London, the youngsters split from Zara and spent the morning cruising the shops in Oxford Street. Kyle got a couple of CDs he'd been after for ages, James got the latest FIFA game for his Playstation and Lauren got T-shirts and a couple of squeezy toys for Meatball's rapidly expanding collection.

Mac had booked a table in a swanky restaurant at Piccadilly Circus, but the kids arrived to find a message telling them not to wait around: the Prime Minister was running behind schedule and Zara and Mac were going to have lunch with him.

The crowd was mostly business people in suits and the kids got odd looks as the waiter took them past a spectacular waterfall bar to a window table well away from all the other diners. It looked down eight storeys on to the bustle of shoppers and tourists in the paved square below.

'Glad I'm not paying,' James said, as he read down a list of main courses, the cheapest of which was twenty-one pounds.

In the end, James and Kyle both satisfied their meat cravings with thirty-five quid's worth of rib-eye steak and French fries, while Lauren ordered roast vegetables in peanut butter sauce.

'You're really serious about this whole veggie deal, aren't you?' James said, as the waiter put their meals down on the table. 'You're gonna end up pasty and thin, like all the other vegetarians.'

'Shut up and eat your dead cow,' Lauren tutted. 'If you think that a giant slab of red meat is going to be better for you than what I'm eating, you're even stupider than I thought.'

'Hey,' Kyle said firmly. 'This is supposed to be our day off. So how about I get a day off from you two digging at each other and we change the subject?'

'How's your chest today?' Lauren asked.

James shrugged. 'Bit stiff, that's all. I *told* Zara it was nothing. Eight hours we sat around in that hospital and I ended up with a bottle of painkillers that she could have picked up in the village shop.'

'Better safe than sorry though,' Lauren said.

'I suppose,' James shrugged, as he watched a pigeon land on the window ledge outside.

'I wonder how Zara's getting on,' Kyle said. 'It must be *so* weird meeting someone that important. Especially for a job interview.'

'It sounded like she was hurling up in the toilet this morning,' James said.

'Morning sickness,' Lauren giggled, as she bit a roast

parsnip off her fork. 'Maybe she's pregnant as well.'

'I always get the *worst* diarrhoea when I'm nervous about anything,' Kyle said.

James started to laugh. 'Isn't this nice? We come to a swanky restaurant in the middle of London, we order a hundred quid's worth of food and drink and sit at the table talking about puking and crapping.'

'You know what?' Lauren said. 'I wish I'd bought those camouflage trousers now. Do you reckon we'll have time to go back?'

'No *way*,' James said firmly. 'I know what you're like. We'll spend half an hour traipsing back to the shop and when we arrive you'll try them on and change your mind again.'

'When would I ever do that?' Lauren said, grinning mischievously.

'Besides, I don't want a camouflage-wearing vegetarian for a sister.'

'If you don't shut it I'll dye my hair black again.'

'I thought your hair looked nice when it was black,' Mac said.

The three youngsters had been looking out of the window and hadn't noticed Mac and Zara being led to their table. The waiter asked if they needed anything as they sat down.

'We'll wait for the kids to finish their main courses,' Zara said. 'Would you mind fetching us some dessert menus? Then we can all have dessert and coffee together.'

The waiter nodded efficiently and walked away.

'So?' Lauren said, once he was out of earshot.

'It was *good*,' Zara said, checking that there was nobody within listening distance before breaking into a grin.

'I was at Geoff Cox's interview yesterday and it was very formal,' Mac explained. 'He spoke with the ministers about schools and education policy and a little bit about his time in the intelligence service.

'Zara's interview was totally different. The PM was hooked when she told him about the mission she was working on and how you two boys infiltrated the AFA before anyone had ever heard of it. He even asked Zara about her family and ended up looking at pictures of Tiffany and Joshua. After sitting through both interviews, I'm confident that Zara has nailed it.'

'Way to go!' James grinned. 'Just remember that you and I are old mates when you're dishing out the punishments.'

'No special treatment,' Zara said, shaking her head. 'You'll just have to behave yourself. Besides, I know it went well, but I'm not popping any champagne corks until I've got a letter of confirmation in my hand.'

The waiter strode purposefully across to the table and handed out five dessert menus. James was pigged out from his steak, but couldn't resist a look.

'Steamed chocolate pudding with blood orange compôte,' James grinned. 'I've *got* to have a go at that.'

'So, it's a big day for you boys tomorrow,' Mac said. 'I'll be taking a keen interest in how you get on.'

'So will the Prime Minister,' Zara added. 'He asked the intelligence minister to make sure he gets a briefing on how it goes.'

Lauren noticed the uncomfortable look on her brother's face and made a *de-dum, de-dum* sound, like a heart beating. 'Feeling the pressure James?'

Kyle laughed as he wrapped an arm around James' back. 'We're not worried, are we, mate? All we've got to do is travel to some unknown location, foil some unknown plan and bring down a well armed, well funded and highly dangerous terrorist group.'

'And make sure nobody gets hurt in the process,' James said.

Mac laughed as Lauren started doing the heartbeat noise again. James put his arm around Kyle's back and pulled him in tight.

'You know what I think, Kyle?' James asked, as he grinned at his best friend.

'What?' Kyle asked.

'I think we're *totally* screwed.'

29. PICKUP

Jo called Kyle on Tuesday night and it looked like the AFA intended to keep security tight. The boys were told to wear accurate watches and set them to the correct time before leaving. They were asked to wear ordinary casual clothes and carry one small bag or backpack. The packs were supposed to contain one change of clothes, a towel, a small quantity of personal toiletries and – optionally – one book or magazine which Jo said should be *suitable for reading on a long journey*. IPods, mobiles, or any other forms of electronic gadget that might contain a hidden listening device were banned.

The pickup point was the dilapidated barn where they'd met up with Zebra Alliance activists before vandalising the police cars a month earlier. James and Kyle noticed Tom's MG as they approached and found the two lads around the back, squatting on the edge of an upturned water trough.

Kyle stepped up and gave Tom a long kiss. Viv gave James an almighty slap on the back, his trademark greeting for anyone he liked.

'Hey, cop killer, long time no see,' Viv said, before looking across at Kyle and Tom. 'I know what you're thinking, kid. I mean, how can *that* possibly be better than what I got up to last night with Sophie?'

James started to crack up laughing. 'So how's your arse?'

'Fully recovered,' Viv said. 'I was really pissed off to miss the action on Monday. Tom said it was an amazing night.'

'Certainly wasn't dull,' James smirked, as a horn blasted on the other side of the barn.

The boys wandered around the front to see a long-wheelbase van rolling up the drive. A woman in sunglasses stepped out of the cab and James realised it was the one who called herself Jo the second she opened her mouth. She wore combat trousers and judging by the bulge, there was a handgun tucked into them.

'Hey boys,' she said. 'You must know how this works by now, so step into the barn and start stripping off your clothes.'

Another woman had climbed out the passenger side of the van. She was in her twenties, good looking, with red cheeks. James thought she looked like the sort of girl who'd settle down and squirt out half a dozen kids.

*

Adelaide Kent, Lauren thought, almost dropping her camera in shock.

Lauren was staked out in the bushes twenty metres from the barn. She wasn't invisible, but you'd have had to look hard to see her and if she was caught she could push the matchbox-sized digital camera down the back of her underwear and pretend to be nothing more than a kid sister sticking her nose where it didn't belong.

As James, Kyle, Tom and Viv stepped into the barn to be searched by the two women, Lauren crept up through the bushes until she was directly in line with the rear of the van. She could easily be spotted from this distance, but it was the only way she'd get a shot inside the van when the rear doors opened.

She flipped the tiny camera into video mode, propped it on a branch and tied it into position with the neck strap. When this was done, she dashed back to her original spot and slid a tiny remote out of her pocket.

James was the first to emerge a couple of minutes later. He pulled down his tracksuit bottoms and started peeing against the side of the barn. By the time he'd finished, the others were heading towards the rear of the van. Lauren hit record on the remote as Jo opened the rear doors.

*

'Looks comfy,' James grinned, as he stepped into the back of the van. There were cushions and beanbags piled up inside the long metal box. There were no windows in the back or sides, so they wouldn't know where they were going, but the vehicle had started life as a security van and the escape hatch in the roof had been ripped out to let in fresh air and light.

The only other person in the back of the van had made himself comfortable, stripped down to his shorts and sprawling over two beanbags. He looked about twenty years old.

'I'm Jay,' he said, touching fists with the four new arrivals as Jo slammed the back doors and plunged them into gloom.

Once they'd all settled in, Jay put on The Beatles' white album and offered everyone a choice of Coke or mineral water from a cooler box.

'You better appreciate the music,' Jay grinned. 'I

waged war to bring this boom box – I told the girls there was no way I was sitting in a van for four hours staring at metal.'

'You couldn't read for that long,' Kyle said. 'Especially in this light.'

The long wheelbase gave all five lads space to stretch out and James got comfortable on a big cushion, with a smaller one propped behind his head. He was nervous about the next forty-eight hours, but Tom, Viv, Jay and Kyle all started chatting and he found it hard not to pick up the buzz of five young men going on an adventure.

The only trouble was, it was high summer and they were trapped inside a poorly ventilated, metal-sided box. By the time they reached the motorway, everyone had copied Jay and stripped down to their shorts.

*

Lauren gave the van a minute to clear the area around the barn, before grabbing the camera and sprinting off across the fields towards the cottage. Zara was waiting at the kitchen table with her laptop open.

'What did you get?'

'I took pictures,' Lauren gasped. 'More important, I recognised one of them: Adelaide Kent, from when we rescued Meatball. She seemed so gentle with the dogs and putting her little sisters to bed and that . . .'

'You should know better than to judge people based upon one meeting,' Zara cautioned, as she wired Lauren's camera up to the laptop. She copied the whole lot on to the hard drive and e-mailed the pictures to CHERUB campus before taking a look herself.

'Run the video,' Lauren said. 'I wonder if we'll be able to make out anything inside the van.'

Windows Media Player popped up on screen. The first few seconds of picture were washed out, as the little camera adjusted its exposure settings from the sunlight reflecting off the back of the van to its gloomy interior.

The next bit showed legs and bums as the boys clambered into the van, but Lauren finally spotted something useful as they settled on to their cushions.

'That's Jay,' Lauren said, tapping the screen. 'Adelaide's boyfriend.'

'Can you remember his surname?'

'Buckle, like a belt,' Lauren nodded.

'Good stuff, Lauren. Hopefully the names and the picture of the mysterious Jo will help us fit together a picture of the AFA.'

Ryan had taken to spending all of his mornings in bed and was heading into the kitchen, dressed in a set of striped pyjama bottoms.

'Morning,' he said, reaching into the fridge and grabbing the carton of orange juice. 'Did I overhear you talking about Jay and Adelaide?'

'Eww,' Lauren gasped. 'Don't drink out of the carton, Ryan. You're as bad as James.'

Ryan grinned as he grabbed a glass out of the cupboard, but Zara's tone was serious. 'James and Kyle went for their pickup and Lauren positively identified Adelaide Kent.'

'You're kidding me,' Ryan said, his eyebrows shooting up so fast that Lauren thought they might fly clean off his head.

Zara tapped her pen on the screen. 'Look for yourself.'

'She's my god-daughter,' Ryan gasped. 'The stupid, *stupid* little girl. Do you know where they're going?'

'No idea,' Lauren shrugged. 'Do you think Anna and Miranda might be involved too?'

'I doubt it,' Ryan said. 'Then again, if you'd said Adelaide was involved ten minutes ago I would have said you were off your trolley. Jay seemed like a nice young fellow too. He's studying film and television at university with Adelaide. He was telling me all about a work placement he was doing on a big car-chase movie.'

'Eh?' Lauren gasped. 'Where are they making the movie?'

'He didn't say, but there's a big studio complex near Bath, it's probably out there.'

Zara looked at Lauren. 'What are you getting at?'

'Well,' Lauren said, 'for a big car-chase movie, they've got to be wrecking, modifying and painting lots of cars for stunts and stuff. So, what if Jay got some of the dudes working there to modify the Rapid Trak van that James and Kyle took up to Wrexham the other night?'

'I've heard worse theories,' Zara said, as she tapped *Bath film studio* into Google. 'Got it,' she said, reading from her laptop screen. '*Currently filming at Walker Studios near Bath, Wild Ride II is the sequel to the surprise hit of summer 2004. This time the gang plot to steal the crown jewels from the Tower of London using a fleet of antique racing cars . . .*'

'It's got to be worth checking out,' Lauren said.

Zara nodded. 'I'll pass the information along to campus and one of our research assistants can start digging.'

30. COOKS

The five lads tried making the best of a van ride that took up most of the day: listening to Jay's CDs, talking about life and fighting the heat by drinking endless Cokes and bottles of mineral water. Jo had scheduled a single toilet stop in an unidentifiable field, but as the second half of the journey dragged on she refused to make another even though the lads were all busting.

Viv's solution was to piss into an Evian bottle and lob it out through the hatch in the roof. James cracked up laughing and couldn't resist the urge to copy. Seconds later, the boys got thrown around as the van stopped abruptly at the side of the road.

'Which one of you *idiots* did that?' Jo steamed, as she ripped open the back door of the van.

James sheepishly raised a finger.

'Then you're a stupid little prick,' Jo spluttered. 'We're not heading to summer camp, you know. What would have happened if that bottle hit another car? What if someone pulled our numberplate and the cops stop us further up the road?'

Viv butted in angrily. 'Hey, Miss High 'n' Mighty, it's OK for you, sitting up there in air-conditioning. We're cooking back here. We've been drinking gallons and I've asked for another toilet break loads of times.'

Jo swiped the gun out of her trousers and pointed it at Viv's head. 'I'm not stopping you from peeing in the bottle, moron. But there's no need to throw it out through the roof. Was it you that threw the first one?'

'What, are you gonna shoot me for urinating?'

Jo clearly wasn't used to being backchatted. She jumped inside the van, clicked off the safety and pushed the gun against Viv's head. 'If you balls this operation up, I'll ram this gun in your mouth and spray your brains over the nearest wall.'

'Hey, hey, hey,' Kyle said, raising his hands. 'We're all hot, we're all bored and this is just a misunderstanding. So let's calm down, eh?'

'We're all on the same team,' Tom added.

'I've got my eye on you, Viv,' Jo snarled, as she slid the gun back into her trousers.

'Join the queue. A lot of women have their eyes on me,' he responded, though James thought he looked uncharacteristically subdued.

Jo shook her head with contempt as she jumped off the back of the van and punished the boys' eardrums by slamming the door as hard as she could.

Tom scowled as he whispered to Viv, 'These are serious people. Are you ever gonna learn when to keep your trap shut?'

Viv was rattled and made a pathetic attempt to disguise it.

'I can handle myself,' he sneered, sounding like an eight-year-old who'd just lost a fight.

*

Zara came off a twenty-minute phone call and wandered out to the back garden. Meatball was allowed outdoors now that he'd had his vaccinations and was celebrating his newfound freedom by licking bugs off a tree trunk. Lauren sat in a sun lounger reading a book called *The Complete Idiot's Guide to Beagles*.

'So, what's the news?' Lauren asked.

'MI5 identified Jo from your photograph. Her real name is Rhiannon Jules. She's the daughter of Joe Jules.'

This last name was clearly intended to mean something, but Lauren didn't have a clue.

'Before your time, I guess,' Zara grinned. 'Joe Jules was a singer-songwriter. Shot down by Los Angeles police during a cocaine bust in eighty-two. Rhiannon is his only daughter and his albums still sell, so you can bet she's worth a few bob.'

'Enough to fund the AFA?'

'Definitely,' Zara nodded. 'Remember the EAA?'

Lauren twisted up her face as she racked her brain. 'Extreme Animal Action . . . Is that the group Kennet Marcussen was involved with in the eighties?'

Zara nodded. 'Most EAA members were women who lived in a commune. One of our research assistants found out that the commune was situated in a large country house, which once belonged to an American singer-songwriter . . .'

'Joe Jules,' Lauren grinned.

'How'd you guess?'

Lauren shrieked as Meatball reared up and licked the

bottom of her foot. 'That *tickles*,' she giggled, as she gently nudged him away. 'Any news about the film studios?'

'There certainly is,' Zara grinned. 'Your hunch was spot on. They typed *Jay Buckle* into the police computer. He's been arrested twice at animal rights demonstrations, both times with Adelaide Kent. Two weeks ago he was arrested on the set of *Wild Ride II* and questioned about a Volkswagen Transporter that had disappeared a few days earlier. The charges are still on file, but the police haven't got enough evidence to charge him.

'At the time the van was stolen, it was loaded up with three hundred grand's worth of TV cameras, studio lights and other equipment being used to shoot a documentary on the making of *Wild Ride II*. And the cherry on the cake is that the theft of a respraying rig and a pressurised metal cylinder used in car stunts has also been reported to Avon police.'

'So, it was worth me hiding out and taking those photos,' Lauren grinned.

Zara nodded. 'We're starting to put together a really solid picture of the AFA. There's already enough evidence to move in and make arrests. Just one huge spanner in the works: at this moment James, Kyle and all of the main AFA suspects have headed off to some unknown location with no intention of resurfacing until they've pulled off some kind of terrorist spectacular.'

'Yeah,' Lauren said, 'and I wonder what they want with all that TV equipment.'

*

The van finally arrived at a semi-derelict farmhouse, with a dozen rooms spread over two storeys. The lads were told to dump their stuff in a bare room with sleeping bags and pillows spread over the floor. Down in the kitchen, two men were cooking up a vegan roast to feed at least a dozen.

Jay and Adelaide had equipment to set up inside the house and Viv was asked to join them shortly after they arrived. That left James, Kyle and Tom to stroll the isolated farm and wonder what they'd let themselves in for.

'Wherever we are, it's a long way from civilisation,' Kyle said.

The sun was setting and he looked out over hills bedded with heather and rocky peaks in the distance.

'Pretty though,' James said. 'What do you reckon, Scotland?'

'I'm not sure we went that far,' Kyle said. 'Maybe northern England. Northumberland or somewhere like that.'

As James turned back towards the house he spotted Mark – a.k.a. Kennet Marcussen – wading through the long grass and waving his arms.

'Get back here,' he shouted. 'Everyone's waiting for you.'

Mark led them into a huge dining-hall, with a vaulted ceiling and dark patches on the walls where paintings had hung many years earlier. One end of the room had been set up as a TV studio, complete with cameras on wheeled tripods, bulky studio lights and a video production suite.

The stage set consisted of pale blue background panels with two trendy black chairs and a man-sized cage at its centre. The cage had been designed for show rather than security, with chromed bars and a neck brace dangling inside.

Jo stood at the opposite end of the room, in front of a

giant flipchart on which she'd written the detailed plans for the operation. As the crowd gathered around her, Viv approached James, Kyle and Tom. He'd changed into a smart suit, matched to an expensive-looking tie.

'Did you and Jo make up and decide to get married?' Tom grinned.

'Looks the business, doesn't it?' Viv said. 'I've just had my screen test. I'm presenting the show.'

'What show?' Kyle asked.

Jo clapped her hands together before Viv could answer. She looked sweaty, like she'd been hefting stuff about, and as always the gun bulged at her waist.

'Can I have everyone's attention please,' she said sternly.

James counted eleven people besides Kyle and himself as the room went quiet.

'OK,' Jo said. 'Thank you all for coming. I'm sorry that the journey was an undignified one for so many of you, but absolute secrecy is required for this operation to succeed. I'm sure none of you need reminding that while you're here, you're strongly advised not to divulge your surnames or any unnecessary personal details to people you don't already know.

'The launch of the AFA a few days back proved a spectacular success. The latest news is that Clyde Wainwright is still in a critical condition and unlikely to resume his job as the Chairman of Malarek UK. But the general public are still not paying attention to our message. Animal rescues aren't even local news these days and even the most spectacular property destruction gets scant attention.

'We live in a society that cares little about religion and

even less for the politicians and businessmen that lead it. But there's one group of people in which the public still has an extraordinary degree of interest: celebrities.

'In less than twelve hours, we're going to have a celebrity guest in the cage at the opposite end of this room and our very own TV show going out live on the Internet.'

Jo looked pleased with herself as she paused to build up the suspense. 'For twenty-four hours, this room is going to be hosting the most sensational media event ever staged by liberationists.'

Jo leaned forward and dramatically ripped the front sheet off the flip chart, revealing an A3-sized mug shot of a man instantly recognised by everyone in the room.

'Comrades,' Jo grinned. 'I give you our special guest, celebrity restaurateur and TV chef, Nick Cobb.'

31. STUDIO

Nick Cobb stood at a mirror in his dressing-room. The windowless space had a pastel pink sofa straight out of 1985 and shiny black marks trodden into the ragged carpet. Cobb could remember when all this stuff was new and – depressingly – the mirror seemed to indicate that he'd aged no better than the furniture.

He'd come a long way since those first television appearances at Tyneside Studios, standing in for the resident chef on a long forgotten magazine show. He now owned eight restaurants, had eleven bestselling cookery books under his belt, hosted the longest running cookery show on United States television and owned a major stake in The Gourmet Network satellite channel.

Cobb strolled across to the drinks cabinet and thought about a shot of vodka, but it was ten in the morning and he couldn't face the dusty bottles and fingerprint-smudged glassware. His publicist, Amanda, knocked on the door and stepped in without awaiting an answer.

He was about to ask why they'd agreed to come back to this dump, when a set of grey tyres inched into the room.

The kid in the wheelchair was thirteen, with twigs for arms and metal braces on her legs. He'd heard her sob story, but could only remember that he'd been too tired to argue when he'd agreed to let her visit the dressing-room.

'Hello there, young lass,' Cobb said, turning on the charm with an accent pitched awkwardly between Tyneside and California. 'You must be Gaynor.'

The girl smiled and said something, or rather gargled because of the breathing tube sticking out of her throat.

Fortunately, Gaynor's mother could translate. 'She's baked you cakes,' the mum explained, as she reached into a basket beneath the wheelchair and picked out an airtight box.

Gaynor was weak and it took her half a minute to peel the lid off. Cobb eased the silence by asking his publicist to fetch a pot of tea.

'Clean china cups,' he added, instantly wondering if the demand made him sound like the kind of celebrity prick he was always telling himself he hadn't become.

Cobb took one of the little sponge cakes out of the box and bit it, expecting the worst.

'That is one *fantastic* bit of sponge cake,' he beamed.

And Cobb wasn't lying; the cake got everything right: fluffy without being too dry and just enough vanilla to stop it from being dull. But once he'd commented on the cake he couldn't think what else to say and the perfect sponge somehow made the presence of the grinning Gaynor even more dismal.

He'd seen more than his share of dying kids over the years, but still felt as uncomfortable as when he'd encountered the first, eighteen years earlier. What were you supposed to say? *Hey Johnny, how's the whole dying of cancer thing coming along?* But ignoring the presence of death and talking about something else seemed impossibly awkward: like taking a swim while trying to ignore an alligator at the other end of the pool.

'*Soooooo,*' Nick said, sucking air through his teeth as he helped himself to another magnificent cake. 'Did you come here by car? Was the traffic OK?'

Then he glanced at his $16,000 Patek watch and wished that Amanda – a master of small talk – would hurry back with the tea.

*

After an edgy night sleeping on bare boards, James had been woken up at 5 a.m. Kyle helped him dye his hair brown and spike it up with gel, while they discussed the possibility of ambushing the AFA operation before it got underway. But there were eleven AFA members, several of whom carried guns; the two cherubs had no idea where they were and no way of communicating with the outside world. They decided to play along with the operation and hope that an opportunity arose to stop it before anyone was seriously hurt.

After another hour stuffed in the windowless rear compartment of a van, James ended up in the front row of a studio audience, getting slowly cooked by the lights hanging over his head. Mark and Adelaide sat on either side of him.

The AFA had taken every reasonable step to make James unrecognisable. His usual tracksuit and football shirt was replaced with a punkish look: tatty black boots, drainpipe jeans with rips over the knees and black hoodie with *The Ramones* written across the back. Mark and Adelaide had received a similar makeover for the benefit of live TV.

Nick Cobb grinned at the cameras from a smart blue couch, while husband and wife presenters Wendy and Otis Fox fed him easy-to-answer questions. The excitable audience lapped up every word from the local lad made good.

'So, Nick,' Wendy Fox grinned, as James marvelled at the quantity of make-up plastered over her face. 'You've written this mammoth biography – eight hundred and fifty-six pages of it – why did you feel that now was the right time in your life to do it?'

Nick smiled yet again. 'I've sold a lot of cookery books and I've had publishers chasing after me to write an autobiography for many years. But when I first spoke with my co-author, Penny Marshall, I realised that I'd finally met a person with the talent to help me get my life down on the page.'

'Well it is an absolutely *fascinating* read,' Wendy Fox grinned. 'Now, I understand that the proceeds from the book are going to charity?'

'Absolutely,' Cobb nodded. 'I hit fifty a couple of years back. The wives have all left me and my boys are at college, so I decided it was time to work on something other than my own bank balance. The royalties from sales of *Word on the Cobb* are going to support a basket of organisations, including Oxfam, the Red Cross and the Chef's Trust. That's a local charity here on Tyneside that runs a catering school for underprivileged youngsters.'

Cobb lapped up a round of applause as James' watch ticked over to 11:54. James pushed his sunglasses up his nose, pulled his hoodie over his head and drew on the string to tighten it around his face. At the same instant, Adelaide and Mark were going for the guns hidden inside their jackets.

'Nobody move,' Adelaide screamed, pulling her gun as she leapt out of her seat.

There was an air of disbelief amongst the audience – a student prank maybe? But Mark cleared away the doubts by shooting at the ceiling.

The round tore through one of the giant lamps on the overhead gantry. Members of the audience screamed beneath a shower of hot glass, as James and Adelaide charged on to the stage.

'I need your radio mic,' Adelaide demanded, as she waved her gun at Wendy Fox.

James took the little microphone from Wendy and clipped it to Adelaide's bomber jacket.

'I'm sorry to interrupt your daytime viewing,' Adelaide said, her voice trembling. 'But the Animal Freedom Army will not stand by while men like Nick Cobb make millions of pounds through the enslavement and torture of animals.'

While Adelaide unfurled a banner with the Animal Freedom Army's web address on it, James stepped up to the astonished Nick Cobb and ripped a set of handcuffs out of his jeans.

'Show us your wrists.'

Cobb grinned dumbly, unwilling to comprehend the gravity of his situation as Otis Fox made a clumsy lunge at James. Unfortunately, the closest the tubby presenter had come to exercising in the past decade was a stroll on the golf course and James dodged easily, before coming back with the handcuffs bunched in his fist and smashing them into the bridge of the presenter's nose.

Wendy Fox made a pig-like squeal, as Otis crashed off the end of the sofa with blood streaming down his face.

'Don't mess us about,' James ordered.

'Anyone else pulls a stunt like that, I'll shoot a member of the audience,' Mark yelled, swinging his gun around so that it pointed at Gaynor's wheelchair in the front row.

The audience was eerily quiet, apart from the sobs of a woman burned by the falling glass. Cobb finally held out his wrists so that James could fit the blood-spattered handcuffs as Mark stepped back from the audience and pointed his gun towards the cameraman nearest the studio exit.

'Open it up.'

James told Cobb to start walking as daylight broke into the studio. He was the last to step out into a drizzly morning and set off at a run across a parking lot towards two Honda touring bikes.

Mark opened up the pannier on the back of the nearest motorbike and tossed James a crash helmet and riding gloves. Adelaide buckled up her helmet and locked her gun away before planting a helmet on Cobb.

'I can't shoot and ride,' Mark said, as he handed his gun to James. 'Safety's off.'

With the gun in his hands, James had the power to free Cobb, but Kyle was with Jo and he reckoned she'd shoot him if he betrayed the AFA.

'How am I supposed to hold on?' Cobb protested, jangling his cuffs.

Adelaide realised that this was a glitch in the AFA's carefully laid plan. She grabbed a small key out of her jeans and undid the cuffs before pointing at James. 'Try any funny stuff and the boy will shoot you.'

A couple of studio employees had ventured out on to the first-floor fire escape and one of them filmed bravely with a camcorder. James waved the gun at them before jumping on the thickly padded rear seat of the giant bike and locking his arms around Mark's waist.

'All set,' James said.

Adelaide and Nick roared off first. She hit sixty miles an hour on the slip road out of the lot, before taking a quick glance over her shoulder and surging on to a lightly trafficked section of dual carriageway. James had ridden dirt bikes across tracks in Idaho, but he'd never experienced a bike at high speed.

The AFA had deliberately provided tight clothes, but even on a touring bike with a big screen to prevent buffeting, his trousers flapped like crazy and he struggled to breathe as the two Hondas doubled the 60mph speed limit.

The bikes kept in close formation as James glanced back for any sign of a police car. According to Jo's plan, the nearest station was fifteen minutes away, but you could never be certain that there wasn't a patrol car somewhere closer.

Dodging between traffic, with the wind rushing and the blur of tarmac a few centimetres from his boot was one of the most frightening experiences of James' life. He wasn't wearing properly padded motorcycle leathers and had no idea how much experience Mark had of riding a heavy bike on a damp road. He tried not to remember the horrific images of skin grafts and shattered bones he'd seen in his motorbike magazines, but they kept popping into his head as the sweat drizzled inside his helmet.

Mercifully, the trip was short. Mark and Adelaide covered eight miles in under five minutes, before pulling off for a final stretch at saner speeds, shooting along a deserted side road past boarded-up warehouses.

They ended up at an abandoned container terminal on the edge of the River Tyne. Two vans and two cars awaited them. One van had its rear doors open with Jo and Kyle sitting on the ledge. Kyle slid out a metal ramp and the passengers climbed off the bikes, before the riders drove them inside and cut the engines.

The helmets and riding gloves were tossed in after the bikes, then Kyle and James turned the metal ramp on to its edge and shoved it noisily back inside. Jo pointed her gun at Cobb and ordered him to walk towards a blue van parked twenty metres away.

James checked nobody was within earshot before whispering to Kyle, 'I've got Mark's gun. Do you reckon we can take them down?'

'Not a chance,' Kyle said, shaking his head. 'Jo's got a gun, so's Adelaide. There's another guy with a gun in the van around the corner. Tom's up on the roof keeping lookout.'

'Shit,' James muttered. 'Even if we *could* pull that off, it'd be a bloodbath.'

A police helicopter blasted overhead. Everyone looked up in shock, but it was flying high and fast, probably heading towards Tyneside Studios.

Mark was walking towards the boys. 'Heart missed a beat there,' he grinned, as Kyle slammed the van doors.

'Are you driving this one, Kyle?' James asked.

Kyle nodded, before pulling James into a hug. 'See you, dude.'

'Keep safe,' James said, as he felt Kyle slip a piece of paper into his pocket.

A blue van with Jo at the wheel and Nick Cobb handcuffed in the back roared past, with spray shooting off its back wheels.

Mark jangled a set of car keys in front of James. 'Better shift,' he said. 'Adelaide's changed already. We need to get to the safe house.'

As Kyle stepped into the driver's seat of the van with the motorbikes in the back, James and Mark strode briskly towards a small Renault parked around the corner. Adelaide gave a quick wave as she skimmed past in a Mini. Tom had jumped off the roof as soon as he'd seen the hostage leave and Kyle drove away with him a few seconds later.

Mark opened the back door of the Renault. He kicked off his shoes and began a quick change into a tracksuit and white canvas pumps. James stripped off his punk gear, revealing a white Nike tennis shirt with blue shorts underneath, then took a pair of white trainers out of a bag containing rackets and balls on the back seat of the car.

The clothes, shoes and sunglasses they'd used in the raid were all stuffed into a black bin liner that would be incinerated later. Mark told James to zip the handgun inside a plastic case covering a tennis racket.

James glanced at his watch again as they pulled out of the dockyard: 12:07. Thirteen minutes earlier they were masked punks waving guns around in a TV studio. Now they had different wheels and looked like a father and son heading off for a knockabout on the local courts.

32. HUMMINGBIRD

James, Mark and Adelaide's role in the kidnapping was over, but Jo had laid down strict rules for their conduct. They'd worn disguises, but there was a chance that someone might have recognised them on TV and she wanted the trio out of the limelight until the operation was complete. She'd ordered them to hole up together in a safe house where they could keep an eye on each other. They weren't supposed to go outside, or make any attempt to communicate with friends or family.

The Mini and the Renault arrived a few minutes apart, parking outside a terraced house in the coastal town of Whitley Bay. Each floor was a small, furnished flat. James raced upstairs to the top flat and dumped his overnight pack before rushing towards the toilet. Unfortunately the door was bolted.

'Shan't be a minute,' Adelaide yelled.

Mark deadlocked the door at the bottom of the stairs before striding through to the living-room and flipping on News 24.

'We're the top story,' he yelled happily.

James was torn between needing to pee and wanting to watch the news, but Adelaide was already coming out. She flicked water off her hands before grabbing James and surprising him with a hug.

'You were bloody great, kid,' she said, as her lips smacked his cheek. 'Bloody great.'

'Thanks – you weren't bad yourself,' James grinned, as he bolted the bathroom door.

There were towels on the rail and a grubby sliver of soap on the sink. So they were clearly borrowing someone's home, and it wasn't a palace.

James grabbed the piece of paper out of his pocket. He'd been driven out of the farm in the back of a van and still had no clue where it was, but Kyle was driving so he had to know where he was going. The were just four words in Kyle's immaculate handwriting: *Hummingbird Farm near Rothbury.*

It was the information James had hoped for, but getting it to the outside world wasn't going to be easy. The AFA plan called for James to stay in the flat for twenty-eight hours, when Mark would drive him to the station and put him on a train back towards Bristol. James didn't have his mobile, the door at the bottom of the stairs was deadlocked and Mark and Adelaide both had guns.

James reckoned he'd be able to take Mark and Adelaide out and make a run for it, but he'd be putting Kyle in danger if word of his betrayal got back to Hummingbird Farm.

Once he'd peed, James went into the living-room to find the TV turned up loud. Mark and Adelaide sat on the sofa and an excitable newsreader spoke over footage from Tyneside Studios. The pictures showed the kidnapping, with

TV CHEF KIDNAPPED rolling across the bottom of the screen.

Although the two camera operators on the stage floor had panicked and stopped filming, the Wendy and Otis Show's director had remote cameras positioned around the studio and kept his show on air, cutting expertly between different angles as the drama unfolded.

'That's gotta hurt,' James grinned, as he watched a replay of his mercifully unrecognisable self punching Otis Fox's lights out.

Then the camera cut to a close-up of Gaynor, crying in her wheelchair as Mark's gun hovered in her face. The newsreader spoke sternly over the images.

'These pictures were taken forty minutes ago inside Tyneside Studios near Newcastle. TV chef Nick Cobb was kidnapped live on air and taken away on the back of a motorcycle at high speed. Police currently have no idea as to Cobb's whereabouts and have mounted a search for the three kidnappers.

'The Animal Freedom Army have claimed responsibility for the kidnapping and have issued a statement saying that they will run a live webcast with Nick Cobb, starting at one p.m.'

*

The drive from the banks of the Tyne to Hummingbird Farm took just under an hour. Two vans travelling at speed in a rural area might have raised eyebrows, so the one with Jo driving and Nick Cobb held at gunpoint moved quickly, while Kyle and Tom took the scenic route.

A stocky woman called Chase opened the gate for Kyle when they arrived. She had an assault rifle slung over her shoulder and as far as Kyle could tell, this was the only automatic weapon in the AFA's small arsenal.

'Take the van around the back and park beside the barn,' Chase ordered, then she grinned. 'Better get a move on, they're about to start the webcast.'

Kyle's heart was pounding as he stepped out of the van, making a point of keeping hold of the keys.

'Excited?' Tom smirked, as the two lads stopped by the back of the van and looked at each other.

'Half excited, half scared,' Kyle said uneasily.

They stepped close and kissed. Kyle's feelings were all tangled up: Tom was great fun, he had a great body and was everything Kyle wanted in a boyfriend – apart from the difficult to ignore fact that he was one of the bad guys.

'We should go on holiday together when this is over,' Tom said. 'Just you and me. I've got enough cash for a couple of cheap flights down to Greece and we can go camping for a couple of weeks. Do you think your mum could handle that?'

Tom's plan made Kyle sad. There was nothing in the world he wanted to do more than bum around the Med with Tom, but it wasn't going to happen.

'If she won't let me, I'll run away with you,' Kyle said.

'I'll book tickets when we get back,' Tom said, before glancing at his watch. 'Wanna go watch Viv's TV debut?'

The studio lights made the dining-room unbearably hot. The ancient electrics inside the house weren't up to the demands of all the equipment and bundles of cable ran out through the windows to a diesel generator standing on the back lawn.

Two women manned the cameras. Jay sat at a fold-out table, in front of three screens and enough buttons to launch a space shuttle. He yelled orders at a couple of teenage flunkeys who were making last-minute adjustments to the lights and microphones hanging over the tiny set.

Viv stood centre stage. Tall, young and well spoken, he looked every bit the aspiring TV presenter, except for the black Balaclava over his head. Jo handed identical Balaclavas to Kyle and Tom, before shaking their hands.

'Keep 'em on in the studio, just in case a camera turns around and catches you,' Jo said. 'Bang-up job this morning, by the way.'

'Where's Cobb?' Tom asked.

'He's in the other room. I'd prefer him not to see the set until we're up and running. I want the camera to film his reaction when he first sees the cage.'

'So, who can pick up this broadcast?' Kyle asked.

'It's going out live over the Internet. The public site might get swamped if too many people try to download our video, but we've just sent all the big media organisations access codes for a high-bandwidth website, which guarantees they'll be able to download broadcast-quality video.'

'Can they trace our signals from the Internet back to here?' Kyle asked.

Jo shook her head and smiled reassuringly. 'Don't worry yourselves, boys. I've been working on the technical side of this for over three years. We're sending the images from here via an encrypted satellite link and then uploading them to web servers spread all over the world. There is a risk that someone will shut our servers down and stop us broadcasting, but the only way we'll physically get caught in here is if the police followed us or someone tips them off.'

'OK, let's have some quiet,' Jay yelled, 'on air in five, four, three, two, one.'

*

'Hello,' Viv stuttered, tripping over his first few words as he imagined the thousands – perhaps millions – of people watching the AFA webcast. 'Welcome to Liberation TV, broadcasting live over the Internet from . . .' Viv paused for effect, 'Well, maybe I'd better not tell you that.

'Today's show is brought to you by the Animal Freedom Army, who believe in ending all forms of cruelty towards living creatures and using an animal-free lifestyle to create an environmentally sustainable future for our planet.'

Jay flipped the switch and Liberation TV cut to a computer graphic:

CRUELTY FACT N° 1.
Last year, 600,000,000 sheep, cows, pigs and chickens were bred to be slaughtered and fed to domestic cats and dogs.
The vegetables fed to those farm animals would have been enough to feed every malnourished child on the planet.

'But you're not here for facts,' Viv said brightly, when Jay cut back to him. 'You're here to meet our very special guest, Mr Nick Cobb.'

Cobb was led on to the set, dressed only in a knee-length T-shirt with a picture of a rabbit on it.

'Take a seat and let's hear a big round of applause.'

A few dabs of applause broke out across the dining-room, as Viv and Nick sat on the trendy chairs.

'Thank you *so* much for coming,' Viv said, grinning sarcastically beneath his Balaclava. 'What would you like us to call you? Cobb, Nick, Nicky Poos, Cobbykins?'

'I'm not playing your games,' Cobb said angrily. 'I'm being held against my will and you'll all be caught and locked up.'

The soft California twang had disappeared from Cobb's accent and he sounded like he wanted to put up a fight.

'Nick, you are but one man,' Viv sneered. 'Billions of your fellow creatures are being held in much nastier conditions than this room in farms and laboratories around the world.'

'Give over, you pompous prig,' Nick said dismissively.

Viv broke out laughing. 'Cobby *darling*, I know you've been on a lot of chat shows recently talking about that dreary autobiography. One of the things that you *don't* mention in your book is your Cobb Cleanse range of kitchen cleaning products. Sadly they're not available here in the UK, but I understand they're quite a hit across the pond.'

Nick glared defiantly at his tormentor.

'But my friends in the Animal Freedom Army found out some interesting facts about Cobb Cleanse sink and worktop cleaner. Back in 2003, a three-year-old girl in Alabama drank some Cobb Cleanse sink and worktop cleaner. Now, it goes without saying that this made her very, very, sick.

'Sadly, the little girl was only able to drink from the bottle because of a batch of faulty safety caps and her parents sued your company, Cobb Cleanse Inc, for sixty-six *million* dollars. Now, Mr Cobb, perhaps you could tell our audience what you did when you found out that you were being sued?'

Cobb didn't answer, so Viv leaned forward in his chair

and faced him off. 'Cobby, I know you're used to going on chat shows and having it all your own way. But it's exceedingly boring if you don't answer our questions and if you're boring on Liberation TV, you might find that we decide to liven things up by shooting you.'

'You're a toffee-nosed little twerp,' Cobb snarled. 'Spoilt brats like you know nothing about the real world and to be honest, I'd sooner be shot than listen to any more of your left-wing tripe.'

The onslaught made Viv uncomfortable, but he was determined not to let Cobb get the better of him. 'Well, Mr Cobb, hopefully the viewers at home will have a chance to see us shoot you a little later, but I'll finish my story first.

'You see, viewers, when Nick Cobb's lawyers found out that the little girl's parents were suing for all the damage to her digestive system, they decided to defend the case on the grounds that the amount of damage done by the Cobb Cleanse was being grossly exaggerated by her lawyers.

'To prove this fact, Cobb Cleanse Inc paid Malarek Research's US laboratory twenty-three thousand dollars to run an experiment. In the tests Nick Cobb commissioned, one hundred and eight rabbits were made to drink Cobb Cleanse sink and worktop cleaner. Once the cleaner was administered, the rabbits were left for three days while their insides slowly burned away. They weren't even allowed a sip of water. At the end of three days, eighty-one rabbits had died from internal bleeding and the remainder were gassed. Their bodies were then cut up to examine the extent of the damage done by Cobb Cleanse.'

Jay cut to another graphic:

Viv shook his masked head grimly. 'Do you know, Mr Cobb, I think that authorising those tests makes you an evil man. The Animal Freedom Army has brought you here today to avenge those one hundred and eight dead bunnies.

'We're going to put you in our cage and give you a nice refreshing drink of Cobb Cleanse sink and worktop cleaner. Then, we're going to point our cameras at you and let all our viewers watch you suffer for twenty-four hours. Doesn't that just sound absolutely yummy?'

33. NETWORK

CNN, ITN, BBC, NBC and even the business news channels showed the live feed of Nick Cobb being dragged across the set. James, Mark and Adelaide were squeezed together on a sofa in Whitley Bay, watching the story unfold.

'*This is terrorism meets reality TV and the power of the web,*' the commentator said. '*Appalling and yet compelling in a way that makes you utterly unable to look away from the screen.*'

James watched as Cobb was forced into the cage by Viv and two masked teenagers he'd met briefly the night before. Cobb's neck was locked into a brace so that his head poked between the bars and the door was slammed shut.

'*This is exactly how they did it with the bunnies, Cobby,*' Viv explained. '*And I'd just like to emphasise that my colleagues and I have no medical training, just like the laboratory assistants at Malarek Research.*'

The cage door slammed as Viv was handed a pint glass and a bottle of Cobb Cleanse.

'*Mmm – pine fresh,*' Viv grinned, as he squeezed the viscous blue liquid into the glass. '*Doesn't that make your tummy* growl when you look at it? Maybe the viewers at home can place bets on whether you'll live or die? Or if you're watching via our website, why not vote in our online poll?'

Cobb moaned desperately as Viv pinched his nostrils together to force him to breathe through his mouth, while one teenage assistant tried to prise his jaws apart and the other moved in with a feeding tube and funnel.

'*Come on, Cobby Wobbly,*' Viv said exuberantly. '*Be a good bunny and eat all your din dins.*'

The picture on the little TV blacked out for a second, before cutting to the face of a slightly startled newsreader. '*Well, it appears that our director has cut away from those deeply disturbing scenes. But we will continue to follow this rapidly unfolding story.*'

Mark flipped through all the news channels, but every news director in Britain and America had drawn the line at seeing a celebrity having a feeding tube forced down his throat.

Adelaide tutted. 'We're only showing a procedure that happens to thousands of lab animals every day.'

'Can we get the Internet?' James asked.

'Not in this flat,' Adelaide said. 'There's not even a telephone.'

James shrugged. 'Does anyone fancy another cup of tea?'

'Definitely,' Adelaide grinned.

'Count me in,' Mark nodded. 'Three sugars.'

James squeezed off the middle of the couch and wandered through to the kitchen. He filled up the kettle and tried to think as he watched it boil. He realised that he'd got too wrapped up in Liberation TV and hadn't put any serious thought into his main task: finding a way of getting the information about Hummingbird Farm to Zara without endangering Kyle.

Nobody at the farm had been in contact since they'd arrived at the flat. James figured that they were all busy making the webcast and looking after their hostage – and besides, why would they need to contact three people sitting in a safe house watching TV?

As the kettle rumbled, James realised that a couple of factors were working in his favour. First, there was no landline in the house and because mobiles can be unreliable, the crew up at Hummingbird Farm probably wouldn't be suspicious if they couldn't get in touch with Mark or Adelaide. Second, Kyle was a top agent. He'd given James the location of the farm and would surely be taking steps to protect himself in the event that things went wrong.

By the time James had poured the water in the teapot and grabbed the cups, he'd decided to move on Mark and Adelaide. The biggest problem was their guns. He knew Mark's gun was still zipped up in the bag of tennis equipment, which now sat beside the nest of tables in the living-room. This meant James couldn't get hold of it, but Mark wouldn't be able to get his hands on it quickly either.

Adelaide's gun was trickier. James had no clue where it was, or even if she'd taken it out the back of the motorbike. He decided to deal with her first.

As the tea brewed, James searched through the kitchen drawers and found scissors and a ball of chunky nylon string. He gave it a good tug to make sure it was strong, before slicing off half a dozen two-metre lengths. He made each length into two loops and formed a noose at the top. Next, he grabbed the tea towel off its hook and soaked it under the tap, before wringing it out, folding it into quarters and leaving it on the countertop next to the string.

The living-room curtains were pulled to stop the afternoon sun bleaching out the TV picture. James strolled into the gloomy space and handed over the hot mugs.

'Cheers, James,' Adelaide said.

'Anything happening?' he asked.

Mark shook his head. 'They're not showing any live footage. Just old farts sitting in the studio speculating over what we're gonna do next.'

'Adelaide,' James said, 'I think I've got this rash on my head, from the hair dye or something. Would you mind having a look at it?'

'Sure,' Adelaide said, as she stood up.

James headed through to the kitchen.

'Where are you going?'

'It's lighter in the kitchen,' James explained.

Adelaide huffed reluctantly, but followed after him. 'If your skin's reacting to the hair dye, it's probably easiest just to dive in the shower and wash it out.'

Adelaide was exactly the same height as James and he didn't think she'd be difficult to take down. The tricky part was doing it without Mark overhearing.

'Sit in the chair or something then,' Adelaide said. 'I can't see your head from all the way up there.'

'What happened to your gun, by the way?' James asked. 'Did you leave it in the bike?'

Adelaide looked surprised at the abrupt change in subject

matter. 'It's here,' she said, lifting up her shirt to reveal it tucked into the waistband of her sweat pants.

As soon as James saw the gun, he grabbed the sodden tea towel off the cabinet top. He snatched Adelaide's wrist and twisted her arm up behind her back with one hand, while bundling her forward and clamping the wet cloth over her mouth with the other.

She ended up pressed against the wall with James holding her in an arm lock. A sharp backwards kick hit James in the knee, but it wasn't enough to knock him back.

'I can snap your arm like a twig,' James whispered nastily, tightening the painful lock to make his point clear. 'Open your mouth.'

As Adelaide opened up, James forced the cloth into her mouth until it was completely crammed. Once he was sure the cloth wasn't coming out, he let go and pulled the gun out of Adelaide's waistband.

'Put your wrists together.'

James tucked the gun in the pocket of his shorts as he grabbed one of the loops of string off the countertop. He hooked a loop over each of Adelaide's hands, before pulling the nooses tight and securing it with a constrictor knot. He glanced out into the corridor to make sure that Mark wasn't on the move before whispering in Adelaide's ear.

'I won't hurt you if you do what you're told, OK?'

'Mfff,' Adelaide nodded.

'Walk into the living-room with me, sit your arse in the armchair and *stay still*.'

James grabbed the remaining loops of string off the countertop before shoving Adelaide towards the door.

'What the hell,' Mark yelled, looking startled as he saw Adelaide with the soggy tea towel sticking out of her mouth. His eyes darted between James and the sports bag alongside his seat.

'You won't reach it in time,' James said, gesturing with the gun and using the firm but slow voice he'd practised in training. 'Take this and tie Adelaide's ankles together.'

'Listen James,' Mark said. 'I know you're young and I guess seeing it all on TV has made you scared. But running away from us isn't going to help. The best way to stay out of trouble is if everyone sticks to the plan.'

'Thank you for your input,' James said. 'Now take the piece of string and tie Adelaide's ankles together or I'll shoot you.'

Mark put his arm up on the back of the couch and smiled confidently. 'There's no shame in being scared, James, but this is silly. None of us is going to get caught so long as we stick to the plan.'

The TV pundits were droning in the background, '*The police have asked us not to broadcast any live footage from the Animal Freedom Army webcast at this time, but we can tell you that Nick Cobb has had a tube forcibly inserted into his stomach and has been force fed approximately one pint of cleaning fluid. At this stage, we're not clear how damaging the fluid will be, but our doctor here in the studio has indicated that the dosage could be fatal if he doesn't receive medical treatment within two or three hours . . .*'

The words made James realise that he didn't have time for a debate with Mark.

'Fine,' James yelled as he lunged forwards. 'I've tried being nice.'

It's extremely awkward to hit a person who is sitting on a low couch, especially if they've got gangly arms and legs in the way. James propped his knee on the sofa and swung the gun at Mark's head. But the punch missed and Mark managed to get an arm around James' back.

The badly aimed punch might have cost James against a powerful opponent like Viv, but Mark was scrawny and James managed to wriggle out of the clumsy hold and land a better punch with his empty hand.

It connected with the side of Mark's head, and the follow-up loosened a couple of teeth as the gun smashed into his mouth. But Mark wasn't unconscious and he struggled as James threaded loops over his hands and secured his arms behind his back.

'Now look at the state of you,' James said angrily. 'And whose fault is it?'

James stood up and realised that his tennis shirt was spattered with blood. He found Mark's phone stuck between two sofa cushions and waved the gun at his bound-up victims before heading out into the hallway.

'I've been nice so far,' James warned, 'but if I hear so much as a squeak, I'm putting bullets through both your heads.'

James went out into the hallway. He flipped open the mobile and dialled Zara.

'James, thank god. Are you safe?'

'For now,' James said, as he noticed beads of blood welling up on his knuckles. 'I'm in some flat in Whitley Bay. Nick Cobb is being held at Hummingbird Farm near Rothbury and Kyle's up there too.'

34. BLOOD

It was the vilest thing Kyle had ever seen. Nick Cobb threw up as the feeding tube came out of his throat and hadn't stopped retching in the hour since. At first he'd brought up food, mixed with Cobb Cleanse, but now he was bringing up blood as the powerful cleaning solution burned its way through his digestive system.

Viv basked in front of the cameras. He poked a microphone between the bars, continually tormenting Cobb about the pain he was in; and even read out a recipe for rabbit pie from a Nick Cobb cookbook.

Cobb was defiant at first, but as the pain grew he swallowed his pride and begged for water.

'You paid to make a hundred and eight rabbits suffer exactly like this,' Viv taunted. 'They didn't get water and neither will you. The AFA wants *everyone* out there to know – farmers, scientists, supermarket executives, laboratory workers and shoppers – this is just the beginning. When the AFA gets you, we're going to make you suffer in whatever way you made animals suffer.'

Kyle and Tom sat together on a woodwormy bench at the

rear of the dining-hall. Jo steamed through the door behind them with a mobile at her ear.

'We're off air,' she announced, flipping her phone shut angrily. 'I'm not sure how they've done it, but none of the remote sites are receiving our satellite signal.'

The room filled with moans, as Jay turned away from his control console. 'Do you want us to keep filming?'

'Might as well,' Jo shrugged. 'We can use the footage later, but it's not gonna have anything like the same impact that it does going out live.'

Over on the set, Viv noticed a glimmer of hope in Nick Cobb's eyes.

'Go ahead and smile, bunny rabbit,' Viv sneered, kicking the bars. 'You're still gonna die in that cage.'

Cobb raised his head off the ground to be sick again. There was nothing left in his stomach and all he could do was retch before slumping back to the floor of the cage.

Tom stood up and headed briskly out of the room. Kyle followed him down a wood panelled hallway and out on to the front lawn. The morning cloud had burned off and it had turned into a hot July day, with the hum of the generator fighting the sound of birds and crickets in the surrounding countryside.

'What's up?' Kyle asked.

Tom looked upset. 'Do you think my brother's enjoying himself just a little bit too much up on that stage?'

Kyle nodded solemnly. 'I think he's loving every minute.'

'Do you think this is right?' Tom asked.

'I . . .' Kyle said, unable to think of anything worth saying.

He couldn't imagine how Tom could think this was anything but wrong.

'This whole eye for an eye deal. You kill bunnies so we kill you,' Tom said, wrapping his hands around his head and looking stressed. 'And seeing a man tied up in a cage, puking himself to death. I thought we'd be blowing up a building or something. I wish we'd never got involved in this shit.'

Kyle felt a huge surge of affection: he'd always thought that Tom was basically a good person and the confirmation made a tear well up in his eye.

'This is a big bloody mess we've got ourselves in,' Kyle said, grinning wryly. 'I guess we could grab a van and try making a run for it, or something.'

'Viv wouldn't leave; he's in his element in there.'

'Screw Viv,' Kyle said. 'I'm talking about *us*.'

'We can't,' Tom said, shaking his head as his eyes welled up. 'If we walk out on Jo now, she'd definitely find a way to stitch us up – grass on us for the arson attack or something. The only way we'll come out clean is by seeing this through.'

Jo stepped out on to the front lawn. 'Hey, you two lazy asses,' she yelled aggressively. 'We need a hand.'

'Doing what?' Tom asked.

'I don't know why communications have gone down, but I know I don't like it.'

Kyle was confused. 'I thought you said they might shut the websites down.'

'The websites are working fine,' Jo explained. 'It's the satellite link. It might be a technical glitch, but it could mean that someone is on to us. Either way, I want everyone on alert.

'You two go over and get the three vans ready for a quick departure. I want them driven around to the front of the house and facing the gate, with keys in the ignitions. And I want the two motorbikes unloaded from the back of the van and ready to roll as well.'

Tom walked towards the courtyard behind the barn where the vans were parked, as Kyle headed into the house to get the other two sets of keys. Kyle wondered if the satellite had been shut down as a result of James getting the information about their location out to Zara, but he doubted it. Blocking a satellite signal is easy once you know where it's coming from, but it also puts your opponent on high alert.

'Has anybody got van keys?' Kyle asked loudly, as he walked into the dining-room.

He was surprised to see seven masked terrorists gathered around the cage, debating furiously. Nick Cobb had coughed up more blood and lots of it. He lay in the middle of the cage convulsing violently. Kyle could hardly bear to look.

'Get Cobb out of there!' Jay yelled.

'Screw him,' Viv said. 'So what if he's not lasting as long as we expected? We knew there was a chance he might die. If he pegs it, we'll still be making our point and we can pack up early and be home in time for *Neighbours*.'

Nobody was interested in Kyle's request for keys, so he decided to use the set he already had in his pocket and headed out towards the courtyard.

'What happened?' Tom asked.

'It's going pear-shaped in there,' Kyle explained. 'Looks like Cobb's gone into shock.'

'Great,' Tom said, shaking his head miserably.

'I'll get the other keys in a minute when they've calmed down,' Kyle said. 'I might as well drive our van up to the exit gate in the meantime.'

'What am I supposed to do?'

'I dunno,' Kyle shrugged as he climbed into the van. 'Have you checked to see if they've got the keys in the ignition already?'

'Good point,' Tom nodded.

Kyle considered his options as he reversed the van out of the courtyard and trundled up the rutted path towards the gate.

He didn't fancy taking on nine people and until now he'd been relying on James getting the information about the farm out to Zara and sitting tight until the cops arrived. But with Nick Cobb's health declining faster than anyone expected, this option looked increasingly like a death sentence for the TV chef.

Kyle's first thought was to squeeze the gas pedal, plough through the gate and keep going, but Chase was on guard duty with her British army assault rifle and if anything, the combination of his escape with the satellite signal going down might make Jo even more paranoid and push her into a violent standoff with the cops.

As Kyle stopped the van and pulled on the handbrake, he realised that Nick Cobb's only decent chance of leaving Hummingbird Farm alive would be if he rescued him.

*

Back at the cottage in Corbyn Copse, Zara had barely been off the phone in the half hour since James rang through with the information on AFA headquarters. She'd taken down all the details of the farm layout from James, as well as who the activists were and what weapons they had, before relaying it all to the headquarters of the national anti-terrorist unit in Milton Keynes.

One problem with CHERUB operations is that you have to cover your tracks if agents behave in a way that makes it clear that they aren't ordinary kids and James' situation at the safe house was one of them: Adelaide and Mark were surely going to wonder how a fourteen-year-old boy had overpowered them, before disappearing without trace.

But that was only one of Zara's problems. She was on the phone to CHERUB's liaison at the anti-terrorist unit and she was absolutely furious over the mix-up with the satellite uplink.

'I have a sixteen-year-old agent on that farm,' she yelled. 'I don't care what your director says about the importance of cutting off the oxygen of publicity to terrorists. I'm concerned about the safety of my agent and when I pass confidential information up to you, I expect you to make intelligent use of it, not to put them at risk.'

'It's out of my hands,' said the voice on the other end of the line.

'I know it's not your fault, Joseph, but the local police say it's going to be at least another hour until they can get their armed response teams out to Rothbury and ready to move in on Hummingbird Farm. The absolute last thing you should have done is cut the satellite relay and put the AFA on a higher state of alert.'

Lauren was dealing with the calls Zara couldn't take and came running out of the kitchen with her mobile at her ear.

'Give us a second,' Zara said into her phone. 'I've got to speak to Lauren.'

'I've got campus on the phone,' Lauren explained. 'They've contacted MI5. They have a team on an operation in Gateshead who can drive over and sort out the situation with Mark and Adelaide.'

Zara nodded hurriedly as she covered the microphone of the phone in her hand. 'Good work, Lauren. Can you ring the details through to James yourself? The number's written on the notice board in the kitchen.'

'Right,' Lauren nodded, before dashing back to the kitchen and turning down the volume on the portable TV. Meatball was jumping up and down, wanting to play.

'Sorry mate, I'm a bit busy,' Lauren said, giving the dog a quick stroke while dialling Mark's mobile.

'Zara?' James asked anxiously.

'It's me,' Lauren said.

'Hey, sis. I've been stuck here for an hour awaiting instructions. Can you tell Zara to sort something out pronto?'

'She's busy dealing with Kyle,' Lauren explained, 'but I've just got off the phone with the control room on campus. I've got your instructions. Ready?'

'Yeah,' James said. 'And say it quick, I keep getting the low battery warning on this phone.'

'MI5 are sending out a unit to your flat to tidy things up, but they don't have high enough security clearance for CHERUB operations, so you've got to be out of there before they arrive. Have you got a car or something?'

'Choice of two,' James nodded.

'Right, pick up your stuff, get in a car and make your own way back to campus.'

'So how will they cover for me?' James asked.

'The MI5 dudes will inject Mark and Adelaide with enough tranquilliser to knock them out for twelve hours or so. They'll wake up in a police station in a state of total confusion, and be told that they were arrested following an anonymous tip-off from a suspicious neighbour. They can claim that you tied them up if they want, but nobody's gonna believe them.'

'Good stuff,' James grinned. 'What about me?'

'They'll say that you scarpered out of a window when the cops kicked the door in.'

'I'l grab some car keys and shoot off then,' James said. 'See you back at campus, I expect.'

The phone made another low-battery bleep as James flipped it shut. He wandered into the living-room, where Mark and Adelaide were now blindfolded, gagged and expertly trussed.

'Hope you're nice and comfy there,' James grinned, as he reached into Adelaide's trouser pocket and grabbed the keys to the rather spiffy looking Mini Cooper parked outside. It was a long drive back to campus, so he decided to take all the paper money from Adelaide's purse in case he needed to stop for something.

After diving into the toilet for a quick slash, James stuffed the two guns and a bottle of mineral water into a carrier bag. It took a leap of the imagination for James to pass as someone old enough to hold a driving licence, so he looked down at the pavement as he hurried out to the car and stepped into the driving seat.

Once inside, he flipped on the air-conditioning to conquer the stifling heat before fumbling around, looking for a road atlas or map under the seat or in the glove compartment. All he came across was a pair of sunglasses, which he put on in the hope that they made him look older, or at least made it harder to see that he was only fourteen.

With no atlas, James figured that he'd head south for a hundred miles or so and then buy a map and work out the finer points of his route somewhere along the motorway.

35. HERO

Kyle stepped out of the van and wandered across to Chase.

'What's up?' the stocky woman asked.

'Jo sent me over,' Kyle lied. 'She told me to take over so you could go back to the house for a cup of tea and a bite.'

'Thanks,' Chase grinned. 'I'm busting for a pee, actually. It's undignified having to squat in the bushes.'

Kyle cleared his throat as she started walking away. 'Sorry Chase, but I don't reckon I'll make much of a guard if I'm left to fend off the enemy with my bare hands.'

Chase burst out laughing. 'God I'm daft.' she giggled, as she unhitched the strap from her shoulder and passed the rifle to Kyle. 'Do you know how it works?'

'As a matter of fact, I do,' Kyle said, expertly clicking off the safety and raising the heavy rifle so that the muzzle pointed at Chase's head. 'Start walking back towards the house, quickly and quietly. Be a good girl or I'll have to shoot you.'

Chase's eyelids fluttered like she'd heard a tasteless joke, until Kyle's grim expression made it clear that he wasn't joking.

It was two hundred metres to the house and Kyle gave his hostage a couple of shoves in the back to make her pick up the pace: he had no cover and it would only take someone looking out of a window to turn the whole show into a shoot-out.

Keeping his finger on the trigger, Kyle cut behind the house, hoping to find Tom in the courtyard; but it looked like he'd gone searching for keys. He did find a four-wheeled trolley with pneumatic tyres that had been used to shift some of the heavier studio equipment the day before.

Kyle looked at Chase. 'Take it.'

'You're off your skull,' she sneered.

'You might well be right,' Kyle said, too nervous even to force a grin, as part of him wished he'd taken the simple option of driving out of the gate and leaving the tricky stuff to the cops.

Rifle poised, Kyle led into the house through the chunky back door, with Chase and the squeaking trolley wheels behind him. He leaned into the kitchen and was relieved to find it empty, then cut across the hallway and peeked inside the giant dining-hall before looking back at Chase.

'Leave the trolley. You go in first.'

Kyle counted eight AFA members in the room: Chase, Viv, Jay, Jo, plus the two teenage lads who'd been working as stage hands and the women who worked the cameras. Tom was the only absentee.

Apart from Chase, they were all standing close to the cage. Kyle clicked the gun into single-shot mode and fired a round at the wall to grab everyone's attention.

'Hands up everyone,' he shouted.

Kyle reckoned that Jo, who had a gun, and Viv, who didn't, were the most likely to give him trouble. He closed Jo down with the gun aimed at her head and tried to sound as friendly as his nerves would let him.

'I think we've made our point, Jo,' Kyle said. 'Let Cobb out of the cage and I'll take him to hospital. You'll be long gone by the time the cops get here.'

'You haven't got the guts to shoot us,' Jo hissed. 'And don't you care about the animals?'

CHERUB training teaches you to study the dynamics of the group you're trying to infiltrate. The AFA's were simple: Jo was the boss and the others were all scared of her. Kyle reckoned he'd have everyone except Viv under his thumb once Jo submitted.

'Jo, if I back off now you'll either pull your gun and kill me on the spot, or stick me in the cage with Cobb. So I might not be a cold-blooded killer, but I'm smart enough to know that shooting you may be my only option at this stage.'

Jo mulled over Kyle's words, before slowly pulling her gun and handing it to him backwards.

'Thank you,' Kyle nodded, managing a brief smile before looking around at Chase. 'Wheel the trolley up to the cage.' Then he looked back at Jo. 'Open it up and get the boys to lift Cobb on to the trolley.'

Kyle was fairly certain that Jo was the only one with a gun, but kept his eyes open, looking for any sudden movements.

The cage clanked open and Cobb made a low moan as the two stage hands lifted him on to the trolley. His hair glistened with sweat and his giant T-shirt was a mass of puke and bloodstains.

'Who has the keys to the blue van?' Kyle asked.

'I always knew you were a soft prick, Kyle,' Viv shouted angrily. 'Your kid brother James has more balls than you.'

'Soft prick with an SA80 pointing at your head,' Kyle grinned, feeling much more confident now that he had Jo under control. 'Someone give me the keys.'

'Your boyfriend took them away,' Viv sneered.

Kyle cursed his luck. Tom must have been cutting around the front of the house towards the courtyard as he'd come in the back with Chase.

'I need your phone, Jo,' Kyle said, trying not to let on that he wasn't sure what to do next.

Jo handed it to Kyle without any fuss. He stuffed it inside his trousers and started backing up towards the door.

'I want you all to stay in this room and keep calm. Once you hear me drive away, you can do whatever the hell you like. Chase, you pull the trolley. Jay, come with us to help lift Cobb into the back of the van.'

Kyle thought about ordering Chase to wheel the trolley up to the white van parked near the gate, but even if the trolley made it up the rutted path, the bumpy ride would knock the stuffing out of Cobb.

Kyle couldn't fetch the van back himself, because he wouldn't be able to control the others from two hundred metres away and he reckoned Jo had more weapons stashed upstairs. If he asked someone else to go get the van, they'd most likely use it to escape.

With hindsight, Kyle realised that the best plan would have been to put Chase in the van and reverse it back towards the house. Now he was left with no choice but to go out the back and hope that Tom would hand over the keys to one of the other vans.

'Roll him out,' Kyle ordered.

Kyle checked that Tom wasn't waiting outside, before Chase pulled the trolley with Cobb on it along the hallway and out into the sun.

'You out here, Tom?' Kyle yelled, trying to sound casual, as he wondered what might be going through his boyfriend's mind, or if Tom even realised that he'd taken the others hostage.

As Chase and the trolley squeaked across the lawn towards the courtyard, Kyle kept his finger on the trigger and Jay walked alongside him. It took half a minute to reach the two parked vans.

Kyle shouted again, 'Tom?'

He walked away from the trolley and looked around and under the two vans. He shook with fear as he tore open the back doors of the blue van and pointed his rifle at the cushions and junk inside.

'Tom, what's the matter, mate?' Kyle asked as he crept around the side of the van.

As he walked parallel to the open window on the passenger side, Tom popped up out of the footwell and aimed a revolver through the window frame, fifty centimetres behind Kyle's head.

'Drop the rifle,' Tom ordered.

Kyle turned slightly, so that he could see Tom's shaking hands reflected in the door mirror.

'I did this for you, Tom,' Kyle lied. 'You said it isn't right. We can leave together, dump Cobb at the local hospital and get the hell out of here.'

'I told you that the only way we'd get away with this is if we went through with it,' Tom said angrily. 'You've just made a bloody enormous mess.'

'I thought . . .' Kyle said, wondering how he could talk his way around Tom as he shifted the gun across his chest.

'Hold *still*.'

'I thought you and me had something special,' Kyle said, trying to sound needy.

'Kyle, I don't . . .' Tom faltered. 'I can't believe you *did* this, dude. I don't want to shoot you, but I don't want to get nicked either.'

'I guess I'm an idiot,' Kyle said, looking down submissively, like he'd given up hope. 'If you're not coming with me, I can't see any point.'

Kyle reached across his chest to unhook the shoulder strap holding up the gun. He could see how scared Tom was and guessed that he'd fly up like a jelly if it went off.

Keeping one eye on Tom's reflection in the door mirror and with the dangerous end of the rifle pointing harmlessly towards the ground, Kyle pushed the strap off his shoulder, but grabbed the trigger with his opposite hand as the rifle fell.

The round punched harmlessly into the dirt, but it made Tom jolt, exactly as Kyle had hoped. As Tom's revolver pointed at the sky, Kyle plunged his hand inside the van. He pushed Tom's hands against the roof and twisted the gun from his grasp, as Chase dived for the rifle.

Kyle launched a savage backwards kick, hitting Chase in the guts and knocking her into the dirt. With Tom's pistol in one hand, he spun a hundred and eighty degrees and pressed his shoe against Chase's ribs as he tore the rifle away.

Kyle screamed at Tom, 'Get out of there and help Jay load Cobb into the back.'

As the two young men lifted Cobb from the trolley on to the cushions inside the van, Kyle looked in the front and was relieved to see keys dangling out of the steering column. Once Cobb was laid out and the back doors had slammed, Kyle threw the rifle across the passenger seat and started the engine.

The van juddered, almost stalling as he headed for the road. He left the engine running as he jumped out and swung open the gate at the top of the drive, all the while keeping a wary eye on the house in case someone had found a gun and decided to come after him.

Once he was safely back inside the van, Kyle pulled out into a country lane and worked his way up through the gears before grabbing Jo's mobile out of his pocket. He dialled the CHERUB campus emergency line.

'I'm coming out of Hummingbird Farm,' Kyle screamed. 'I need urgent directions to the nearest hospital.'

Kyle recognised the voice of Chloe Blake, a recently promoted mission controller. 'Are you badly injured?'

'I've survived worse,' Kyle said, as he checked in the mirror to make sure nobody was following him. 'But I've got Nick Cobb in the back and I have absolutely no idea if he's gonna make it.'

36. TRANSIT

Things had calmed down at the cottage in Corbyn Copse: James's situation had been sorted and Kyle was dealing directly with the control room on campus.

Lauren had settled on the living-room couch next to Ryan and marvelled at the way twenty-four-hour news channels manage to keep waffling on about a story without ever actually saying anything new. She was in half a mind to go out the back and throw a couple of balls around for Meatball, when Zara came charging in.

'Kyle's safe,' Zara grinned. 'Cobb is with him, but he's haemorrhaging blood. As soon as the police know Cobb has been released, they'll send all their units into the area around Hummingbird Farm to sweep up the terrorists. James and Kyle are both going to be identified and the police will trace them back to this cottage. We'd better disappear before that happens.'

'Now?' Lauren asked.

'Absolutely,' Zara nodded. 'We'll pack our own stuff, then we'll go into the boys' room and do theirs.'

'What about me?' Ryan asked.

'I want you out too,' Zara said. 'I'll book you into a hotel until we sort you out a flat, unless you've got a friend you want to stay with.'

'What about my parole?' Ryan asked anxiously. 'This is my registered address, I'm not supposed to stay anywhere else.'

'Don't make any contact with your parole officer. Call me at campus tomorrow and tell me where you are. I'll square your parole situation and transfer a few thousand into your bank account to keep you ticking over for a couple of months.'

Lauren looked warily at Zara. 'What about Meatball? I'm not allowed pets on campus.'

'I guess we'll have to take him with us. You'll have to give him to one of the red shirts, unless Ryan wants him.'

Lauren's heart fluttered as she imagined Meatball disappearing with Ryan and never being able to see him again.

'I can't see that working,' Ryan said, to Lauren's massive relief. 'I expect I'll be moving around on Zebra Alliance campaigns and I can't keep arranging a dog sitter.'

Zara looked down at Lauren with a smile. 'Why are you still standing there? Come on, get packing.'

*

'Right,' Kyle yelled into the phone, as the blue van steamed through a red light at the end of a street of terraced houses. 'This one is definitely King Edward Place. Now what am I looking for?'

Chloe's reassuringly calm voice came back down the phone: 'It should be the second turning on your right.'

Kyle got a horn blast as he slowed sharply to make the

turn, then had to slam the brakes on as he spotted the no entry sign.

'It's a one way,' Kyle yelled, as he heard Cobb moaning with pain in the back. 'Hang in there Nick. Not far to go.'

'According to the map on my screen, any of the next three turnings will get you there,' Chloe said. 'Take another right when you reach the bottom and you should be able to see the hospital.'

Kyle heard a police siren coming up behind him as he pulled away. Plain clothes police had been scouting the area around Hummingbird Farm. It looked like they'd seen him leave and sent their colleagues after him.

'I've got a blue and white on my tail,' Kyle yelled. 'But I'm not pulling over before Cobb is in the hospital.'

'Roger that,' Chloe said. 'I'll try getting a message through to the local police telling them not to stop you before you arrive.'

The next street was one way as well, but there was no traffic and it looked wide enough to pass even if there was. Kyle made the turn and hit fifty-five mph, but the police cruiser still closed in his mirrors. As he neared the bottom of the road, a set of lights changed and he found a line of cars turning towards him.

The lead car pulled up as Kyle blasted the horn. He swerved on to the pavement, but still tore the front bumper off a little Toyota as he turned into a busy main road, with the police siren blaring directly behind him.

He slowed up to pull on to the slip road of something that looked uncannily like a hospital, but it turned out to be an adjoining retirement home. By the time he'd realised, the police car had swung into the opposite lane and attempted to cut him off by turning into his path. But Kyle knew that trick from his advanced driving course and managed to get on the accelerator and use the weight of the van to barge the nose of the police car out of his way.

Kyle spotted a couple of ambulances parked up under a canopy at the entrance to an accident and emergency unit. He warned a couple of pedestrians with the horn as he pulled on to the lot. The police car was directly behind and Kyle screamed to the hospital staff for help as he jumped out.

An ambulance crew and a couple of hospital orderlies ran towards the van.

'Patient's in the back,' Kyle shouted.

By the time the medical staff had the doors open, the two policemen were out of their car and steaming angrily towards Kyle. They weren't armed, but he had nowhere to run to and he was completely exhausted, so he raised his arms to surrender.

'Up against the van,' the cop said, drawing his baton.

A couple of metres away, an ambulance woman stepped inside the van as a trolley was wheeled up to the back doors.

'It's Nick Cobb!' the woman shouted.

'Turn to face the van,' the cop said nervously. 'What's that you've got sticking out of your pockets?'

'A Smith and Wesson revolver and an automatic pistol.'

The policeman looked shocked as he stepped forward and pulled the guns out of Kyle's pockets. 'Is that all you've got?'

'There's an assault rifle on the passenger seat.'

As the other cop walked around to check the front of the

van, a message burst out of his radio. *'Units six-two and one-eight-eight. One of you stay and look after the van. The other officer to escort the van driver to Newcastle airport.'*

*

It took half an hour to load up the people carrier. Lauren felt sad as she did a final check under the beds and in all the wardrobes and drawers. As she came out of the loo, she bumped into Ryan at the top of the stairs.

'Hey,' she said, looking up and feeling her eyes start to moisten.

'What's the sour face for?' Ryan grinned. 'I wouldn't be upset if I was you. Wherever this CHERUB campus is, it sounds pretty fantastic from what I've heard.'

'It's cool,' Lauren nodded. 'I'm looking forward to seeing my mates and that, just . . . Do you remember the first time I saw you? You said how you were never going to have a family and how you'd probably end up dying in prison, well . . .' Lauren paused to rub her nose on a tissue. 'Well, I really hope you win against Malarek and that you live until you're ninety-nine and die with about twenty kids and grandkids sitting around your bed.'

Ryan was touched. 'I didn't know you cared,' he smiled, giving Lauren a hug and rubbing her back as his own eyes misted over.

'If I've made a few kids like you think about what they put in their mouths and get them to stop eating meat and wearing bits of dead animals on their feet, maybe it will have been worth it,' Lauren quoted.

'Blimey,' Ryan sniffed. 'Well remembered.'

Lauren grinned. 'I'm not eating meat ever again. Well, I

might have to if I'm working undercover, but apart from that I'm staying vegetarian.'

Ryan leaned forwards and gave Lauren a bristly kiss on the cheek. 'You're a cool kid, Lauren. I really hope you stick to it.'

'I will, I swear. And I'm gonna download all those leaflets about factory farming off the Internet, make photocopies and try persuading all my mates to go veggie as well.'

Zara was at the bottom of the stairs, holding Meatball in a makeshift dog carrier that consisted of the washing basket with a couple of towels folded up in the bottom. 'If you're ready, we'd better run. Do you need a ride anywhere, Ryan?'

'I'll be all right,' Ryan said, as Lauren ran down the stairs, dabbing her face with the tissue. 'I'll stay with Lou for a few days until I sort myself out. He's coming over to pick me up when he finishes work.'

Lauren stroked Meatball for comfort as the car pulled off the driveway and the little cottage receded into the distance. She saw a few familiar faces holding placards as they drove past the gates of the Malarek Research compound for the final time and felt sadder still when she realised that she hadn't said goodbye to Stuart.

*

James had learned to drive, busted out of a drug dealer's compound in a Range Rover and driven across Arizona and California with thousands of law enforcement officers looking for him. But this was the first time he'd ever actually got in a car for the comparatively simple purpose of driving home.

As the car crawled through the rush-hour jam on the motorway outside Leeds, he listened to the drama unfold over the car radio. He'd heard the dramatic news that Nick Cobb had been delivered to hospital by a young terrorist, then that two vanloads of AFA members had been arrested by armed police as they attempted to escape a farm near Rothbury.

Next it was announced that one of the women arrested was the daughter of eighties pop star Joe Jules and to cap it all a seventeen-year-old suspect named Kyle Wilson had killed himself with a concealed knife while sitting in the back of a police car taking him to a Tyneside police station.

James was particularly amused by this detail and wondered what excuse they'd dream up for his own disappearance. His mood was only dented by his dead mobile and the flickering low-petrol light on the dashboard.

He pulled in at the next services and couldn't decide if he was getting stared at for looking suspiciously young as he filled up. Fortunately, the forecourt was almost empty and the sour-faced cashier was only interested in the microwaved chicken and mushroom pie he was cramming down his neck.

After refuelling, James parked outside the food and shopping area. He bought a map in the gift shop and studied his route back to campus while he sat in Burger King eating a Double Whopper, special-ordered without mayonnaise. Before leaving, he called Kerry from the payphone to tell her that he was OK and that he reckoned he'd arrive home at about eight o'clock.

37. HOME

Zara glanced at her watch when the people carrier got close to campus. It was just past seven.

'Do you mind if I stop by my house for a few minutes?' she asked. 'Ewart will be putting the kids to bed about now and I've not seen much of them lately.'

Lauren was half asleep in the middle row of seats and rubbed her eyes as she told Zara that she didn't mind. The Askers lived in a secluded bungalow about two kilometres from campus and Ewart brought his son and daughter on to the doorstep as he heard Zara pull up.

Tiffany could only manage a few steps unassisted, but Joshua ran out dressed in a Buzz Lightyear pyjama top with matching shorts.

'Is this home now, Mummy?' the toddler asked.

'Yes, I'm back home now sweetheart,' Zara grinned, as she picked her son up and gave him a kiss.

'Where's my present?'

'Ahh,' Zara said uncertainly. 'I'm afraid I couldn't go to the shops today. So how about I take you to the shops tomorrow and let you pick your own present?'

'No,' Joshua whined, screwing up his face. 'I want it *now*.'

Luckily, Lauren had put Meatball on his lead and was taking him out of the car to stretch his legs.

'Nice dog,' Joshua grinned, pointing at the ground to signal that he wanted to get down and play.

Meatball looked suspicious as Joshua came towards him.

'Stroke him nicely,' Lauren said. 'Don't make any sudden noises or you'll scare him.'

As Joshua ran his hand along Meatball's back, the little dog tipped his head forward and licked Joshua's toes. Tiffany screamed because she was missing out on the action, and Ewart held her up by her hands so that she could walk towards Meatball and her big brother.

'He's a beautiful little beagle,' Ewart said admiringly. 'I had a golden retriever when I was a red shirt.'

Lauren thought of something as she watched Zara's family making a fuss of Meatball. 'Why don't you take him?' she asked. 'Meatball's quite sensitive after all he's been through and I don't fancy having him pulled around by a bunch of red shirts. Some of those little kids are lunatics, especially the boys.'

Zara and Ewart exchanged a look.

'What do you think?' Ewart asked, as he crouched down and gently bounced his daughter on his knee. 'We did talk about having a dog; and you won't be away so much once you're made chairman.'

'*If* I'm made chairman,' Zara said pointedly.

Ewart smiled. 'Mac seems sure you've got the job.'

Joshua had cottoned on to the conversation. 'Can I have him?'

Zara and Ewart smiled at each other.

'You know Lauren, that's a really kind offer. We'd love to take Meatball,' Zara said. 'And we live near enough to campus that you can still visit him and take him out for walks and things.'

'Cool,' Lauren smiled. 'Can I bring Bethany over too? She's heard about Meatball, but she's not seen him yet.'

Ewart crouched down and looked at Joshua. 'What do you say to Lauren for giving you Meatball?'

'Thank you,' Joshua grinned.

'Oh, there's one condition though,' Lauren said. 'He's not allowed to eat meat.'

'Eh?'

'I've got a few packets of vegetarian dog food in the car and there's places on the Internet where you can buy more if you can't get it in the supermarket.'

Zara gave Lauren a smile. 'Don't worry, I'll make sure Ewart doesn't sneak him any scraps of steak.'

*

James got lost a couple of times and finally arrived at the gates of campus shortly before nine. He parked the Mini outside the main building and blasted the horn a couple of times in the hope that someone would come downstairs and check out the car.

At this time on a summer evening, he'd expected to see older kids still out on the tennis courts and football pitches, but everywhere seemed empty.

'Where are they all?' James asked, as he stepped up to the reception desk inside.

'Charity five-a-side tournament in the gymnasium,' Violet,

the elderly receptionist, explained. 'I hardly recognised you with the brown hair, James.'

James grinned. 'Does it suit me?'

'I'm sure you'd look handsome whatever you did with your hair, but you don't smell so great. I'm not sure about the blood on your shirt either.'

'Oh,' James gasped, realising that he hadn't showered since leaving Corbyn Copse two days earlier. 'I'd better go up for a quick scrub before I go find the gang.'

'Aren't you forgetting something?' Violet said, as James headed for the lift.

'Am I?'

'I'll have the car keys, thank you *very* much. We wouldn't want you joyriding with your mates, would we?'

'Would I do a thing like that?' James grinned, feigning innocence as he dumped the key fob on the reception desk.

'I'm sure butter wouldn't melt,' Violet said. 'And all those appointments in Dr McAfferty's office have been the result of simple misunderstandings.'

'Exactly,' James nodded, as he noticed the lift doors opening and jogged off.

He headed up to the sixth floor. Most of the rooms were open because it was warm, but nobody was inside. He was especially disappointed when he leaned into Kerry's empty room, but it still gave him a rush seeing all her things, breathing her smell and knowing that he'd be seeing her as soon as he'd scrubbed up and put on clean clothes.

He realised Zara and Lauren were already back when he found his room unlocked and his hurriedly-packed holdall and a bag of dirty washing standing in the doorway. As he turned through his door, he noticed Kyle, spread across his bed in the room directly opposite.

'Hey,' James said, leaning into Kyle's doorway. 'You got back quick.'

Kyle propped himself up so that he could see James. 'Helicopter from Newcastle airport; dropped me down on the pad at the back of the rugby fields.'

James realised that Kyle didn't look too happy. If he hadn't been crying, he was close to it. 'What's the matter?'

'Just . . . Tom,' he said.

'You spent a lot of time hanging out with him, didn't you?'

Kyle nodded solemnly. 'Remember when you said that Kerry wasn't the most beautiful girl in the world, but that she was special because everything clicks when you're together? Well, that's how it felt when I was with Tom: driving around the countryside in his little MG, going to the cinema—'

'Romping on my bed while I was stuck in school,' James interrupted.

Kyle laughed. 'One time.'

'Don't worry about it,' James said, shaking his head. 'I never said sorry for how I acted that day. From now on, absolutely anyone can use my bed, just so long as they keep their underwear on.'

Kyle grinned half heartedly. 'One thing I won't miss is that titchy cottage. The way we were all crammed in there, I'm amazed nobody came to blows.'

'That's true,' James nodded. 'I'm gonna take a quick shower and head over to the gymnasium to find the gang. You wanna come with me or are you happy being miserable?'

'Might as well,' Kyle said. 'Can't spend my whole life sitting around feeling sorry for myself, can I?'

38. JET

Two days later

Provided they behave themselves, every cherub gets a five-week break at the CHERUB summer hostel on the Mediterranean island of C——. Kids who are late back from missions are flown out on regular, scheduled services, but the main flights that take half the population of campus in one go are put on by the Royal Air Force in one of its dilapidated Tristar jets.

Designed for carrying soldiers, every expense had been spared. There was no entertainment system, the basic seats had torn covers, they didn't recline and the bare metal floor was covered in sand and mud from soldiers' boots. It was best not to put anything into the seatback pockets because years of accumulated orange peel and crumbs had sprouted mould and the ashtrays were still full, even though smoking on RAF jets had been banned years earlier.

Not that any of the 116 cherubs on board cared. They wore shorts and T-shirts and were already tearing into the bagged lunches they'd been handed as they boarded the plane. There was screaming, shouting and occasional choruses of *why are we waiting?*

They were stuck on the tarmac because one of the coaches bringing them to the airport had broken down and it had taken over an hour for the stricken passengers to be picked up in a stream of taxis. James and Kerry were among the last group to arrive and Lauren spotted them running up the steps from her window seat.

'Looks like those two have finally come up for air,' Lauren grinned.

Bethany nodded her head, which had a paper crown and streamers dangling off it. 'I saw them three times yesterday, and they were snogging every single time.'

'Lucky James,' said Rat, who was in the aisle seat.

'Kerry looks *so* fit these days,' Bruce added, from across the aisle.

James stepped inside the plane and caught a none too pleasant odour from the toilets. As he walked down the left-hand aisle, he spotted a few people he hadn't seen since arriving back. Bethany's brother Jake grabbed his arm.

'Thanks for helping us out in training,' Jake said.

James stopped walking and looked back at him. 'I heard that you and Rat passed,' he said. 'Well done.'

'Basic training's a piece of cake,' Jake grinned, dismissively waving his hand in front of his face as one of his little mates held out a PSP.

'You didn't look so confident when I last saw you,' James smirked as he walked on.

'Hold up,' Jake said urgently. 'Watch this clip, I guarantee you'll love it.'

'What is it?' Kerry asked, as James grabbed the PSP off Jake and hit the play button.

The little screen showed the familiar set of the Otis and Wendy Show. Otis made his lunge and the director zoomed in as James threw the punch at his nose. James was impressed by how brutal it made him look.

'That was some *bad* punch,' Jake smiled.

James showed Jake and his friends the circular cuts where the handcuffs had cut his fingers. 'And I've got the marks to prove it.'

'Not as bad as the state of Otis Fox's nose,' Jake's friend giggled.

'I've got my PSP in my bag,' James said. 'Can I make a copy of that clip when we get to the hostel?'

'Course you can.'

Kerry gave James a disapproving look as they headed on down the aisle towards Lauren.

'What have I done now?' James asked.

'Those two are only ten,' Kerry tutted. 'You shouldn't be encouraging them.'

'Jake doesn't need any encouragement,' James grinned. 'He's a total nutter already.'

When they reached the row with Lauren, Bethany and Rat in it, James gave Rat a congratulatory high five for passing training as Kerry wished Bethany happy birthday.

'Oh yeah, happy twelfth birthday,' James said half heartedly. 'Has Lauren talked you into becoming a veggie yet?'

'Yes, as a matter of fact I have,' Lauren grinned. 'And Rat's thinking about it too.'

'Am I?' Rat gasped.

'You told me you were going to read the leaflets,' Lauren said.

'Yeah, but only to stop you from going on and on and on about it,' Rat laughed.

James nodded to Bruce, as Kyle stood up from a seat in the row behind Lauren. 'Saved 'em for you,' he said.

'Put my bag in the overhead,' Kerry said to James, handing it to him as she shuffled into the middle seat.

'Anything else, madam?' James sneered. 'Duty free, hot towel, tea and crumpets?'

As James opened the flap of the overhead compartment, a piercing scream hit him in the face. Several camera phones popped up and snapped his shocked expression as he stumbled back and dropped his bag.

'Bloody hell,' James gasped, clutching his chest with fright.

Cheers erupted as a little red-shirt girl called Lyra dangled her legs off the side of the overhead bin and jumped down on to the metal floor.

'Gotcha James,' Lauren grinned, as Lyra collected half a dozen chocolate bars from James' mates in return for the ten minutes she'd spent crammed into the overhead locker.

'Show us,' James said, grabbing Lauren's phone and looking at the picture of his gawping mouth on the screen.

He could see the funny side as he settled into his seat and buckled his belt.

'Zara's coming up the steps,' Kyle announced. 'Looks like she's the last one.'

Lauren glanced out of the window and saw Zara carrying

a stroller up the steps. Ewart walked behind her with Joshua and Tiffany in his arms.

'I wonder who's looking after Meatball while they're away,' Lauren said.

'Probably Mr Large,' Kyle said. 'He lives in the bungalow next to the Askers and he's already got dogs.'

'*What?*' Lauren gasped. 'Large's dogs are dirty great massive bloody Rottweilers. They'll *eat* him.'

James giggled, 'Large will have Meatball up at four o'clock every morning, making him run a little doggy assault course and doing doggy push-ups.'

'Shut *up*, James,' Lauren said, clearly worried.

Kyle spoke reassuringly, 'Seriously Lauren, don't get upset about it. Large and his partner have got five or six dogs. I've seen them in town with their daughter and a little Jack Russell.'

'Besides,' Bethany said, 'he's hardly gonna let Thatcher and Saddam eat the chairman's dog, is he?'

James tutted. 'Lauren, you weren't supposed to go blabbing about that to Bethany.'

'I didn't tell her anything,' Lauren said indignantly. 'They announced that Zara's the new chairman at dinner last night. You would have found out if you hadn't been over at the lake with Kerry.'

Kerry didn't have a clue. 'Zara's the new chairman?' she grinned.

'Yep,' Kyle nodded.

'That's *so* cool. I thought it was going to be some old fart from outside.'

As Zara stepped on to the plane, everyone started clapping,

cheering and chanting *chairman, chairman, chairman*. Zara broke into a big smile and turned bright red.

'I hope you're all this enthusiastic when you get in trouble,' Zara said. 'Thank you.'

'How can she be the chair*man*?' Rat asked.

Lauren shrugged. 'Maybe she'll be the chairwoman.'

'Or she could have a sex change,' James said.

The pilot's voice came over the intercom. '*Good morning, everyone. I've just been told that all our passengers are on board. The stairs are being rolled back and the cockpit doors are closing as we speak. Could all passengers fasten their seat-belts, secure their tray tables and remain seated until we've reached a cruising altitude. We've been given an immediate take-off slot, so we should be taking to the air in under five minutes.*'

A big cheer went up as the plane started to roll. They were flying out of a small military airfield near to CHERUB campus and it took less than a minute to taxi to the beginning of the runway. After a jarring halt and a brief pause, the pilot opened the engines up to full blast and all manner of interior fittings began flapping and groaning as the aged jet belted down the runway.

'You know it's so cool,' James grinned to Kerry. 'You, me, Lauren, Kyle and Bruce all getting to go to the hostel at the same time this year.'

'Pity about Gabrielle getting a mission at the last minute,' Kerry said. 'But I still reckon it's gonna be the best summer ever.'

In the next row forward, Lauren reached into her Nike gym bag to pull out a *Just Seventeen* magazine and noticed a mysterious dark object at the bottom. It felt greasy to the touch and she immediately pulled it out and scowled back at her brother through the gap in the seats.

'James,' Lauren screamed over the roar of the engines. 'What the *hell* is this?'

'Looks like lamb chop to me,' James said, as Kyle smiled and Rat burst out laughing.

'It's not funny you know,' Lauren yelled. 'That was a beautiful, living animal.'

'Beautiful with mint sauce and gravy,' James smirked.

As the aircraft left the ground, Lauren aimed the chop at her brother's head.

'You just wait till that seat-belt light goes off, James. I'm gonna kick your arse.' Then she turned around and thumped Rat on the arm. 'It's *not* funny.'

James looked at Kerry, but got a disapproving look.

'Great start,' Kerry huffed. 'You and Lauren will probably be on punishment for fighting before we even arrive.'

James smirked at Kyle, who thought James was mean but couldn't help laughing.

'You think she's angry now,' James whispered. 'Just wait until she finds the chicken nugget hidden inside her swimming costume.'

EPILOGUE

RHIANNON JULES, a.k.a. JO, was one of twenty-three people brought to trial in connection with the Animal Freedom Army's kidnapping of Nick Cobb. Following a three-week trial she was sentenced to eighteen years in prison. KENNET MARCUSSEN a.k.a. MARK, ADELAIDE KENT and VIV CARTER were each sentenced to twelve years in prison and JAY BUCKLE was sentenced to nine. Because of his youth and relatively slight role in the kidnapping and torture of Nick Cobb, TOM CARTER received a sentence of four years.

Subsequent police investigations into Animal Freedom Army members revealed deep-rooted links to the original target of the CHERUB mission, the Animal Freedom Militia. Several militia members were tried and convicted, including two men who received seven-year sentences for blinding Christine Pierce.

There have been no recent attacks by the AFM and police believe that the group has now disbanded.

RYAN QUINN's stormy relationship with Zebra Alliance leader MADELINE LAING led him to quit the group in September 2006. A few weeks later, Ryan launched a website and fundraising initiative for a new, non-violent, liberationist group called Zebra 06. It is believed that Ryan's new outfit will closely resemble the original Zebra 84 group, with tightly focused campaigns run by a small but loyal group of activists.

Of the seventy-three BEAGLE PUPPIES rescued by the Zebra Alliance, four were destroyed by the vet because they were suffering from serious infections brought on by the unsanitary conditions at RIDGEWAY KENNELS.

The sixty-nine dogs who survived the clean-up process were distributed to sanctuaries and homes around the country. RIDGEWAY KENNELS closed down briefly before being sold to new owners, who have improved conditions and demolished the isolation shed where animals were bred for experimentation.

The original kennel owners were fined £850 and banned from breeding animals for ten years. The Zebra Alliance described the sentence as '*derisory*,' and called for all people convicted of cruelty to animals to serve a minimum of five years in prison.

In late 2006, MALAREK RESEARCH announced that it would be winding down its facility at Corbyn Copse over an eighteen-month period. After striking a lucrative deal with a property developer to turn the site into more than three hundred homes, a statement to Malarek shareholders said that it would commence construction of a new, state-of-the-art animal laboratory at an undisclosed location in East Asia.

The company said that: '*The new facility will enable Malarek Research to carry out vital scientific research in a lightly regulated, low wage environment, with the full support of the local government and a licence to run our own security force to protect our business from the ongoing threat of terrorism.*'

NICK COBB survived, but the effects of drinking Cobb-brand sink and worktop cleaner caused irreversible damage to his digestive system. Following seven operations in the UK, Cobb flew to an exclusive private clinic in Switzerland to complete his recuperation.

Cobb Cleanse Inc eventually settled out of court with the three-year-old girl from Alabama. The exact amount of damages paid was not disclosed, but sources close to Cobb have described the settlement as '*an eight-figure sum*'.

July 28th 2006 marked DR TERENCE MCAFFERTY's last day as the chairman of CHERUB. With over half the population of campus holidaying at the summer hostel, he spent the morning writing up guidelines for Zara in his office before taking his usual lunchtime jog around campus.

Mac said he didn't want a leaving party, but he did call a few members of the senior staff into his office after lunch for a farewell drink. The following day, he set off on a four-week Caribbean cruise with his wife.

Mac expects to return to campus in September 2006, along with more than five hundred other retired CHERUB agents, to celebrate the sixtieth anniversary of the organisation founded by his father.

Read on for the exclusive first chapter of the
next CHERUB book, *The Fall*.

SEPTEMBER 2006

A Ford Focus pulled up amidst a line of deserted parking bays as a powerful wave crashed against the adjacent sea wall. The spray turned into an ankle-deep wash that swirled across the wooden promenade, while a line of partially submerged huts fought for survival on the pebble beach below.

The man behind the wheel was fifty years old, with a beer gut and a bloodshot face that gave him a look of permanent sunburn. His name was George Savage.

'Some storm,' George said, raising his voice to make himself heard above the rain pelting the metal roof. 'Haven't seen one go off like this in donkey's years.'

The young woman in the passenger seat wore the same uniform as her driver: black trousers and a white shirt with epaulettes bearing the words *HM Customs & Excise*. She pulled a hefty torch out of the glove box before reaching between the seats and grabbing a waterproof jacket off the rear bench.

'Are you coming with?' she asked, though she already knew the answer.

'No point both of us getting drenched, is there, Vet?' George grinned.

Yvette Clark hated her partner. George was old, lazy, smelled like a night in the pub and took particular delight in never using her proper name. She was Vet, Vetty, Vetto, Vetster, sweetheart and even occasionally cupcake, but if the word Yvette had ever passed George Savage's lips, she hadn't been there to hear it. She could have happily kneed George in the balls, if it wasn't for the dent it would put in her three-month career as a customs officer.

The wind practically tore the waterproof coat from Yvette's hands as she stepped out of the passenger door into the darkness. By the time it was zipped up, her shirt was soaked through and she had a horrible vision of George leering at the black bra that would show through when she got back in the car.

Yvette felt sorry for herself as she stepped up to the sea wall. She'd joined customs straight from university, expecting to spend her days uncovering serious fraud and hunting down drug dealers. The recruitment brochure hadn't mentioned ten-hour shifts patrolling the coastline with an obnoxious pig for company.

And just as it seemed life could get no worse, the wave hit. Bigger than its predecessors, its tip crashed over the wall and kept on coming. Yvette turned to run, but was outmatched and quickly found herself wading in icy water. She lost her footing on the slippery promenade, and grazed the hand she put out to save herself as the receding tide swelled over her shoulders and all but covered her head.

As Yvette gasped from the cold and staggered back to her feet, George triumphantly blasted the horn. It was 1 a.m., but the promenade was illuminated with strings of bulbs and Yvette got a good view of her colleague roaring with laughter from his cocoon behind the flapping windscreen wipers. She wanted to steam over and tell George exactly what she thought of him, but knew that a tantrum would only enrich the story he'd tell everyone back at the office the minute he got the chance.

Close to tears and with salt water burning her eyes, Yvette stumbled back to the wall and slid the powerful torch from her pocket. Anticipating another blast of water, she gripped the railing atop the wall before pointing the beam of light out to sea.

Much to Yvette's surprise, she spotted the very thing she'd come looking for.

*

The narrow strip of water between Britain and France is the busiest waterway in the world. At any given moment there are over a thousand ships in the English Channel, ranging from 100,000-tonne supertankers down to one-man sailing boats. With so much traffic, accidents are frequent – and when one of the big boats hits one of the little ones, the little boat always comes off worst.

Three hours before George and Yvette pulled up on the seafront near Brighton, a 15,000-tonne catamaran with two hundred and thirty passengers onboard radioed the coastguard after colliding with a small motor launch. The launch appeared to be damaged and a lifeboat and a French naval helicopter were sent on a rescue mission. Despite the fact that the launch was listing badly and taking on water, the captain refused help and tried making a run for it. He clearly had something to hide.

The helicopter tracked the crippled boat for ninety minutes as it headed for the safety of international waters, but eventually had to fly back to base for fuel. Under normal circumstances, a naval patrol would have intercepted the launch by this time, stopping it by force if necessary. But the awful conditions had left other boats in distress and resources were stretched to the limit.

As a last resort, the coastguard was asked to track the stricken launch on radar. But tracking a small boat through a stormy sea is close to impossible and the coastguard put out a radio request asking other ships to report sightings of a crippled white launch.

Just after midnight, the captain of a container ship radioed in to say that she'd passed a vessel matching the description. It appeared dangerously close to sinking and was making a desperate attempt to reach the English coast.

With nobody available to intercept the boat at sea, police, customs and coastguard units along a ten-mile stretch of coast were told to head for the seafront and search for the stricken motor launch.

*

George Savage sounded put out as his dripping colleague leaned inside the car. 'Bloody hell, are you sure?'

Typical George, Yvette thought. He was clearly annoyed that his peaceful night had been spoiled.

'There's a boat tied up at the end of the jetty. It fits the descriptions and it's listing badly.'

'Could just be moored there,' George said thoughtfully, as he dragged a finger over his stubble.

'There are lights on inside, George. I think it's the one . . . I mean, you'd *have* to be desperate to moor a boat outside of a harbour in this weather.'

'We'd better wait here. I'll call for backup.'

This pushed Yvette over the edge. 'For all we know they've only just tied up,' she screamed. 'The bad guys could be out there *right now*.'

'Smugglers carry guns, sugar plum. We don't know what we're up against.'

Sugar plum . . .

'I'm sick of you!' Yvette banged her hand on the top of the car. 'I tell you what, George; you sit on that giant arse of yours and wait for backup. I'm going to walk up there and try doing my job.'

'Temper, temper.' George grinned, as he reached for the radio mic. 'I've been at this game a lot longer than you . . .'

Yvette knew she'd only get madder if she stood around listening to another lecture on the benefits of thirty years' experience. She flicked the torch on and set off briskly down the promenade towards the steel jetty.

The rusting structure went fifty metres out to sea and was less than three paces wide, except at the head where it widened out to enable a ship to come alongside. The jetty had been built decades earlier to accommodate pleasure cruisers, but nowadays it only served anglers and a few brave swimmers who used it as a diving platform.

Despite the foul weather and the sheets of water

crashing over the jetty, the lampposts that ran its length were working and Yvette had a decent view of the boat. It appeared to have been hurriedly lashed to a single mooring point.

The crew had scarpered without even turning off the lights, leaving the raging water free to slowly wreck the launch. The windows along one side were shattered and the rear jutted out of the water, as if the bow was flooded. Only the length of rope lashing it to the jetty kept it above the water.

Part of Yvette wanted to encounter the crew and make her first arrest, but her sensible side was relieved to find the baddies long gone.

And then she heard a scream.

Yvette thought she was imagining it, but the noise had coincided with a particularly fierce wave engulfing the head of the jetty. She heard the high-pitched noise again when the water cleared away.

'Hello,' she yelled. 'Is anybody out there?'

A gust of wind ruined her chance of hearing any response, but her shout had apparently reached an audience. Yvette sighted a skinny figure with her arms wrapped around a lamppost. It looked like a child, no more than twelve years old.

'Holy Father,' Yvette said to herself, panicking as she fumbled for her radio. 'George, are you out there? There's a young girl at the end of the jetty. She's holding on to the railings for dear life, too scared to move.'

'I'm coming down,' George shouted. Even he couldn't ignore a stricken child.

But Yvette couldn't imagine her partner being of much help. 'What about our backup?' she asked.

'Negative,' George said. 'At least, don't hold your breath. There's tiles coming off houses, trees down in the road and the nearest cop car is dealing with a major accident on the A27: articulated lorry turned over by the gale. Serious injuries.'

'Roger that,' Yvette said. 'I'll have to go get the kid myself.'

'Keep your head on your shoulders and wait till I get there,' George said. 'That's a *direct* order.'

But despite thirty years in the service of Her Majesty, George had never been promoted and had no authority over his partner.

Yvette was drenched and knew she ought to be shivering, but the tension made her face burn. She wrung her hands as she watched the raging tide, trying to pick a moment to run on to the jetty. She imagined that it might be like the video games she played with her young nephew, hoping for some magical pattern that would allow her to run along the jetty, grab the child and escape unscathed.

But there were no breaks. All Yvette could do was set off quickly and grab the handrail when the waves tried to knock her off. Figuring that bare feet were better than her flat-soled shoes, she slipped them off along with her socks and raincoat. She was already soaked and the waterproof fabric would drag as it billowed in the wind.

'Hold on there, sweetheart,' Yvette shouted, as the wind caught the abandoned coat and whipped it into the air. 'I'm coming to get you.'

She took a deep breath and considered a prayer, but

George was coming towards her in the Focus. She didn't want him to stop her, so she settled for a quick kiss of the gold cross around her neck.

When the swirling tide dipped, Yvette vaulted the three steps at the front of the jetty, grasped the metal railing and began to run. The first wave to hit barely broke over the wooden decking, but the fierce wind gave it impressive force and Yvette had to curl her toes into the gap between planks to stop her legs being washed away.

The next wave was huge and swept across the jetty from the opposite direction, pressing her back against the metal railings as the surging water forced its way up her nostrils. She hacked and spat as a break in the wave allowed her to dash another thirty metres, almost making it to the head of the jetty before the next blast.

When the water cleared, the stricken boat was less than five metres away and the child was in clear view. It was a girl, with long blonde hair. She wore leather boots, leggings and a soggy polo neck. Although the girl had been too petrified to let go of the post and make a dash towards the shore, she'd managed to protect herself by wedging her leg into a gap between the post and a rubbish bin.

'Are you OK?' Yvette shouted.

The girl shook her head and said something in a language Yvette couldn't understand. The girl's pale skin and cheap but warm clothing suggested that she hailed from Eastern Europe.

Yvette realised that the runaway boat had been smuggling illegal immigrants. The terrified girl must have become separated from her companions as they escaped along the jetty, and they'd either thought she'd been washed out to sea or not cared enough to go back and rescue her.

Yvette's next move was the hardest: the head of the jetty was designed for boats to dock and had no handrail. She'd have to wait for a break in the waves and then dash to the girl, grab her and run back. If she timed it wrong, she'd be swept away to certain death: either drowned or brutally smashed against the legs of the jetty or the sea wall.

The sea looked black and the erratic gusts made it hard to time the waves. Yvette tried giving the youngster a reassuring smile, but as she crouched down holding on to the last section of railing, her heart banged like it was trying to hack its way through her chest wall.

She dipped her head as a massive wave reared up. The metal structure made a groan like whale song, then shuddered as the launch strained at its mooring post. Its plastic hull thudded into the side of the jetty.

'Here I come,' Yvette shouted.

It took less than three seconds to reach the girl and wrap an arm around her waist. The youngster's teeth chattered and her skinny body felt eerily cold. Yvette realised that the girl was in the early stages of hypothermia and would be unable to support her own weight.

As Yvette twisted the girl's leg out of the gap, she saw a colossal wave break over the end of the jetty, almost at head height. The water knocked her on to her back, but she managed to keep one arm around the girl.

Yvette felt pure terror as the water lifted her body off the wooden decking and shoved it towards the edge. She heard the hull of the boat slam again, then something heavy hit the decking directly in front of her.

'Grab hold,' George shouted.

Yvette reached out for the object, which she now realised was a tethered life preserver. George had one leg wrapped around the railings and the nylon rope coiled around his chunky wrists. He struggled to hold on as the wave tried to push the two females over the edge.

Yvette and the girl both screamed, coming up for air as the last of the wave drained between the wooden planks. Still clutching the girl, Yvette rolled on to her chest and was horrified to see how close she'd come to going over the side.

She rushed towards George and the relative safety of the railings.

'I told you to wait,' George shouted furiously, before they all ducked down, grabbing the railing as a modest wave washed over the deck.

'I didn't want you to stop me,' Yvette said, close to tears and coming to the awkward realisation that she now owed her life to a man she detested. Maybe she'd never like George, with his sexist jabs and nicotine-stained fingernails, but he'd proved himself to be a better man than she'd realised.

As more water rushed over them, Yvette huddled herself around the girl and felt oddly reassured by the fat hand pressing against her shoulder. The nylon cord had sliced George's wrists and blood streamed along his fingers.

When the last of the water had drained away, Yvette looked through the railings and saw that the sea around the jetty had taken on an eerie calm.

'Lull before the storm,' George said hurriedly. 'Spot of

high pressure, but the big buggers will come back in a minute.'

The wind howled against the structure of the jetty as the break in the waves gave them a clear run back to shore.

CHERUB: The Recruit

So you've read *CHERUB: Man vs Beast*. But how did James Adams end up at CHERUB in the first place?

CHERUB: The Recruit tells James' story from the day his mother dies. Read about his transformation from a couch potato into a skilled CHERUB agent.

Meet Lauren, Kyle, Kerry and the rest of the cherubs for the first time, and learn how James foiled the biggest terrorist massacre in British history.

CHERUB: The Recruit available now from Robert Muchamore and Hodder Children's Books.

CHERUB: Class A

Keith Moore is Europe's biggest cocaine dealer. The police have been trying to get enough evidence to nail him for more than twenty years.

Now, four CHERUB agents are joining the hunt. Can a group of kids successfully infiltrate Keith Moore's organisation, when dozens of attempts by undercover police officers have failed?

James Adams has to start at the bottom, making deliveries for small-time drug dealers and getting to know the dangerous underworld they inhabit. He needs to make a big splash if he's going to win the confidence of the man at the top.

CHERUB: Maximum Security

Over the years, CHERUB has put plenty of criminals behind bars. Now, for the first time ever, they've got to break one out . . .

Under American law, kids convicted of serious crimes can be tried and sentenced as adults. Two hundred and eighty of these child criminals live in the sunbaked desert prison known as Arizona Max.

In one of the most daring CHERUB missions ever, James Adams has to go undercover inside Arizona Max, befriend an inmate and then bust him out.

CHERUB: The Killing

When a small-time crook suddenly has big money on his hands, it's only natural that the police want to know where it came from.

James' latest CHERUB mission looks routine: make friends with the bad guy's children, infiltrate his home and dig up some leads for the cops to investigate.

But the plot James begins to unravel isn't what anyone expected. And it seems like the only person who might know the truth is a reclusive eighteen-year-old boy.

There's just one problem. The boy fell from a rooftop and died more than a year earlier.

CHERUB: Divine Madness

When a team of CHERUB agents uncover a link between eco-terrorist group Help Earth and a wealthy religious cult known as The Survivors, James Adams is sent to Australia on an infiltration mission.

This time James isn't just fighting terrorists. He's got to battle to keep control of his own mind.

CHERUB: The Fall

When an MI5 operation goes disastrously wrong, James needs all of his skills to get out of Russia alive.

Meanwhile, Lauren is on her first solo mission, trying to uncover a brutal human trafficking operation.

And when James does get home, he finds that his nightmare is just beginning . . .

And don't miss the rest of the CHERUB series: *Mad Dogs*, *The Sleepwalker*, *The General*, *Brigands M.C.* and *Shadow Wave*.

HENDERSON'S BOYS: THE ESCAPE

The very first CHERUB adventure is about to begin . . .

Summer 1940.

Hitler's army is advancing towards Paris, and millions of French civilians are on the run.

Amidst the chaos, two British children are being hunted by German agents.

British spy Charles Henderson tries to reach them first, but he can only do it with the help of a twelve-year-old French orphan.

The British secret service is about to discover that kids working undercover will help to win the war.

www.hendersonsboys.com